The Closest Thing to a Normal Life

Michael Méndez Guevara

PIÑATA BOOKS
ARTE PÚBLICO PRESS
HOUSTON, TEXAS

Praise for *The Closest Thing to a Normal Life*

"With humor and undeniable charm, Michael Méndez Guevara navigates the complexities of grief and shows how our deepest relationships ultimately shape our understanding of ourselves and the world around us. *The Closest Thing to a Normal Life* reminds us what it means to find one's place in the midst of chaos and change."
—Matt Mendez, author of *The Broke Hearts* and *Barely Missing Everything*

"Alarmed that your students are reluctant to pick up a book? Tempt them with the first pages of *The Closest Thing to a Normal Life,* and I predict they will be fighting to be the first to get their hands on your copy. The narrator takes readers on the roller coaster ride of his senior year—ups and downs that are testament to his gumption and resilience. Ethan-Matthew's search for 'normal' is a contemporary odyssey."
—Carol Jago, associate director of the California Reading and Literature Project at UCLA, taught high school English for many years and is past president of the National Council of Teachers of English

"High school is hard enough without having to start over in a place that was never supposed to be home, living a life that was never supposed to be yours. Ethan-Matthew Cruz Canton wasn't planning to spend senior year in his dad's childhood bedroom, pretending he's totally fine (spoiler alert: he's not). After losing both parents at once, he's stuck in a school where friendships go back to the sandbox, just trying to survive. But then come the unexpected connections, tangled emotions and a pull that makes him question everything. *The Closest Thing to a Normal Life* is heartbreakingly real, laugh-out-loud funny and for anyone who's ever felt lost, out of place or unsure of where they belong."
—Annie Jenson, host of The History Solarium Book Club

The Closest Thing to a Normal Life is funded in part by grants from the Texas Commission on the Arts, the Alice Kleberg Reynolds Foundation and the National Endowment for the Arts. We are thankful for their support.

Piñata Books are full of surprises!

Piñata Books

An imprint of
Arte Público Press
University of Houston
4902 Gulf Fwy, Bldg 19, Rm 100
Houston, Texas 77204-2004

Cover design by Ryan Hoston

Library of Congress Control Number: 2025933397

∞ The paper used in this publication meets the requirements of the American National Standard for Information Sciences—Permanence of Paper for Printed Library Materials, ANSI Z39.48-1984.

The Closest Thing to a Normal Life © 2025 by Michael Méndez Guevara

Printed in the United States of America
April 2025–June 2025
5 4 3 2 1

For all my former English and journalism students who said, "Mr. G, you should write a book."

For Veneé, Zachary, Zane and Zion—my favorite Guevaras who inspire me and survived my creative endeavors.

For Andrew Smith—this wouldn't have happened without your help.

ACKNOWLEDGEMENTS

Thanks to the students who had me as a teacher with whom we would write every day in class and share our writing with each other. Over two decades of teaching, students would often say to me, "Mr. G, you should write a book." After a nod and smile of appreciation, we would go on with our learning and that would be the end of it—until it wasn't. Thank you to my former English and journalism students whose stories, experiences and encouragement have fueled and inspired my writing. I will always believe student journalists are some of the bravest people for putting their words out in the world for others to consume and critique.

Thanks to Veneé, Zachary, Zane and Zion—my favorite Guevaras—I know I upended all your lives when I came out during the process of writing this book, which was the only way I was able to finish it. You have continued to love me, support me and inspire me. I know you will see traces of yourselves in my words.

Thanks to Andrew Smith for telling me people would want this story and for showing me how to start this journey. Thanks to my Abydos Literacy writing colleagues, particularly Dr. JAC and Cindy Tyroff, for all I've learned from you. Thank you, Cyndi Piña, Christina Iltis and Sharri Peterson for your support and advice on all my writing projects. Thanks to Dr. Nicolás Kanellos, Marina Tristán, Dr. Gabriela Baeza Ventura and all the wonderful people at Arte Público Press, for your dedication, support and all you did to bring this work to life. Thanks to Shari Maurer, my agent, for taking a chance on me and for believing this was too beautiful to suppress.

This is for every person struggling to embrace their true identity, I hope it doesn't take you as long as it took me. Peace, love and Rock Chalk.

1

This room never used to creep me out.

I've spent lots of nights in this room over the years. I've drooled on the pillows in this room, bled on the carpet in this room when I discovered the absolutely wrong way to close a pocketknife. I've forked over teeth to the tooth fairy in this room, and I've hurled my guts out in this room after protesting that one more Christmas cookie never hurt anyone. I also discovered what it means to be a man in this room so many times that I had to learn to do my own laundry to keep the effects of my raging hormones between me and my socks.

Grams and Gramps just thought I was the most industrious child ever. "Aren't you just the sweetest thing? So willing to help. You just set those filthy things right there, and I'll take care of them," Grams would say.

"No, Grams. I want to do them. You always do so much for me," I'd say quickly.

I can't imagine trying to explain to her how my socks managed to get so crusty. Dad, of course, smirked at every one of those conversations between me and his mother. Grams would throw shade at him and insist I was just darling.

Honestly, I think Dad knew exactly what was going on, but he had the decency to feign obliviousness. After all, he was the one who insisted Mom stop barging into my room back at home and that she knock before entering. Dad was cool about that stuff, so you would think with so much of my DNA literally and figuratively in this place that I would feel right at home in my dad's childhood bedroom. But I don't. I shouldn't be here right now. I've never been here at this time of the year, and I hate it.

Three months from now for sure, I would lie here in this bed watching YouTube videos late into the night until falling asleep and then roll out of bed the next day when I got tired of sleeping. I'd stumble into the kitchen in nothing but my boxers and house shoes, and Mom would mutter some half-hearted edict about marching back to the room to get some clothes on. The piles of pancakes or waffles or breakfast tacos—those are a thing in Texas—would do their Sirens and Odysseus thing on me, and I would stuff my face until I felt the need to go back to my room for more videos and a nap.

Gramps would eventually knock on the bedroom door and say some cheesy-old-person thing like "Daylight's burning" or "Only lying dogs sleep in this house." Then he'd get me up to join him in watching whatever marathon series was playing on the History Channel, or we'd toss the frisbee in the backyard, or shoot hoops in the driveway. About three miles up the road from their house was a Catholic university that strung lights in every tree on campus, and each year we'd pick an evening to stroll through campus oohing, aahing and taking pictures.

As a typical teen, I wasn't supposed to like any of that stuff. I was supposed to rebel against my grandparents dragging me to yet another drive-through live Nativity scene put on by the local Lutheran church, but I looked forward to it every year. Nothing beat Christmas break with Grams and Gramps.

Except it's not Christmas break, and now I live in this room.

My dad used to lie in this bed in this room in this very spot and stare up at the ceiling just like I am doing now. He used to lie in this bed and do the same things I do in this room, which is a little weird to think about your dad doing that, but everyone has always said how much alike we are. I guess that's why this room now creeps me out. It was never supposed to be my room. Now it is, and all I can say about that is that it sucks.

Senior year, when you're an only child, is supposed to be somewhat akin to a coronation. Your first- and only-born child achieves the monumental accomplishment of completing compulsory education, picks up some athletic or academic accolades along the way—Best Haiku, 7th grade—and you spend the annual budget of a micro country announcing to family, friends and the guy who sat next to you in a cubicle two years ago that your child will receive a diploma along with ten of his closest friends and 400 acquaintances. Parents eat that up.

Granted, my high school accomplishments extended well beyond the borders of the compulsory, but none of that matters anymore because I begin my senior year of high school at a completely new school.

Yes, first-world-problem-party-of-one. Lots of kids transfer high school their senior year, survive and manage to live almost normal lives. Of course, most of those kids don't transfer their senior year to live with their grandparents in the house their dad grew up in to go to the same school their dad graduated from because both of their parents died at the same time. Right?

Yeah, didn't think so.

2

They have this thing at my new school called "Gear-Up Day." The week before school starts there is one day where each grade has an assigned time to go up to the school and register for classes. You get your textbooks, have your school picture taken if you aren't a senior, order your yearbook and turn in all manner of forms.

For students, it's the first official opportunity to come together as a class, to see all those people you didn't see over the summer. You get to see the teachers you like and the ones you hope to never see again—unless it's their mug shot on the evening news. Mostly, though, you go to Gear-Up Day to get your schedule of classes, to see who you got for what and which of your friends got it with you.

From the looks of everyone around me, this is supposed to be a big deal, but I don't care about any of it. All my life I heard stories of my dad's high school experience and this community. I heard about this small enclave tucked in the middle of the much larger city as its own separate school district. Generations of families linked to the history of the city itself called this community home. My dad went to kindergarten through 12th grade in this district, and that was the norm here. In this tight-knit community, kids grew up together, they had cotillions together, moms Junior-Leagued and lunched together while dads golfed and fished for tuna in Scandinavia together. But Dad kept me away from all that, from this place where everyone knew everyone—well, almost everyone.

"Name?" asked the woman in front of me, her fingers poised and ready to search the plastic file box in front of her. Before getting to me, I watched her hand schedules to kids in front of me without having to say a word, but with me she looked baffled, curious and possibly annoyed that I interrupted her system. She looks like the kind of person who takes pride in knowing something you don't know.

"Ethan-Matthew Cruz Canton."

Her raised eyebrows have all the subtlety of an eyeroll and a dismissal. Yep, outsider, party of one, that's me.

The schedule she hands me doesn't surprise me. It has all the classes I would have taken at my old school. I don't know anything about my new teachers, but how different can things be? I'm in the newspaper production class, which is about all I can manage to even remotely care about. So, stick with the plan, just move down the line, get your textbooks and get out of here. Simple.

I missed senior picture day for the yearbook, but Grams and Gramps have already scheduled a make-up appointment to avoid the dreaded "Photo Not Available" label over my name for posterity. I do get all my textbooks. Basically, I'm as geared up as I'm ever going to be.

Grams and Gramps live less than half a block behind the school. I can pretty much walk to their house and barely break a sweat, even in a Texas heat that can melt your shoes if you stand still for too long. I should probably stop calling it their house and start calling it home, but I'm not ready for that. I'm not sure I'll ever be.

The house is so close to the football stadium that Grams and Gramps can probably hear the sound of the coin toss hit the astro turf from their living room. Bright lights from the stadium, the blare of the band rehearsing every night and cars flooding the street in front of their house every Friday night might be enough to make normal people want to move some place less hectic, like, I don't know, a NASCAR track. But it's football, it's Texas and they love it.

On the way to their house, I walk by the field where the drum line bakes in the relentless summer sun of San Antonio, sweat streaming down bodies and pasty skin transitioning from varying stages of pink to red—and it's only 10 in the morning. The entire scene at the stadium looks like something straight out of a Disney teen flick. Cheerleaders stack themselves into pyramids of dizzying heights, band members march in place and random students spread paint across banners the size of small billboards.

There was no American football at my former school. Everyone played *fútbol* (soccer in Spanish). We didn't have cheerleaders nor any of the hoopla. Aside from *fútbol*, things were almost exclusively academic. We did have some sports and found ways to have fun and get into the kind of trouble you're embarrassed to confess to your college and adult friends later in life because you realize how lame you were, but the overall consensus was you went to school to learn.

The hoopla fascinates me, though, and I'm not ready to go back to the house. I stop to observe. I find a spot in the bleachers shaded by the press box. I take out my journal and start scribbling notes. My journal goes everywhere with me. It's a habit you can't help but pick up when your parents are—or rather were... I have to pay more attention to my verb tenses now. Anyway, carrying a journal for notes is something you pick up when both your parents *were* journalists.

Maybe this can turn into my first editorial of the year.

Perfectly coifed ponytails bob to the rhythm of a cheer on the track at the south end of the football field. On the north end, the drumline beats out cadences with precision and flair.

School doesn't begin for another week, and already students (find out when they started practice) have begun sacrificing to the golden calf of the well-rounded student.

But does it really get them anywhere?

After high school, most of them will never split/perform another hurkie (or is it hurkey—gotta look this up or ask a cheerleader. Correct terminology?) (Sidebar or feature idea—where does the name herkie come from? What's the new herkie?) Most will never march another half-time show or score any kind of point or goal in a school uniform (look up statistics on how many high school athletes go on to play college sports.)

So why do it?

Parents ~~spent a shitload~~ invest thousands of dollars on lessons, fees, camps and coaches hoping for the next virtuoso, prodigy, superstar. But by the time kids get to high school, both the parents and kids have to know this is the end of the dream (or maybe here ends the dream?).

Sure you have your Michael Jordans, who contrary to popular belief (too cliché? Mythos maybe?) wasn't cut from his high school team but spent a season on the JV squad before going on to professional success and GOAT status, but you're not MJ and exceptions to the rule are like snow days in South Texas—they don't happen. Often.

"What are you writing?" I hear a voice say to me.

I was so pleased with my snow day simile that I didn't notice someone had entered my space.

"Just some observations, things I notice in the world around me." *Omg—how cheesy did that sound?*

"You're a regular Jack Kerouac there."

Right now, there is a pinging in my head. All my synapses are firing into overdrive. I'm impressed by the Kerouac reference but don't want to look like I'm impressed by it. I want her to know I get the reference without looking like a tool for being impressed that she knows it.

"Well, if you can't be on the road, chillaxing on some metal bleachers in a high school football stadium is the next best thing."

My witty retort dutifully awaits her bidding. Will she ignore it, mock it, roll her eyes or do the right thing and recognize me as a born raconteur? (Dad loved describing himself as a "born raconteur.")

And then, she does it. Even if she didn't do it, I would know she's a cheerleader because she's dressed exactly like the other girls down on the field clapping in exaggerated unison. Her hair, long, thick and the color of espresso is pulled back in the most perfect ponytail, and, well, her deeply tanned legs, *cafecito* with *un poquito de crema*, look like the kind of legs every cheerleader throughout the history of cheerleading has aspired to have.

She tilts her head to the right with a sprightly pop that makes her ponytail dance. I swear, they must teach that head pop move at cheerleader camp or hot girl school. She thrusts her hand confidently forward with all the precision of a Buckingham Palace guard and officially announces her presence.

"Hi, I'm Carmelita Cortínez, but everyone just calls me CC."

Her boldness throws me for a moment, along with her name. I've never known a Carmelita. Before I realize what I'm doing, I answer with my full name, like I'm some debutant being announced at a charity ball.

"I'm Ethan-Matthew Cruz Canton. Matthew isn't my middle name, Cruz is. That's a thing with some Mexican families, where you get your mother's maiden name as a middle name. But my first name is Ethan-Matthew, still two words but one first name. It was a thing with my parents."

About a half second into my name diatribe, I want nothing more than to stop myself from delineating my family history and just say, "I'm Ethan." But Mom always used them both, wanted them both, so I couldn't do anything to stop this name train from barreling off the tracks and down into a canyon below, just like in *Back to the Future Part III*, which is, in fact, the worst of the franchise. They should have stopped at two. Dad guilted me into a *BTF* marathon with him one weekend Mom was away on assignment.

"That's a lot of name going on there, Ethan-Matthew Cruz Canton." She looks at me with the look I've learned to read my whole life, the you-don't-look-Mexican look. "You're either a law firm in the making or new here."

"I'm new."

"Well, Einstein," she says just before giving me another of those perfect cheerleader head snaps, "I'll see you around." Then she be-bops down the bleachers and back to her flock.

Einstein? What the hell was that? School hasn't even started, and I already have a nickname. I think that's a good thing.

I finish writing my editorial when I get back to Grams' and Gramps' and then read through all the flyers shoved into my hands by every group, organization and association represented at Gear-Up. With no friends in town, I have only YouTube, my books and my writing to buffer me from the constant doting of my grandparents.

    I really can't blame them for wanting to dote on me. My therapist, who specializes in grief, trauma and adolescents, keeps reminding me that it's natural—he doesn't like the word "normal." It's natural for me to feel overwhelmed, losing (I hate that word) both of my parents at the same time and the way it happened, and moving to the States and moving in with my grandparents and leaving my school and friends and on and on. He reminds me that Grams and Gramps are in mourning too. I lost my parents, and they lost their only child and the daughter-in-law that they loved as if she were their own child. I guess, they think they have to be strong for me because everything in our new lives together is all about me. Mom and Dad had a well-articulated fend-for-yourself approach to parenting, not neglectful in any way. Speaking of over-protecting, I swear Grams has been ironing my boxers before she puts them away in the chest of drawers for me. This has definitely complicated other matters for me. Sometimes, I just want to tell her to back off and give me some space, but it's a small price to pay to give Grams something to take her mind off how much it sucks to lose your son and become a parent all over again.

3

My first day of senior year at my new school begins when my alarm goes off at 5:30 a.m. Cross country practice starts at 6:15, but since the house is so close to school, I can walk out of the house at 6:05 and make it to practice with time to spare. I'm thinking that I'll definitely sleep until 5:45 for day two of school. But first, downstairs for coffee.

Light melts out of the kitchen into the hallway, my eyes squinting as they try to adjust from the darkness of a long sleep and an especially early morning. Of course, Grams and Gramps got up with me, despite my insistence last night that I can get off and out of the house without them having to do anything extra for me.

For the last three years, I would get up and fly out of the house with some semblance of breakfast in hand and a cursory but sincere goodbye to whichever parent happened to be home. Sometimes, it was both of them but depending on what was going on in the world, it could have been one or the other of them or neither. I mean, it was obvious I loved my parents, they really were super cool, and I liked having them around. But I also liked my independence, being alone for stretches of time, but that probably isn't good for me these days.

Lately, I'm prone to emotional outbursts that can range from fits of anger to bouts of crying to painful resentment, which is why I'm super glad I'm barely awake, or who knows which outburst I would have when I walk into the kitchen. Not only have my grandparents clearly been up long before me and are dressed and drinking coffee when I stumble into the kitchen, but they also have a back-to-school send off on full display. There's an elaborately decorated first day of senior year photo op poster ready to go for me and a collection of *cositas* decoratively arranged on the table. Who knew Grams and Gramps would be out scrounging for Star Wars and zombie collectables, Doctor Who bookmarks, a Flash T-shirt, a Spider-Man T-shirt and a Ninja Turtles pencil bag? There are boxes of Pop Tarts in just about every conceivable flavor forming a tower with a five-pound bag of Hot Tamales candies at the base. It's like Grams and Gramps had rummaged around inside my head.

Standing there in just my boxers and an over-sized Northwestern T-shirt, I have to rub the sleep out of my eyes and say something. Even though I'm kind of pissed they've ignored what we talked about, and all I wanted was to slink out of the house without fanfare, this is pretty cool.

"Wow, you guys didn't have to do all this. I love it—oooh, brown sugar cinnamon. These are my favorite."

Contrary to popular adult theory on teenage boys, we don't all speak in grunts, scratch ourselves and tune out anything around us not tied to a hormone. I mean, yeah sometimes, but not always. I'm fairly well versed in social graces (thanks Mom and Dad) and, when not surprised by hot cheerleaders or over-the-top expressions of love, I'm usually quite eloquent.

As I browse through the eclectic collection of things to show they love you, I know I have to say something more than, "Wow, this is cool." The occasion needs something more winsome and sincere.

"Grams and Gramps, you guys are the best. I really appreciate all of this, well, really appreciate like everything you've done for me. I don't want to sound like some ungrateful hooligan (I intentionally threw in some old people lingo to represent), but you don't have to get up with me and do all this stuff to make me feel welcome here and show that you love me. I already know that." Not close to my best work, but it is 5:37 in the morning.

Grams and Gramps turn and look at each other. Adults always seem to turn and look at each other before speaking to kids. It's like they communicate telepathically or something before they hand down their punishment or aphorism. Grams does most of the talking. Gramps masterfully plays the strong, silent role.

"Ethan-Matthew..." They love calling me Ethan-Matthew, which probably explains my parents, "... don't you worry your gorgeous little head about your ol' grandparents at all. What the hell do we need more sleep for, anyway?"

Grams can get pretty salty.

"We want to take a picture before you leave.... So run along and get dressed for practice because your penis is poking out of your boxers."

How I manage to turn and exit gracefully without looking like I'm wielding my tool like a light saber still baffles me. As I'm slinking out of the kitchen, I hear Gramps say, "He gets that from my side of the family."

Holy shitbombs, my grandparents think I have a large penis!

4

It might be the first day of school, but cross-country practice is fully operational. Coach Barajas has us out running before I can even absorb much of anything. His one instruction this morning is, "You new guys just follow behind 'til you learn the routes." Two things are clear: these guys are serious runners, and getting up early isn't going to be the only reason I'll be tired for the rest of the day and probably the entire season. Coach Barajas so far looks like he can win the first day of school in the teacher department. At 6'5", he looks more like a power forward than a cross-country coach, but the way kids flock around him like ducklings imprinting on their mother, I know he has to be a baller.

By the time I make it into my first class, I'm already tired. My AP Bio teacher looks like a newly hatched bird with bits of shell still clinging to him, and his speech pattern follows some kind of X-Men mutation of morphing from stuttering to stream of consciousness. His class feels like it will be challenging but not murderous to the GPA. My AP Calculus teacher sounds like a hippie and dresses like she practices sustainable farming and yoga at the same time. I won't be surprised if she starts talking about chakras and the power of crystals in the middle of class, but she reminds me of lots of other teachers—quirky, odd, idiosyncratic, but decent and good hearted with the misfortune of dealing with kids like me who would give anything to be somewhere else. In my case, it's my old school I miss, but I can't really hold that against her.

Nothing could have prepared me for my advanced journalism newspaper production class. Ms. Gillis has hair so gingery ginger that I swear she's been using chemicals in the photo lab during each passing period to keep it looking that way. It doesn't even pretend to look natural. Everything about her screams pomp and plastic. Her extra-long nail art is much more dogs playing poker than "Mona Lisa," and anything on her that can be rhinestone-ornamented is. But, hey, if you love a look, rock that look.

Standing outside her classroom door, she's wearing a bedazzled school shirt, a denim skirt and boots even more bedazzled than her shirt but also with fringe. She speaks with a twang that can neutralize lemons, and the way she hugs every boy coming into the room, and there are quite a few of them, gives me the impression that she indulges in everything from cupcakes to compliments. Not knowing whether she will hug a complete stranger and also not wanting a hug from a complete stranger, I sneak in behind her when she breaks free from her spot at the door to hug a girl walking down the hall wearing the same boots.

Inside, the room is an homage to gingerhood. There's a large poster of a frolicking, smiling red bear that reads *Ginger Bear and Grin It*. Another poster with a kind of Powerpuff Girls vibe reads *Gingers Do it Redder*, and there's a life-sized cutout of Tina Louise—Ginger from *Gilligan's Island*. My dad loved that show, said he watched it every day after getting home from elementary school, and Mom got him the complete DVD set for Christmas one year. Behind the teacher's desk stacked with piles and piles of papers, which seems unusual for the first day of school, are two large bulletin boards plastered with picture upon picture of this teacher posed with student after student.

Everyone in the room looks completely comfortable and familiar in the space. They're gathered together in various little clusters around the room. Computers are lined up around three of the walls of the room in a U shape. There aren't any desks, just tables spread across the room that's at least the size of two classrooms. I recognize InDesign open on a couple of computers where someone has started laying out newspaper pages. There's a refrigerator in one corner of the room next to a corkboard wall covered with pushpins and calendar pages. On the opposite side of the room are two more large bulletin boards. One is labeled "Yearbook," the other "Newspaper." Finally, I'm in a place that feels familiar.

"Okay, y'all, pipe down while I call ro-well," her twang long and extended. Murmurs of dissent begin to fill the room. "I know, I know. It's just first day formality. They make us turn in these stupid things for accreditation—accredation... oh, you know, record keeping."

I have known this woman for two sentences and already I want her flogged or water-boarded for crimes against language. Still, she looks like she's probably a lot of fun once you get to know her, which clearly everyone in the room does. Ms. Gillis begins her casual run through the list, saying here to herself even before students can answer. And then comes the obligatory pause on the roll call. Generally, this is reserved for an unusual or ethnic name the teacher can't pronounce, but this time the pause comes at my name, something that has never happened to me before in my life, and I've spent all my school years in foreign countries where my parents were on assignment.

"Ethan Canton?"

"It's Ethan-Matthew."

The Closest Thing to a Normal Life 17

"Your last name isn't Canton?"

"My first name is Ethan-Matthew." *Damn it. Why do I keep doing that?*

"Baby doll, I think you're in the wrong class."

Did she seriously just call me 'baby doll'? "I have it on my schedule and my name's on the roll."

"Yes, I know, baby doll…"

Again with the baby doll?

"Your name is on the ro-well, but I don't ah-low new students in my newspaper production class. You'll have to switch to my introductory journalism class. Honeybun, c'mon up here and I'll write you a pass to the counselor for a schedule change."

Holy shitbombs! Not only is it bad enough that every eye in the room is laser locked on the loser new kid, but this woman has a huge-ass, ear-to-ear smile on her face like she's doing me a huge favor.

"Here you go, sweetie pie. Just take this down to the counselor, and they'll get you all fixed up."

"I'm new. I don't know wh…"

"That's fine, honeybun," she says as she escorts me to the door. "You just go straight down the hallway to the stairs. When you get to the bottom or the stairs, you just go left and you'll see the counselor's office. Second door on the right. Good luck, baby doll."

And just like that, I'm summarily excommunicated from the lofty grandeur of high school newspaper production class. Never mind that my parents had been foreign correspondents, had worked in print, radio and television journalism, were journalism graduates from one of the top journalism schools in the country, and that I was practically raised in the fourth estate and read the Associated Press Style Manual for fun. If I had stayed at my last school, I would have been editor. I can't possibly be in any less need of an introductory journalism class. Part of me wants to just keep walking down the hall to the exit door at the end of the hallway and head back to the house with Grams and Gramps. I can tell them I'm feeling overwhelmed. They'll understand and say I can just try again tomorrow.

But I don't. I decide to stay. Grams and Gramps don't need to feel like their first day of school sendoff is a waste of time.

When I open the door to the counselor's office, the voice I've been playing over in my head since Gear-Up Day rings out to greet me.

"Einstein!"

"CC... um, hi, how are you? What are you doing here? This is the counselor's office, right?" *Geez and shitbombs. Could I be any bigger of a turd splash in front of this girl?*

"You're in the right place. Are you in need of counseling?" CC asks with just the right mix of sincerity and kidding.

Of course, she can't know that I have been seeing a therapist, once a week for the last two months. An honest to goodness, real-life shrink with degrees on the wall and an actual couch in his office. I've only ever sat on the couch, and it's a little weird to think of myself in therapy, but I also don't completely hate it.

"No counseling today. I just need a schedule change."

"Oh, well, sign in and have a seat, but you're out of luck. They don't do schedule changes on the first day. They probably won't do any until next week at the earliest."

"Are you the resident schedule change expert?" I ask, trying to be as chill as possible as she plops down in the waiting room chair next to me.

"As a matter of fact, I am. I basically run this office, and really this whole school by myself."

The woman, sitting behind the desk CC had been leaning on, probably the receptionist for the office, smiles and gives her a little wink, which almost makes it seem like CC is very much at home in this office.

"So, ya gotta just chill in whatever class you're trying to get out of for at least another week."

I explain to CC that it was the other way around. The class is getting rid of me, that after hugging every boy in class except for me like she was their Tía Josefina at the family reunion, Ms. Gillis kicked me out of class for not knowing the secret handshake. Of course, I say it much more diplomatically.

"Dude, Ms. DeSoto has got your back. Just tell her what you want to do, and she'll make it happen."

"And how do you know this, queen of the..."

"Goddess."

"Oh, my bad. And how do you know this Goddess of Schedule Changes?"

"Because she's the cool counselor, and I'll ask her to."

"And she'll do it just because you asked her to?"

"That's right, Einstein." There's that nickname again, which, so far, still seems like a good thing.

"Just like that?"

"Just like that."

"Why?" I ask genuinely curious and wondering if she does actually run the school.

"Because I told you, she's the cool counselor, and she's my mom."

"Oh, so you just hang out here all day?"

"No, I just didn't feel like going to chemistry today, and they can't officially count you absent from class until after you actually show up to class. Besides, today is just all that first school day paperwork and get-to-know-each other games. I've been in class with all these kids since kindergarten, so I'm pretty good there."

I guess that knowing all of your classmates since before you knew how to color inside the lines can be a pretty cool thing, unless you're the new kid moving in right before everyone else is about to move out. When you're that kid, you feel like every bit of the outsider you are.

"Anyway, I've already sat through two perfectly wretched classes already," CC says, her voice suddenly taking on an exaggerated Southern accent, "where the teacher droned on and on with the same first-day school drivel I've heard since God was a boy."

"*Steel Magnolias?*" I asked, already knowing the answer.

"Oh, a southern charmer," she says, "I add a little Blanche Devereaux for extra flavor."

"That's the one from *Golden Girls*—my Grams loves that show," I say.

"My mom and I are huge LTW junkies."

"LTW?"

"Lifetime Television for Women. We're especially drawn to the crazy cheerleader daughter and mom murder movies. We've even imagined acting out several of the plots here at cream cheese high."

"Carmelita Selena DeSoto Cortínez María de la Peña *de las tostadas con chorizo*, don't give away our family secrets to handsome strangers," announces the woman emerging from her office. "Hi, I'm Ms. DeSoto, CC's mom and one of the counselors here."

Ms. DeSoto looks like a slightly older and heavier version of CC. She's a shade darker than CC and a smidge shorter. They share the same smile, hair and, if it weren't so horribly cliché, I can probably get away with the whole is-this-your-older-sister or super-cool-aunt thing, but I've already been more than cheesy enough with CC. I figure it's a pretty familiar story about why they don't have the same last name, but after what I've been through, I'm kind of learning not to assume anything about anyone's family.

"Mom, you have to rescue Einstein.... You're his only hope."

"Okay, Princess CC. Go to class, and I'll see what I can do to..." She reaches for the clipboard where I signed in and reads my name. "...rescue Ethan."

My first thought is, cool mom, followed almost immediately by the instinct to inform her that my full first name is actually Ethan-Matthew, but something kicks in and keeps me from embarrassing myself again in front of CC, who hops to her feet in what feels like a very cheerleaderesque move and pep-steps her way out of the office.

5

Ms. DeSoto is actually really cool. My paperwork isn't in the database yet, so she has the secretary bring in my file. I know the information about my parents has to be in there, but Ms. DeSoto doesn't try to turn me into a lab rat or anything or ask a bunch of probing questions, you know, the cool counselor and mom thing.

"Oh, you moved here from Spain. *Qué suave. Ay cómo me encanta España. Estuve allá durante mi tercer año de universidad.*"

Most people who see me for the first time don't automatically assume I can speak Spanish, at least not in the US. But I guess Ms. DeSoto figures that if I lived in Spain, I could probably understand some Spanish, so I answer her in Spanish.

"*Sí, señora. Viví allí por tres años.*"

"*Muy bien. Entonces vamos a ver lo que está pasando aquí.* So, what's the issue that my daughter wants me to rescue you from?"

I hand Ms. DeSoto the note from Ms. Gillis that simply reads, "Please move student to JI class. Thx." It's punctuated with a little heart smiley face.

I explain that Ms. Gillis told me she doesn't allow new students into her newspaper production class and sent me down for a schedule change. If Ms. DeSoto doesn't want me to see her rolling her eyes, she doesn't hide it very well—or at all. She flips through my file until she comes across my schedule from The American School of Madrid. Now she adds shaking her head to the rolling of eyes.

"Ethan..." There is something motherly in her tone, which makes me feel safe enough to interrupt.

"It's Ethan-Matthew. Ethan-Matthew is my first name. I know it's kinda wei..."

"Ethan-Matthew, we don't do schedule changes during the first week of school, and even if we did, there's no way I'd let anyone put you in the J1 class. Your schedule from your previous school had you enrolled in advanced journalism. Here, we do our best to put you in the class that most closely matches your last schedule, which is the newspaper production class. So, if you want to stay in the class, that's where we will leave you."

Part of me thinks I shouldn't stay in a class where I'm not wanted, but, as weird as it sounds, journalism is the only thing that feels normal to me, so I opt to stay. Ms. DeSoto lets me hang in her office until the end of the period, so I won't have to do the walk of shame back to class or create another scene. I sit in her office as she clickety-clacks an email to Ms. Gillis explaining that the policy of the district is to honor and match schedules from other schools for transfer students. Since my schedule and all my transfer paperwork has an advanced journalism class on it, they have to match it with the newspaper production class. Though I've only just met Ms. DeSoto, judging by how she's shaking her head in a can-you-believe-this-*loca* way, I have a feeling the message she really wants to send goes something like the one I'm composing in my head:

Dear Ms. Gillis,

Regarding Ethan-Matthew Cruz Canton, please put down your scepter, remove your tiara and get over yourself. While you may think the world revolves around you and your class—because why else would you send a student for a schedule change on the first day—it does not. You are lucky to have a student with his talent and work ethic Plus, he's a cutie. We are honoring his schedule from his previous school. Deal with it, *loca*.

Sincerely,
Ms. DeSoto

Gram and Gramps love that I've come home for lunch, but I know they suspect I'm avoiding being the new kid at lunch, but I'm still able to get away with things by playing the orphaned-kid card. Of course, I make it seem like I came home to explain the newspaper production class fiasco, knowing Ms. DeSoto has already taken care of everything.

After convincing Grams she doesn't need to call the principal to complain, I finish lunch and head back for what ends up being a pretty uneventful rest of the first day of school of my senior year.

6

When I head back to newspaper production class on the second day of school of my senior year, I find CC waiting outside the door to the classroom.

"Looked for you at lunch yesterday."

"Yeah, my..." I choose my words carefully here because I really don't want to go into a lengthy explanation of my plight as an outsider. "Um, I met my folks for lunch yesterday."

"Oh, cool. Your pare..."

Had to cut her off. "We live just behind the football stadium, so I just walked over after I finished with your mom."

"Oh, she thinks you are the cutest thing ever. Forget the whole southern charm thing.... You spoke to her in Spanish. She already loves you way more than she loves me. Anyway, I'll meet you right here for lunch."

Before I can muster any kind of excuse to avoid the miasma of high-school lunch, CC's on her way and out of sight. With the tardy bell ringing, I'll have to consider lunch later. Now, I have to contend with the teacher who announced just yesterday to the rest of the class that I don't belong here, but here I am anyway.

The second day of class, and the room already buzzes with energy and familiarity. Everyone zooms around with purpose and the sense that they belong, which they do. I stand lurking in the doorway, even though I know that lurking in doorways is rude. But as the designated interloper, I'm not exactly sure what to do.

Since it seems like Thanksgiving break will come and go while I stand there waiting for Ms. Gillis to notice me and welcome me back to class, I decide to get myself noticed. I reach into my bag and pull out the editorial I started writing after Gear Up Day and walk toward my new journalism teacher.

"Hi, Ms. Gillis, I wrote this editorial I thought we could use in the paper. It's about..."

"Oh, we'll do story assignments later. Uh, I put instructions for your assignment on that computer back there," she says, turning to walk away from me, not even bothering to look at what I wrote. Although I don't think I can feel like more of an outsider, the task she's found for me to do confirms my alien status and ensures she won't have to deal with me until graduation at the earliest.

Archival research is just about as boring as it sounds, even or especially when assigned under the guise of helping me fit in and learn about the traditions at my new school. My assignment: Review the past year's editions of the newspaper (and the yearbook for good measure) and create a spreadsheet of stories written by topic and angle. What editorials have been written over the years? What stances have the editorials taken? What point and counterpoint issues were covered.

I have to review all the different news stories written and create a calendar of recurring school events. I'm also supposed to chronicle topics and trends of feature stories and what human interest stories have been written over the years, as well.

Class drags on. Not a single person in class says a word to me or even walks near my area. The message is clear: We don't need or want anyone new in our lives. I'm sure for most new kids, this would be something really tough to take, but I've already had so much taken from me that a little exile from kids I don't know just means one less thing to hold me here when this school year ends. But damn, these people are committed to ignoring me. I'm sure that by the time the class period ends, a scarlet P for pariah will magically appear on my chest or that Ms. Gillis will remind the class that I have a raging case of not-one-of-us cooties, and everyone will be better off by continuing to ignore me. As loser-ish as it sounds, all I want is for class to end so I can walk to the house and have lunch with Grams and Gramps again. But from what I can tell of her already, CC will be waiting for me right where she said she'd be.

There is an innate sense of time all students have that tells us when class is almost over. Teachers hate it because they are powerless against it. Whether they are speeding through a PowerPoint presentation or juggling chainsaws, students lose all ability to pay attention when class is almost over. It's like our spidey sense. A ripple swims through the room, and we know it's almost time to go and we start the packing up to leave class.

As we start packing up, I catch sight of CC. Through the window of the classroom door, I see her leaning against the wall across from Ms. Gillis' room. Do cheerleaders have special rules for them about coming and going to class? I can't understand how she left me at class right as the tardy bell rang and is now waiting for me before my class even ends. I get lost looking at her, trying to look into her, through her. I am staring at her when the bell rings, and I snap out of the fascination.

I gather up my things and get a parting stank eye from Ms. Gillis as I head out of the room and say to her in the sweetest way possible, "Have a nice day and thanks for all the fish." I'm pretty sure this woman hates me.

CC is already surrounded by a phalanx of other beautiful people. I don't know any of them. It turns out that three of the girls and two of the guys clustered around CC have just been in class with me. It's pretty dickish that a group of kids who only moments ago had ostracized me, like I was the kid who reminded the teacher to give homework over winter break, would soon pretend I mattered because the head cheerleader gives me her seal of approval. The whole thing sucks.

"Einstein," CC calls out to me as I step into the hall. "Let's go, ya'll," she says, hooking her arm around my elbow and leading us out of the building.

Real high schools aren't like the high schools you see on TV and in teen movies. There's rarely just one lunch period and one huge cafeteria where the entire school gathers to eat, with the jocks in one area, the geeks in another, goths and stoners buttressed by cowboys on one side and over-hyped teen girls on the other. No, at Pearl Heights, the cafeteria and outside eating areas are relegated mostly to freshman and sophomores, because juniors and seniors can leave campus for lunch. I still would rather walk to my grandparents' house, but it's not an option today.

If I could have faked an emergency at home, I would have, but day two of school family emergencies are extremely rare and would raise more questions than it would save me from. I suck it up and go to lunch with the beyond-pretty girl and her cast of stock characters. But this whole situation bothers me. Not bothers like the idiots who wonder why there isn't a White history month or a White Miss America pageant but bothered at how someone can so effortlessly float between people like me and the people who effortlessly ignore people like me.

When you have an entire class period to do nothing but flip through past issues of a subpar high school newspaper, doing an assignment you know is nothing but busy work, you have time to mull over all the perplexities of life. Things like becoming an orphan and wondering why the girl who seemingly has everything high school has to offer and who you only met in passing a few days ago has taken such an interest in you.

Granted, my experience in American public schools is non-existent. Still, nowhere in the world do girls like CC show interest in the skinny new guy unless:

- The skinny new guy has cancer and just moved into the house next door to the hot cheerleader who increases her already boundless popularity by pulling off an epic end-of-life celebration for the cancer kid no one would have known about if not for her.
- The skinny new guy is part of a nefarious ruse to befriend him, and then, in a meticulously orchestrated scheme, his future is destroyed by the hot but really mean cheerleader who leaves him tied to a flagpole in his underwear.
- The skinny new guy is being used by the hot cheerleader to teach her asshole quarterback boyfriend to appreciate her, which leads to said boyfriend pummeling skinny new guy and leaving him tied to a flagpole in his underwear.
- The skinny new guy has the perfect antibodies for a cure in him to end the zombie apocalypse and is left by the hot cheerleader tied to a flagpole in his underwear as a sacrifice for all of humanity.

It's pretty sad that cancer boy is the only scenario where skinny new guy doesn't end up tied to a flagpole in his underwear, but these are the realities of life. And then an even scarier reality hits me, aside from worrying I may have cancer. I am hoping we get nowhere near any flagpoles because in my haste to figure out my new routine and make it to cross country practice on time this morning, I forgot to pack underwear for after practice. This was not an issue when I thought I'd be going back to the house for lunch again, but now I have super-hot cheerleader girl draped on my arm, and I'm riding commando.

These situations never end well. But as we make our way to the parking lot and past the flagpole, where I audibly gulp, things feel remarkably normal. To her credit, CC gives no indication that she knows anything about three-fourths of the group completely ostracizing me for the previous 53 minutes. No, she acts like I belong, like I have never not belonged.

Normally, on a second day at a new school, a more intimate lunch group would seem preferable, but hopefully lunch with CC's entourage will keep the focus off me. I'll get to mostly listen, feign interest and nod a lot. Really, I don't expect a single person in this group will want to ask anything about me, which is exactly what I want.

But that's not CC's plan. Damn this girl.

The kids from the newspaper class climb into one vehicle while CC and I, along with a guy I finally recognize from cross country and another girl load into CC's 2005 Toyota 4 Runner. I'm a little surprised when we pull into the parking lot of a grocery store, but once we go inside, everything makes sense. The delicatessen in the store looks like a small village unto itself. Kids scatter to different areas of the deli and gather back at tables with everything from sushi to corn dogs. I end up choosing lunch from the mac & cheese bar. A freaking mac & cheese bar—how awesome is that? I build my entree from the mac & cheese bar with sun-dried tomatoes, bacon, chorizo and shallots. I thought $8.95 was a little steep for mac & cheese, but the mac & cheese bar was really cool.

"Y'all, this is Einstein," CC announces as we settle at tables. "His real name is Ethan-Matthew and then about seven other names after that, but I just call him Einstein. He's new."

There are a few head nods, a little wave here and there, and then everyone drifts off into their little groups. I'm mostly invisible once again, and for a moment I think about stirring up the lunch waters by climbing on the table to say, "I live with my grandparents because I became an orphan in one fell swoop. The five of you completely ignored me in class. I'm not wearing any underwear, and my grandparents think I have a large penis."

But I don't. I sit back listening, observing and taking mental notes. The conversations are mostly about class schedules, who has whom for what and when. They cannot believe the expectations from teachers and utter lots of who-do-they-think-they-are questions. There's a buzz about the hot new physics teacher and jokes about changing schedules to get into his class. One of the girls pulls out her phone to show the picture of his ass that she took. I don't mention he's the teacher I have for physics. There's talk about Friday's game. Like real football talk about offensive lines, passing and rushing yards, four- and five-star recruits. I learn it's a non-district game against a much larger school from a division up. Supposedly, this year's team is really good, and there's talk about how far the team will make it into playoffs. Most of the girls in the lunch group are cheerleaders with CC, and the two of the guys from newspaper class play football. So, if I don't already feel out of place enough, I soon discover that I'm the only one in the group who knows almost nothing about football.

Lunch seems to drag along as slowly as newspaper class, and I can't pretend to be distracted any longer by eating because I've finished my mac & cheese. As I scrape my spork across the bottom of my food boat, I come to the realization that if I were any other person in the group, I would be annoyed by me. I wasn't participating in conversations. I wanted to be anywhere else, and it showed. I wasn't making any more of an effort than any of them extended to me. I looked and acted uncomfortable, which generally makes those around you feel uncomfortable. I have no southern charm.

In my defense, I thought I was eating lunch with CC but ended up in a huddled mass of cool people who all knew each other. Plus, no kidding aside, I am still new to the orphan thing, and I'm not wearing any underwear. Apparently from my therapy sessions, I use humor as a defense mechanism. I think maybe I'm just anti-underwear.

Thankfully, lunch ends without incident or me getting tied to a flagpole when we get back to school. Day two of school comes to another uneventful ending, and I get another day closer to making it through the school year with my head down and just surviving.

On Wednesday, I manage to avoid the lunch entourage with what I hope is a convincing and not rude excuse. I pretend I need to do research for an upcoming scholarship essay. Thank God for librarians who stay open during lunch. I never really used the library at my old school, but when I needed a place to escape to because I had nowhere else to go, I discovered that librarians don't actually run around shushing people, and libraries, at lunch, are a haven for all manner of high school orphans. Maybe I can spend lunch in here for the rest of the year.

7

Grams and Gramps have clearly done the parenting thing before and know the first week of school is going way worse than any of us have anticipated. The journalism thing, my monosyllabic answers to how was your day today and coming home and closing myself off in Dad's room, plus catching me openly sobbing multiple times, prompts them to move my appointment up by a day with Dr. Robles. They pick me up for lunch on Thursday, which gets me away from the lunch entourage for yet another day and gets me out of school for the rest of the day.

Dr. Robles thinks Ms. Gillis is a real piece of work, which he says is his clinical diagnosis. He speculates she wasn't very popular in high school and is now reliving high school vicariously through her students. We talk about CC. He understands my reservations about being tied to a flagpole in my underwear but doesn't think CC is the type. He thinks it'll be a good idea to pack my school bags the night before and suggests packing extra underwear.

I really do like Dr. Robles. He's really easy to talk to, which makes sense in his line of work, but he also doesn't let me off easy. He encourages me to not push people away, including Grams and Gramps. Honestly, I can't really conceive how my plan to ghost my entire senior year would've worked, and now I'm willing to give school my best effort. I mean, I'm only going to be at this school for a year. Surely, I can simply go to class, keep my mouth shut, fly completely under the radar, graduate and then move away like Dad did. Yeah, he kept his connection to Grams and Gramps, but he wasn't tethered to this community the way everyone else seems to be.

The logical, normal—I know Dr. Robles doesn't like that word "normal," but what the hell... the normal side of me knows my plan can never work. Keeping the southern charmer side of me suppressed feels like I'm focusing all my mutant powers on maintaining a human form that will let me blend in with the rest of society but means I'll appear catatonic to everyone around me. I'm pretty sure that's what made Grams and Gramps move up the appointment. I had started off the week pretty convinced it would be no big deal, but by Wednesday I'm actually looking like the zombie. I like that Dr. Robles chooses not to put me on any kind of medication, but he says it's an option if I need it. I know I can't realistically quarantine myself from people for the entire school year, but I also don't want to be anyone's pity friend or the source of everyone's gossip or their freak connection. When you're the person to whom the weird or tragic thing happens, everyone tries to bogart a connection to you. I can hear them gossiping:

"Yeah, I know him. We're good friends. He sits three rows over and two seats up from me in English."

"Oh, yeah, that guy. He walks by my math class every day, and I sit by the door, so we're tight."

"Yes, it's really sad. I saw him once. He was tied to the flagpole in his underwear."

And what's worse, I have to go and meet a girl determined to usher me into her world where people socialize, eat together and attend events. And she's also confused me because she seems so different from the people, she keeps trying to put me in contact with.

I tell Dr. Robles that none of the kids from the journalism class has even said hello to me before shuffling off to lunch with me and that they really don't talk to me in class after that either. He asks me if I've said hello to any of them or tried to talk to them after that lunch outing. Touché, Dr. Robles, touché.

"Ethan-Matthew, losing your parents..." Dr. Robles begins saying.

"'Losing your parents' is a really fucked up thing to say," I retort a bit more aggressively than I mean to. "They're not lost. It's not like I'm going to suddenly find them or something. They're dead. They fucking died on me."

"You pissed off at them for that?"

"No... no, I mean it wasn't their fault."

"Doesn't mean you can't be pissed at them."

"I don't want to be pissed at them. It's not their fault."

"It's not your fault either."

"I know that."

"Do you?"

"Yes, geez, what the hell. I didn't do anything."

"Then, when are you going to stop punishing yourself? You're not a bad kid for wanting to feel happy again. Your parents would want you to be happy, to enjoy your life."

Of course, I know this. Of course, this makes sense. But knowing something is often not enough. The things that make me happy are the things I can't wait to tell my parents about, and then they would tell Grams and Gramps. And now I am worried about disappointing them. Grams and Gramps no longer have the privilege of just getting to enjoy my accomplishments. I've never been a bad kid, but I'm still a kid who forgets to clean his room, who has snuck vodka out of the liquor cabinet and got into a shoving match with Robby Márquez back in Spain when he called me and my parents *basura americana* that spoke Spanish like *campesinos mexi-*

canos. Nothing major, but now that's the kind of shit Grams and Gramps will have to deal with... like getting sent to the counselors' office on the first day of school.

Dr. Robles assures me that my grandparents are well aware of what they signed up for.

He ends the session by giving me an assignment for next time: "Make your presence known to others around you. Surely, in the two weeks before our next appointment, you can pass the salt to someone at lunch, strike up a conversation at practice or ask someone in journalism class if they know Ms. Gillis is the worst ever."

8

By the time cross country practice ends on Friday morning and the school day starts, I'm not sure what planet I've crash-landed on, let alone what high school I go to. When they tell you high school football in Texas is a religion, they mean it.

Game night begins long before night even thinks about showing up. For a non-district game that matters only slightly more than an intra-squad scrimmage, the hoopla surrounding the game feels over the top. Aside from shortened class periods to make room for a mid-morning pep rally, teachers parade around campus in the jerseys of varsity team members. It's how you know who the cool teachers are because each varsity team member hand-picks a teacher to sport his jersey for the day. My skepticism radar is pinging like crazy about this tradition, questioning just what certain teachers did to have players asking them to wear their jerseys. The other thing I'm trying to figure out is why there are so many random adults wandering all over campus.

Half the random male strangers are wearing Wrangler jeans and boots, and the other half are in khakis and golf shirts. The women are also divided by their uniforms. There's the flock who look like they own stock in a sun dress and sparkly sandal company. Another group clomps around in white jeans, wedge shoes and blouses with all manner of arm cut-outs. And the rest meander about in power suits with incredibly high heels. The hallways look like a fashion runway.

It turns out that all these strange adults scurrying around are alums, former players and parents of players and cheerleaders. It's part of a first-game tradition that's been going on for decades. If you're connected to the football team in any way and you can make it to campus for the first game, you're welcomed on campus like Roman soldiers returning from conquering the free world. All of this for a no-stakes practice game.

Before I can jot down any of these random thoughts for a column, I have to shake my head and marvel at the next example of alien culture literally parading down the hallway. Everyone knows second period has officially ended by the sound of the drumline thundering on all manner of percussive instruments as they march through the halls rocking, swaying and banging out cadences. And like rats following pied percussionists, we all fall in line behind them on the way to the gym.

If someone would call the fire marshal, the entire pep rally would be shut down for exceeding occupancy levels, except that I figure the fire marshal is probably already here, because the opening rally cry is given by the speaker of the Texas House of Representatives, whose daughter, I have found out, is one of my fellow seniors.

Everything about this morning is foreign to me. In my last school we had tennis, fencing, gymnastics, *fútbol*, water polo, swimming and cross country. We had larger audiences at recitals and debates than at any athletic competition. But this morning has one thing going for it, something that makes squeezing into the bleachers in the gym like coupon holders vying for a $10 flat screen TV on Black Friday: CC.

Damn, I feel like such a cliché sitting here in what undoubtedly is the underclassmen side of the gym, making puppy-dog eyes at the head cheerleader. But I don't care. I don't care how lame I look, looking at her. I don't care that I never really understood or cared for the cheerleader thing before. I can tell there is way more to CC. Plus, anyone who can back flip and twist with reckless abandon as she soars down from the top of a multi-person pyramid deserves admiration.

The show is just that—a show. There are skits, speeches, video montages, band performances, dance-team performances and, of course, cheerleading. The entire morning plays out like a cheesy teen movie, one where the skinny new guy has to sit with his three-ring binder over his lap while a halo of golden light bathes the head cheerleader as she herkies, high kicks and head bobs in choreographed slow motion.

Then the pep rally comes to an end in the booming kind of chant you only hear at cult meetings or world cup soccer. Everyone, and I mean everyone, joins in this chant that bounces off the rafters and reverberates all around the gym:

Woof, woof, rah!
Woof, woof, rah!
Rah, rah, rah, rah!
Woof, woof, rah!
Woof!

As the crowd migrates out of the gym, pushing me along in its wake, I keep turning back to the gym floor, hoping for one more glance at CC, hoping she sees me and acknowledges my presence. Holy shitbombs, I am literally embarrassed by me at this moment. The only meaningful relationships in my life are with my grandparents, my therapist and a journalism teacher who hates that she can't kick me out of her class. Only one person at this school has had any kind of real conversation with me, and I'm thinking of ruining the chance of having a real friendship because I've gone all sappy for a girl who did nothing more than not dismiss me in the community my dad grew up in, where dismissing people, especially interlopers like me, is a varsity sport.

9

My grandparents living right behind the football stadium, I assume, they would be content to listen to this unimportant game from the comfort of their backyard, feet dangling in the pool and able to go to the bathroom far from the presence of strangers. I'm wrong.

After informing me that we'll be going to the game tonight, Grams and Gramps come out wearing matching Pearl Heights spirit shirts and present me with my very own stadium chair to match theirs. Holy shitbombs, I know they like football, but my grandparents are big-ass Friday night football junkies.

As we make our way to the stadium, Grams and Gramps are met with waves, hugs and air kisses blown from afar. Every few feet they're met by one boisterous greeting after another. Because I consider myself a budding journalist, I hang back and watch it all unfold, making myself inconspicuous, the objective reporter. But, damn, I'm completely gob smacked by how popular my grandparents are. They're freakin' celebrities as they stop at each of the fundraising tables set up under the stadium bleachers, where pom poms and noisemakers and programs are for sale by everyone from the French Club to the Young Democrats. Parents peddle spirit buttons and T-shirts, and Grams and Gramps are treated with reverence and delight as they stop at each table.

Things don't change once we enter the stadium as people of all ages call and wave to them. I should have followed their suggestion that I go to the student section, but since I don't know anyone, I opt to sit with my grandparents at my first-ever high school football game.

They have seats in the reserved section, where the hoopla is definitely a bonus for an observer of life.

"This is our grandson."

"Meet our grandson."

"Is this your grandson?"

Lots of ear-to-ear smiling at me, handshakes, pats on the back. Someone even pinches my cheek. How embarrassing is that? Plenty of people ask if I know their son, daughter, grandchild from school. I feign interest as they feed me the highlight reel of their above-average child. I smile, explain that I'm new and say I hope to meet their child soon.

Tonight is definitely the stuff of Texas Friday night lore. As the stadium fills with families and fans of all ages, the budding journalist in me can't help but enjoy the spectacle. Just to the left of the end zone, near the entrance to the locker room, an inflatable helmet the size of a pretentious RV comes to life for the team to run through in hallowed reverence. A cadre of football dads stakes the inflatable helmet to the ground and arranges smoke machines on both sides of the helmet while a phalanx of football moms marches in front of the helmet with massive cut-outs of their football players' heads affixed to wooden stakes like extra fancy picket signs. On the surface, it's cute in a kind of creepy disembodied head sort of way. Still, it feels good to see Grams and Gramps as the center of attention, but this just isn't my thing. I figure I can come up with a way to avoid joining them for other games.

Just then, amid a flourish of cheers and round-off back handsprings, CC and the rest of the cheerleaders bound into the stadium. Then, the real fun starts.

The Closest Thing to a Normal Life

A voice filled with enough Texas drawl to blanket the entire state booms from the speakers with enough timbre to make the WWE blush: "It's Fri-i-i-i-i-i-da-a-a-a-ay Night! Let's play some f-o-o-o-o-tb-a-a-a-all!" Brick Tyler (his actual name), the voice of Big Blue Lacy football (I've learned our mascot, the Blue Lacy, is the state dog of Texas), takes us through the typical Friday night liturgy of prayers, pledges and patriotism that ends with the band playing the national anthem. There's a coin toss, the playing of each team's school song and the greeting of luminaries: the principal of our school, the superintendent, members of the board of trustees, and then... holy shitbombs, my freakin' grandparents!

"Ladies and gentlemen, please direct your attention to the reserved section and give a Big Blue Lacy welcome to Honey and Huck Canton. Honey and Huck, stand up and give the folks a wave."

All of my budding journalistic sensibilities fail me as the spotlight of Grams' and Gramps' local celebrity floods over me. For all my powers of observation, I've missed any hint of what's going on. Clapping, whistling and woo-hooing reverberates throughout the stadium.

Brick continues: "Honey and Huck Canton, our biggest and bluest Blue Lacy fans haven't missed a home game since 1983, when their son Sawyer Tripp Canton III made the varsity team as a freshman. Today we celebrate the life of Tripp Canton and his wife Marisol who lost their lives in the May 18th, 2016, bombing attack at the Foreign Press Agency where they both worked as news correspondents. To Honey, Huck, and their grandson Ethan, who is here with us tonight as one of the newest members of the Pearl Heights senior class, we offer our deepest sympathies. Please stand and remove your hats as we observe a moment of silence for one of our most outstanding alums and for two of our most loyal Big Blue Lacy football boosters."

It's Ethan-Matthew races through my mind as I try to take in everything that's happening while not looking like an ungrateful dick for being annoyed by the attention. Damn, I've just been outed as an orphan kid over the public address system at my very first Texas football game. Is CC staring at me from her cheer spot on the sideline? Of course, she is—everyone is. I feel pairs of eyes on me from all around, blinking out sympathy and curiosity. I have officially become a freak show.

As soon as the moment of silence ends, my moment in the spotlight begins. Pats on the shoulders resume with the addition of you-poor-thing condolences ping-ponging all around me. I smile, nod and repeat over and again, "Thank you," "You're too kind" and "I appreciate that." No one asks for the gory details, and gory they were—a C-4 bomb makes for soul-crushing devastation—but I know they want to ask.

Thank God for kick-off and a huge return that leads to a Big Blue touchdown four plays later. Part of me wants to be mad at Grams and Gramps. It felt like a pretty shitty thing to do to parade my misery in front of strangers and one hot cheerleader in particular, but watching them in their element, watching them hob knob like A-listers on the red carpet, and remembering Dad was their only son slightly erodes any righteous indignation I'm trying hang on to. Still, I am pissed and tired of the pitiful stares and cheap sympathy for my parents, but when Gramps and I go down to the concession stand for a sausage wrapped in a tortilla and nachos, he explains that they only expected to be recognized for their Big Blue Lacy Loyalty, something that has happened on numerous other occasions. The moment of silence surprised them, but he reminds me that in Pearl Heights, everyone knows everyone else's business, and it would have eventually all come out anyway. Perfect for a budding journalist, not so much for an outed orphan.

10

Showing up at school on a Saturday at 5:45 in the morning for a cross country meet ranks right up there with turn your head and cough, but it kept me from enduring pity stares for the rest of the football game because I got to leave at half-time. Besides, I hear the guys at cross country practice saying that when Coach Barajas says the bus leaves at 6, no exceptions, he means 5:59.

Maybe I'll get lucky and none of the team will have gone to the football game last night, but, from the size of the student section, I figure I won't be that lucky.

It turns out I have nothing to worry about. There is no time for idle chit chat because Coach Barajas has a meticulous pre-meet check list with tasks for everyone. Onto the bus, we load folding tables, boxes and bags of snacks, a trainer's medical kit, ice chests, a canopy, tarps for the ground and a banner with the school logo. There are also checklists and a backup list with each runner's name. If I didn't know and already like Coach B, I would have suspected him as the type who spends his weekends feeding his cats and alphabetizing his pantry.

The best gift of the morning is the morning itself. No big surprise, but 6 a.m. Saturdays and high schoolers don't mix. Before the bus even makes it out of the parking lot at 5:59, earbuds are firmly lodged into ears, and the beauty of being young, and able to sleep in any position under any conditions means my teammates are more interested in sleeping than grilling the newly unmasked orphan for details.

Cross country meets are like renaissance fairs without the medieval costumes and axe throwing. Canopies populate every open space of the venue, and kids mill about as they wait for their races to be called.

The junior varsity girls run first, followed by the varsity girls. The general sense around cross-country meets is probably the most chill of any athletic competition I've ever witnessed. Everyone cheers for everyone regardless of team. When the last few JV runners cross the line, they are met with rounds of cheer and celebration. But mostly everyone is waiting for the main event of the morning: the varsity girls' heat.

By the way everyone not running in the varsity girls' heat clusters to watch the race begin, it's clear something special is about to happen. Victoria Pusateri is a junior who won every cross country meet last year and finished second at the state meet in a near photo finish on a mud-soaked course. Everyone wants to see Victoria run.

As I take my place on the side of the course with everyone else, I pull my journal from my drawstring backpack and can't help but write the lead for the newspaper story of the meet.

> With the temperature pushing nearly 85° at 8:30 in the morning (note to self—double check the temperature) nothing could match the heat of determination burning in Victoria Pusateri's eyes as she waits for the gun to sound for her first step toward a state cross country championship.
>
> Or maybe...

The Closest Thing to a Normal Life   47

Jockeying for position, runners to the right and left of junior Victoria Pusateri cast furtive glances at the toughest competition they will face all year. Sure, they hope they can beat her, but they are probably better off calculating which of them has a better chance at second place.

Of course, I have no assignment to cover the race or cover anything. I have no assignments at all in advanced journalism class other than cataloging and spreadsheeting old news. I also can't help noticing that no Pearl Heights reporter or photog is at the meet, which doesn't surprise me. As archivist-in-chief, I've seen the paltry number of column inches cross country has gotten in past newspapers and yearbooks. When Victoria finished second at state, the only mention in the paper was a picture submitted by Coach B and a caption. While looking through the yearbook from last year, I noticed that the cross country spread in the yearbook was one large team photo and three pictures from practice.

If I wasn't already pissed off by the shafting of the cross-country team in the newspapers and yearbooks, after watching Victoria's race, I'm ready to go ballistic. Maybe I would go with the second lead and add the line:

Turns out it was almost two full minutes. Pusateri finished her three miles with a time of 17:11.66. Second place clocked it at 19:10.65.

I have to finish my imaginary sports story later. My race, JV boys, is next. Initially I was kind of pissed but more embarrassed that I was running JV as a senior, but Coach B used meet times to determine who ran varsity each week, and I had no times to qualify me and only a week of practice. So I cluster with the other Blue Lacy JV boys, mostly freshmen and sophomores, a smattering of juniors, and me, the lone senior. Holy shitbombs, was I ever as young as these freshmen? At least three of them look like they are 10 years old. One looks eight.

Clad in tiny running shorts and tank top, I realize how self-conscious I am about armpit hair as I tower over this herd of prepubescent munchkins. As we spread out in a line of other guys clad in equally short shorts, I replay Coach B's race strategy. He said not to go out too fast and to hang close with the leaders before making a break from the pack in the last half-mile.

Good plan, but I ignore it.

When the gun goes off, something in me goes off. I've already heard the gun twice this morning, but something about this time makes it different. Maybe it's the proximity. Maybe it's proximity mixed with nerves, but when the gun goes off, everything comes flooding back to me. I wasn't there when it happened, but I've seen the footage. I've heard the sound of the bombs going off in the newsroom, the shattering of glass, the screams, the sirens. By the time our neighbors picked me up from school and I convinced them to take me to the office building, the smoke was still billowing out in swirling clouds laced with misery, morbidity and the acrid smell of hate. I wondered if my parents had tried to run when they heard the bombs. I wondered as reporters if they ran toward the explosion. I wondered if they had run fast enough, would they still be alive. I wondered if they had tried to run to each other.

So, I take off. I run as if running faster can change something. I run like I have nothing to lose because I've already lost everything. No race strategy, just pure rage. Rage because someone stole the two best people in the world from me. Rage because the life I loved is no more. Rage because I have no friends, because I walk the halls of my school staring at the floor, a stranger to everyone and everything around me. Rage at being relegated to the corner of a room to do a made-up job because my parents had the fucking misfortune of being killed. Rage at having the contents of my totally undeserved misfortune of a life broadcast to a stadium of strangers.

I run until I think my heart will explode, until I think my legs will crumble underneath me, until I see Coach B flagging me down to stop, my varsity teammates feet behind him, hands raised in celebration of the new guy. Dripping in sweat from every pore of my body, I can feel rivers of sweat flowing from places I didn't know I could sweat. I walk in a big looping circle, both hands on my head, trying to catch my breath, my lungs burning less from rage and more from victory.

With my legs and lungs returning to some form of normalcy, the Blue Lacy guys preparing to run the varsity heat began swarming to congratulate me like they have known me all my life. Hell, next thing I know is someone is picking me up in the best version of a bear hug.

"Dude, that was awesome!" says my bear hugger, who I now recognize as the cross-country kid in CC's entourage.

When he puts me down, I see he's a bit taller than me, but we're roughly the same build, which makes me extra thankful and surprised that he didn't drop me. I'm not quite sure of his name—Reeves or Reese—but I don't much care because someone is finally talking to me by choice.

"Seriously, that was awesome. In a district meet, your time wouldn't count because you're a senior, but you're running varsity next week. Really, that was killer."

Coach confirms that my time won't count in districts, but I still won the whole damn thing, and the varsity guys think I can compete with them. I may not want to admit it—after all my goal was to get in and get out of this school year relatively unnoticed—I'm starting to feel a little something someone might loosely describe as school spirit.

"Hey, Dude," Reeves or Reese says, "gotta jet. I'll catch you after."

And he's gone. I figure he probably doesn't remember my name either, but again, someone is talking to me.

Most of the JV guys have finished the race by now, so with my newly earned stud status, I head to our team area, where there's water, orange slices, bagels, bananas and, most importantly at this point, shade. When I get there, I find way more than I expect. Waiting under the shade of the Blue Lacy's canopy are Grams, Gramps and, holy shitbombs, CC!

"Hi, sweetie," Grams says as she walks up to hug me and kiss me on the cheek.

"I'm kinda gross and sweaty, Grams."

"Oh, I don't mind. We're so proud of you. My goodness, you won the race."

"You saw it?"

"Of course, we did," Gramps chimes in. "CC was our race guide. She took us to all the best places to watch the race."

This, of course, is a cross-country thing. As runners pass one area, the crowd then takes off and crosses over to the next turn to cheer on the runners. As runners pass that area, the crowd then moves on to the next area until they end up at the finish line.

"I can't believe you didn't tell me Grandma Honey and Mr. Huck are your grandparents," CC says.

"I didn't know you knew my grandparents. Grams, Gramps, something you want to tell me?"

"Your grandparents are PH legends. They are the biggest Big Blues. We take a team picture with them every year. Lots of teams do," CC explains like this is the most normal thing ever.

"We'll show you the album when we get home," Gramps says.

"Sweetie, you did so great today. Your dad was a pretty fast runner back in the day, but I don't think he could have kept up with you," Grams says.

Did someone order a side of awkward? Part of me wants to look right at CC to read her face, to try and figure out what she must be thinking, wondering about me. I hope she's here with my grandparents because she wants the lowdown on the real-life me. I just look down at my feet. Sometimes, I actually forget I'm not like every other kid sitting in class, that I'm not just any senior excited and nervous about graduation and wondering where I will end up for college.

I don't want to weird anyone out, so I look up and plant a kiss on Grams's cheek, remembering what Dr. Robles said about them grieving, too. Remembering that even though they are proud of me, this has to be really difficult for them, too.

"Thanks for coming to watch. You guys are the best."

"We're going on a Costco run.... We forgot what it's like having a hungry teenager in the house. Any requests? Pop Tarts and Hot Tamales are already on the list," Grams says.

"I'm good. All my major food groups covered."

"You good on underwear," Gramps asks, a little too much of a mischievous glint in his eyes. Note to self, don't tell Gramps about absurd fears of getting tied to a flagpole in your underwear.

My cheeks flush a little because now it's CC looking down. I aggressively whisper, "I'm not wearing Costco underwear."

"Okay, okay. We'll see you at home later... but underwear in bulk is a good deal."

I give them parting hugs and watch as they march holding hands across the field to their car, which is when I remember

CC and my teammates are all there under the canopy with me. Not at all awkward. Not at all!

Grow some balls, Ethan-Matthew. Ask her, I think to myself. "You wanna go watch the men's varsity race?"

"Yeah, let's go. I know all those guys."

"Oh, okay." Cue the budding journalist in me, along with the slightly jealous teenage boy. "Did you come to watch anyone in particular?" *Smooth, Ethan-Matthew, smooth.*

"Sure did," and off she pep-steps from the canopy toward the starting line.

Smooth, CC, smooth.

Damn this girl.

11

Once the buses make it back to school, Coach B's unloading routine takes a twist, and all the unloading falls to the freshmen. Normally, I am quite the social justice warrior, a bleeding heart who looks out for the little guy, but with my legs still burning from my rage running, I take great comfort in the perks of being an upperclassman. I never found out who CC was there to watch, but she was right about knowing the team. She was like everyone's best friend, kind of like one of the guys.

I did find out the name of my bear hugger, Reid Tibbitts, who finished sixth overall in the varsity heat, which helped the varsity boys finish second overall. Not a bad day for the Big Blue cross-country team. Varsity girls finished first, varsity boys second, JV boys first, and JV girls third. I definitely have to see if I can get something about it in the school paper.

On the bus ride home, Reid becomes my new seatmate. He's a junior who barely missed qualifying for the state meet, has a thing for hiking and has known CC since they got put into the same second-grade class. He tells me how they were practically inseparable until freshman year, when their friend group had a little upheaval because Liam and Sutton broke up and all the kids in the group had to pick sides, like friends of parents who divorce. Since Reid and Liam were tight and Sutton and CC were tight, they split into different lunch groups but texted each other all day long. They'd hang out when they could at school, but as they got older, their schedules and activities worked against them. They still manage to hang out every chance they get but don't feel like they have to be together all the time. Besides, he and CC are kind of a friend-group free agents who rotate to eat lunch with different groups. Reid says he and CC had an epic Snapchat streak going that ended recently when something came up. He didn't say what the something was, but I figured a lover's spat, which makes me feel bad for liking Reid and jealous of him at the same time. If I were a little more sneaky, I'd start a scheme to bring him down right then, but I finally have another person talking to me who isn't an adult or paid to talk to me.

By the time the bus is unloaded, and we get the all-clear to leave from Coach B, I feel like most of Saturday is already history. While most kids spend the first weekend of a new school year chilling with friends and trying to hang on to summer for just a while longer until the reality of a new school year finally slaps you out of vacay mode, I have other plans: research.

I don't have anything else to do, anyway. I have no schoolwork to do, no newspaper assignments, no friends to chill with, no car or a Texas driver's license, so research on a Saturday afternoon it is. Not quite a seventeen-year-old boy's dream, but I have questions.

In the hallway adjacent to the front office of Pearl Heights High School, the walls are lined with panoramic pictures of every senior class in the history of the school. I find my dad's class, I find Grams' and Gramps' classes. On the day of the pep rally, when all those random adults were wandering the campus, I had found myself in front of the panoramic wall staring at faces, wondering what their lives were, what they still are, when a man, thirtyish, tall and hanging on to his athletic past, stopped to peruse with me.

"That's my dad," he said, pointing to one of the portraits on the wall. "There's my mom, my granddad on my dad's side, and there's my mom's dad. That's my grandmother and my wife's grandmother. They roomed together in college and were in the same sorority. My older brother there, and that's me right there."

"My dad's right there," I said and pointed to Dad's picture. The man leaned in for a close look.

"You look just like him. When's your picture going up on the wall?"

"I guess this year. I'm a senior."

"Congratulations. Have a good senior year," the man said and then walked off.

This place confounds me. On the first day of school, in my English class, a kid was telling about breaking his arm at recess in the third grade. As he began recounting details of the event, one of the girls in class began correcting details in his story. Several other students in class chimed in to support her corrections. These kids have been in school together for years. They all know each other. They have all known each other for years. Generations of families have carried on the tradition of school at Pearl Heights.

Not my dad. Dad left this community. Dad didn't raise me here. Did he not want me to grow up where he grew up? Why did he barely talk to me about this place? Everything I know about his past here came from conversations overheard and random questions over the years. How did I not ever hear about his parents never missing a home football game? What would he think about me being at the school he seems to have wanted to forget?

Budding journalists seek answers. Sons trying to understand their fathers seek answers, too. That's why I'm going to research this Pearl Heights to find out why the tradition was supposed to end with Dad.

When you're seventeen with no car and no license, the best thing about research is that you can do it with an iPad and a chilled Topo Chico in the pool at your grandparent's house.

I know the basics about Pearl Heights, that it's a small town within the larger city of San Antonio. Some parts of Pearl Heights are officially Pearl Heights, Texas, while other parts are zoned for the Pearl Heights school district but technically have a San Antonio address. The distinction seems minor. If you go to school in the district, you're Pearlies, which is what people outside of Pearl Heights often call people from Pearl Heights.

Scrolling and clicking around the interwebs, I read about how Pearl Heights, the city, has been around for over a hundred years. It was spurred on by a wealthy brewery owner when the rich and elite moved north of downtown and formed their own community, which grew and perpetuated itself over the years.

Way back in the 1800s, Angus Perls, the son of German immigrants, whose name was written as Pearl when the family first immigrated, would go on to found and open Pearl Stables and Brewery. It turns out, you can make money, lots of money, off the vices of others, which is how Angus Pearl became one of the area's earliest millionaires. As the fledgling city of San Antonio continued to experience flooding from the San Antonio River, Angus Pearl and other families of wealth relocated to higher ground. Pearl eventually sold his grand home and 300 acres of land to the Order of Sisters of Charitable Graces to open a university with the promise that they would preserve his home and maintain the natural beauty of the area. Pearl built a new home and continued to develop more of the land attracting other wealthy families to expand the area into a residential community that became the destination for the burgeoning wealthy class in San Antonio.

Eventually, the city of San Antonio attempted to annex the area to increase its tax base, but the residents of Pearl Heights fought the city's intrusion. It became a municipality that enforced deed restrictions limiting the size and scope of businesses that could develop in the community and required residential building and expansion to preserve the natural beauty of the area and community intimacy. I remember Grams and Gramps driving me around when I'd come to visit and point out all the historic homes in the area. They would discuss the craftsmanship of the homes and tell me about how contractors used the natural stone excavated from the quarry in the area to build those homes.

From what I can tell reviewing records online, the children from wealthy families married the children from other wealthy families and had homes built in Pearl Heights. Generations of families, my family included, call Pearl Heights home and also alma mater.

As the area expanded and families grew, the need for a school followed. A one-room schoolhouse was founded in 1905. Within a few years, the school expanded to eight rooms, until they broke ground on the first high school in 1915. In the early days, the sports teams, all men's teams, competed as the Hill Men, an homage to the higher ground they had moved to when they established their community. It occurs to me that they might have changed the mascot when women's teams began competing for the school, but it turns out that when a Pearl Heights alum, Carter Tibbits, was elected as Texas State Speaker of the House, he drafted a resolution to honor the Blue Lacy as the state dog of Texas. Naturally, his alma mater followed in his fervor and changed the school's mascot to the Blue Lacy.

    In two and half hours of clicking and scrolling, I learn so much about Pearl Heights that I could volunteer as a docent in city hall. However, I don't understand it any better, and I'm not sure I ever will.

12

Seventeen-year-old boys, budding journalists or not, can only do so much research before getting bored. I realize, I don't want to turn into one of those pathetic whiner kids: "Oh, my parents got killed, so I get to mope around and be an asshole to everyone because I'm really, really sad." I mean, I am that lots of days, and Dr. Robles keeps reminding me that I'm allowed to have my feelings, that I'm perfectly entitled to them, but I also know I still have so much to be thankful for, something Dr. Robles keeps trying to help me see.

I mean, yes, my parents had been tragically killed by a group of assholes bastardizing their religion to suit their hatred, and that pisses me off every time I think about it. However, I had seventeen years with the two coolest people I've ever known. I know it's not cool to say that because I'm supposed to be an angsty teen locked in a constant battle of wills with my parents, but my parents were down-right awesome.

My parents were Sawyer Tripp Canton III and Marisol Kennedy Cruz Canton—hell, even their damn names oozed coolness. Dad looked like he stepped out of the pages of *Esquire* magazine, and Mom, well, let's just say, I saw the way guys looked at her anytime she came to campus. It's actually kind of weird and creepy to see guys your age, or really any age, I guess, trying to be all player with your mom, but you eventually become immune to it. They were stylish, smart, creative, talented, eclectic and funny with a huge, especially Dad, dose of goofiness.

We would cook dinner together in the evenings and debate the DC vs. the Marvel universes as if world peace depended on it. Mom and I were DC all the way, but Dad, who must have been dropped on his head as a child (note to self, ask Grams and Gramps about this) was a maniac for Marvel. Over the last year, we had also poured our energy into researching colleges, something still occupying hours of my time in an attempt to keep busy. Mom and Dad, of course, no pressure-pushed Northwestern, where they met, as the only viable post-high school option for me, but they would have supported any of my choices. I may have even taken my DC obsession a little far by also considering the University of Kansas, because that's where Clark Kent studied journalism, which is probably another reason I like Dr. Reyes. He saved all his Superman comics from when he was a kid.

Considering a college based on a fictional comic book character—yeah, my parents were cool with that. Like I said, they were awesome. But I was through with research for the moment. My legs were still sore and thinking about how cool my parents were always ended with me sinking into alternating fits of anger and self-pity.

To say San Antonio in August is hot is an understatement. My grandparents' pool is on my short list of things I'm thankful for. Of course, I've always loved their house, but now that I'm older, I have a new appreciation and perspective for the life they've built. I know it fits the history and narrative of Pearl Heights, which is a little disconcerting because, even considering the flattering reviews of the district for its tradition of academic and athletic excellence, it also has a reputation for being exclusive, elitist, and White. And now, I'm a part of that because of where my grandparents live. I feel like I should feel guilty about it, but they have sacrificed their own grief to give me the closest thing to a normal life and, right now, sitting in this pool feels damn good.

"Sweetie," I hear Grams say as she pokes her head out of the French doors leading to the patio, "one of your friends is here to see you."

What the hell? I wonder. I don't have any friends here, and then Reid Tibbitts steps around Grams, gives her a little bow of thanks, which seems cheesy and endearing at the same time, and comes my way as I start climbing out of the pool.

"Hey, dude. It's cool, don't get out," he says and kicks of his Chacos, sits down at the edge of the pool and puts his feet into the water. "Sorry to just barge on over, but I didn't have your number, so I took a chance you'd be home."

"No, it's cool. How did you know where I..."

"Student Council laced Grandma Honey and Mr. Huck's house for homecoming last year."

"Laced?"

"Oh, it's a school spirit thing, you know, the Blue Lacy thing. Different clubs get a home in the district assigned to them from a fundraiser thing and then they lace the yard—they decorate it. Every group wants to get Honey and Huck's house."

"My grandparents are quite the Pearl Heights rock stars."

"Yeah, they're awesome. Your grandmother wanted to know if I wanted to borrow a pair of your swimming trunks."

"Good luck with that. I've got these and some speedos from my swim team days."

"You're a swimmer?"

"Back in the day. I was on the team my freshman and sophomore years, but I wasn't very fast."

"You're pretty fast on land."

"Well, I hope I didn't peak on my first race."

"Nah, Coach B won't let that happen. I've gotten faster each year I've been on the team."

"Doesn't hurt to have your own personal cheerleader rooting you on," I say, hoping my delivery sounded as subtle out loud as it did in my head."

"Oh, CC? Yeah, she's awesome, but she comes to lots of meets and cheers for everyone. She was on the team our freshman year but couldn't keep it up as she became queen bee of the school."

It looks like Reid is becoming my first non-CC friend, although I'm still not sure if CC and I really are friends. Sure, we've traded some delightful banter, and she's dragged me off to lunch, but she is also Miss Ubiquity at school. I don't know if she's just being nice or just being CC, or even what just being CC entails. I do know I'm kind of crushing on her and that I'm possibly becoming best friends with her boyfriend. Awkward. Cliché teen love story, your table is ready.

"Dude, it's fucking hot," I blurt out, hoping that Reid isn't the uber boy scout or religious type who thinks "fudge," "darn" and "shoot" push the envelope of impropriety. "Hop in. You're almost as wet as I am."

Reid is clearly a man of action and probably not uptight because no sooner have I released the words from my mouth than he yanks off his polo, ditches his khaki shorts, tosses them in the direction of the patio furniture and front-flips over me, landing with a splash that announces him as bring-on-the-fun type of guy.

"Feel better?" I ask.

"Hell yes," he says, dog-shaking water from his chin-length hair that flows in the kind of curls lots of girls would pay a small fortune to have.

"That's cool, so, um, ah, what brings you over?" I try to ask in a tone that sounds genuinely curious without also sounding put out in any way.

"I dunno, nothing really. You're new, you seemed pretty cool on the bus and you had a bitchin' run this morning. So, I thought I'd see if you wanted to hang."

"I think I'm gonna feel that run for a couple of days."

"Dude, at first we were like only half watching—JV race and all—But then, people were all 'look at that dude,' and then we were like what's happening here. Dude's a baller."

And just like that, we're like friends or something.

The next few hours consist of hand stands in the pool, contests holding our breath underwater, diving football catches into the pool and merciless teasing of my football throwing skills. We race from one end of the pool to the other, which I win despite my two years away from the swim team. It's the first time I feel almost normal and like my actual self in months.

When we finally get out of the pool and wrap ourselves in the giant beach towels kept in an outdoor chest, Grams collects Reid's clothes to wash them without hesitating. Been there, done that with her before. Besides, they were drenched from our frolicking in the pool. The whole thing starts to take on the feel of a fifth-grade sleep over when Grams brings us pizza rolls and wings and then insists that Reid spend the night.

In what I'm beginning to understand is Grams' way of making the smallest things seem special, she brings us two ultra-luxurious fluffy robes and sends us upstairs to shower. Sitting in my new room with Reid in a fluffy bathrobe, our fifth-grade sleepover pulls a Megatron transformation to more of a preppy boy spa day. Reid shows me how he can cross each of his toes, and I demonstrate my skill of popping my knuckles, neck, wrists, ankles and toes. We play several hours of some ultra-intense video games where our superhero avatars wage mad-crazy epic battle before Gramps comes upstairs with Reid's clothes and some extra bedding materials.

By the time we decide it's time to turn out the lights and crawl into bed, Reid says he isn't the sleep on the floor type, and he narrates the background stories on most of the guys on the team. I find out Reid is family with the Tibbitts I read about in my research, although he says most people don't even know that story. I learn who has dated whom on the team but can't get confirmation on whether he and CC are just really good friends who talk all the time and also date or are just really good friends who talk all the time but don't date. I learn who the cool teachers are, which ones are complete tools and which ones are cool but also really good teachers. There is, as Reid explains, a difference between teachers kids think are cool because their classes are blow-offs and they can get away with doing nothing, and teachers kids think are cool even though their classes are hard, have high expectations and make you work for everything. Ms. Gillis falls into the first category. No surprise, Coach B falls into the latter.

"Look at the team," Reid says. "Coach B lets anyone run on the team. He takes three full buses of kids to meets every weekend, most of them JV who will never make varsity. He runs the hell out of them five days a week, week after week, and they come back and run for him every year."

"Yeah, that is pretty cool," I say, the slightest hint of a yawn in my voice.

"You'll get to know him. You'll see."

"I guess so," I say and yawn.

"Dude, you did good... but you have to work on your race strategy."

"Hey, Reid."

"Yeah?"

"Do you know why CC calls me Einstein?"

"You really don't know?"

"I really don't."

"She said it fits your name—Em, Ethan-Matthew, c squared, Cruz Canton."
"Damn, that girl is clever. No one has ever called me that."
"Hey, Einstein."
"Yeah?"
"I was at the game Friday night."
Pause.
"I heard about your parents."
"I figured."
Silence
"That really sucks."
"It does."
Pause. Silence.
"You okay?"
Pause. Silence. Pause.
"Sometimes."
Pause. Silence. Pause. Silence.
"Einstein."
"Yeah?"
Pause. Silence.
"You okay now?"
Pause.
"I think I am."
Pause. Silence. Pause. Silence. Pause.
"I'm sorry about your parents."
Pause. Silence.
"Thanks. I'm sorry, too."
"What name did your parents call you?"
"Ethan-Matthew."
Pause. Silence. Pause
"Hey, Ethan-Matthew."
"Yeah?"
"If you're ever not okay, I'm here for you."

Pause. Silence.

"Thanks," pause, silence, pause. "I know."

Pause. Silence. Pause.

In the silence, I hear Reid's breathing slip into the rhythm of sleep. I see the silhouette of his chest rise and fall, rise and fall. I stifle the breath fighting to escape my lungs in short, staccato gasps. I'm thankful for the darkness and sleep that hides the tears rebelliously escaping the corners of my eyes. I drift to sleep as the day ends a little less lonely than it started.

13

They're slight and some of them may be my imagination, but there's no mistaking they're there as I sit in class and as I wind my way from class to class the next week at school. Side glances, stares that linger a little too long and eyes darting back to front and center if they fail at being furtive. No one outright stops and stares at me like I'm a car accident on the freeway or sideshow circus freak, but I'm definitely a spectacle.

Two girls sitting behind me in my physics class whisper much louder than they intend and proceed to fill each other in on the rumors and details they've amassed since Friday night's surprise outing. One girl heard my mom died in my arms. The other heard I would have been killed too had I not argued with my parents that morning and ditched them at the café where the bomb exploded. Clearly, these girls have watched one too many Jason Bourne movies or have subpar Googling skills.

But my new week of school isn't all freak shows and gossip fests. I have become a little bit of a local celebrity myself at cross country practice. The varsity runners, who usually tend to stick to themselves because they're just faster than the newbies, have welcomed me into their midst. Reid, my de facto sponsor to the cross-country inner circle, tells me they weren't trying to keep me out but just didn't think to invite me in, and that, yes, there is a difference. They get so accustomed to their little Pearl

Heights bubble that they can't fathom what it's like to not know that experience. But once you're in, it's like you've always been in, even if always has only been five minutes.

Maybe Reid gave them a heads-up or sent a group chat or something and said not to bring up my parents' tragic death, because nobody at practice brings up a thing about it. Conversation doesn't go beyond a few "heys," bro hugs and the usual questions about what we did last weekend. We get an overview of last week's meet and running instructions from Coach B. I strap on some reflective gear and take off running, with Reid sticking by my side the whole time.

Last week, I didn't know any of the routes or anyone on the team, so I just kind of hung in the back and followed, which, I guess, made me look like a slacker and might help explain why the varsity guys hadn't tried to broach any conversations with me. People tend to gravitate to people who are like them, and by hanging back, I clearly wasn't in their league.

Maybe my plan to get through the school year as the anonymous, photo-not-available recluse isn't such a good plan. Plus, I've already failed at it. CC seems hell bent (that's a phrase I've heard a lot in my few months of living in Texas) on social butterflying me back into the kind of kid I was at my old school, the kind of kid who had inside jokes for everything, who gave nicknames to other kids, who could communicate across a room via eyebrows and head nods and the kind of kid who burst into the raucous laughter where you have to fight to keep snot from snorting out of your nose.

And then there's Reid. I mean who just randomly shows up to the house of a kid he doesn't know and ends up spending the night. I'm a pretty bold person, at least I used to be, but that takes balls to show up like that. Of course, I've actually seen Reid's balls. It's hard not to when the guy is throwing handstands in the pool in nothing but his boxers or animatedly playing video games in the fluffy robe your Grams gave him while she washed his boxers. So Reid, literally and metaphorically, has a set of *cojones* on him.

While I think Reid downplayed his connection to the history of Pearl Heights, he has now ushered me to the front of the cross country and possibly the Pearl Heights pack. Wiley Thorne—seriously his parents had to be spaghetti-western fans to give a kid a name like that—finished 27th at the state meet last year and is clearly the dog everyone else is chasing. Reid, who had sights on making it to the state meet this year, is the hungriest dog in the pack.

Carlisle Maxwell, Gage Yeater and Micah Peavy aren't the same caliber runners as Reid and Wiley, but they definitely aren't also-rans and help the team win and place in meets by clocking healthy times. Carlisle is also locked in tenths of a percentage battle for valedictorian with a girl who transferred in as a junior, so there's a lot of tension about that. Gage is some kind of musical virtuoso juggling music auditions at places like Bard College, The New England Conservatory of Music and The Curtis Institute of Music, which I've never heard of but is apparently more selective than the Skull and Bones Society. Micah, who looks like he'd be more at home on a Malibu beach, is taller than everyone in the group and has his eyes set on vet school after college. I swear, if he doesn't end up marketing himself as some kind of surf god vet on every social media platform available, I will lobby to have him committed as a menace to himself.

Last week, I never saw any of these guys after the initial team gathering on the track that went around the football field. They would take off while I would hang back and follow, but now I'm running with them. Wiley leads the way out. We run behind the football stadium, pass the natatorium and practice fields and then turn on the road that runs in front of the main entrance of the school. Once we cross at the stoplight and make it a good full block past the school, I'm initiated into the rebellious side of the cross-country team. Shirts, in unison, begin flying off in almost synchronized choreography. Reid notes the look on my face and explains that the athletic director for the district is a dick who requires appropriate athletic attire for all team practices on school grounds, because a few years back he got a stick up his butt about all these kids wearing Kony 2012 shirts at practices. Now, students can only wear Blue Lacy logos or plain colored shirts for practice—and you're not allowed to be shirtless on campus while representing a school team. Reid says the football players get away with it all the time because they're football, but Coach B gets regular notices about the cross-country guys violating the rule. Thus, the routine is to pull their shirts off once they are off campus and then leisurely put them back on, usually only sticking their heads through the neck holes, when they get back to campus.

Rebels. Pure rebels.

The whole no-shirt thing makes complete sense, though. What I'm discovering about living in Texas and running during the summer, even before the sun is up, is that no amount of moisture wicking technology can challenge the unrelenting humidity of San Antonio. Last week, when I didn't know of the no-shirt rebellion, I got back from the run with my shirt so drenched that I just started wearing my clothes into the shower and doing what I could to wash the stench out of them. I did notice that lately Grams seems to always have a bottle of Febreze handy, and when she discovered two days' worth of practice clothes abandoned in my bathroom, she threatened to set them on fire if I didn't start leaving them in the laundry room.

By the time we make it to the last stretch of the run, which means sprint to the finish because, according to Reid and Malibu

(I figure if CC can give me a nickname, I can return the favor to Micah), Coach B believes in strong finishes even more than he believes in salsa and *cerveza*. I realize I have some work to do as I try to match pace with Wiley and Reid during the run, but on the sprint to the finish, they are able to reach for reserves I don't have. Reid, his shirt merely hanging around his neck like a scarf, greets me as I come in just behind Malibu, Gage and Carlisle and reassures me I'll be faster by the end of the season. I hope he's right, but for now, I'm content to feel content at school for the first time.

Another good thing that has come from Reid crashing my pity party by spending the night at my house and drawing me into his circle of dudes is that we now realize how often we're in proximity of each other throughout the day. It's like my Reid reticular activating system has kicked into full gear and I see him everywhere. His AP American history class is across the hall from my AP Euro class, and his AP Lang and Comp class is next door to my AP Lit class. But there seems to be something more than proximity going on, a something I can't really define.

There's definitely something about Reid. He comes across as the most jocular of dudes, the bring-on-the-fun type who barges in and front flips over you into a pool and who is perpetually smiling. It would be easy to think that's all there is to him, but in the short time I've known him, I've already seen that he's not just some guy ramrodding through life doing guy things. Now that he is comfortable with me, it feels like he's trying to make other people feel comfortable with me, not for their sake but for mine. Now that Reid has seen me in the hallway, he's making sure everyone in the hallway knows he's spotted me.

"Ethan-Matthew Cruz Canton Carnegie Rockefeller," he bellows. "How are you, ol' chap, you salty dog?" Then he high-fives and chest-bumps me.

Now as I walk into class, I don't know if the stares are because little orphan Ethan-Matthew has arrived or if it's because Reid has come in behind me and jumped into my arms.

"Ethan-Matthew Cruz Canton Bellview von bittie titties, I require your assistance."

"Dude, what is your disfunction?"

"I'm injured. I'm suffering from post-practice shin splints. Walking could permanently damage my shin-tilator maximus. As my cross country protégé, I insist you carry me to class."

When I accuse him of faking, he looks at me like I've eaten his last Pop Tart. My AP lit teacher, Mr. Shoenborn—or Mr. Shin, as everyone affectionately calls him—is a 70/30 mix of serious to cool who dresses in the standard male teacher uniform of well-worn khakis, solid oxford shirt with a not-too-bold necktie and sensible square-toed loafers. He's leaning more to his 30-percent side as the tiniest hint of that pinched look of frustration teachers get begins to form, so I carry Reid out of my class into his. Reid's teacher is a diametric juxtaposition of mine. He's in the trying-too-hard-to-be-cool camp, the kind of teacher who insists students call him by his first name, no matter how much the administration looks down on it, and he dresses like he changed outfits multiple times before leaving home. As I carry Reid into the room and set him down, Mr. Trying-Too-Hard pretends to jump into my arms. I ignore him because he's creepy. I tell Reid I'll see him after class and head back to the much-preferred greener pastures of my 70/30 teacher.

So far, I've survived three classes only hearing minor murmurs and without anyone mentioning my being an orphan, but I should know it won't last. I've semi-prepared for the random kid to blurt out, "Oh my God, you're the kid whose parents were killed by terrorists, what was that like?" It doesn't happen. What I did not expect was the OMG to come from a teacher. Like they're supposed to get training on stuff like that, right? Then again, Ms. Gillis operates under her own set of rules in the little journalism world she's created.

Last week, this woman, after trying to excommunicate me, relegated me to solitary confinement in a corner of the journalism room to do a bullshit task because I dared to breech the inner sanctuary of Gingerville, but today she nearly tackles me when I walk into the room.

"Oh, you sweet baby..."

Seriously, "sweet baby"?

"I'm so sorry about your sweet parents."

Did she know them? I know she didn't.

"Come here, honey."

Holy shitbombs. Less than a minute in this class, and she's giving me a cavity with all this sweetie and honey shit.

And then... and then, she pulls my face to her chest in one of those poor-baby hugs while she pats my head. Not that it isn't awkward and uncomfortable enough, because I'm quite a bit taller than she is, but oh, my yikes... her hefty bosoms and cleavage are in my face. Am I supposed to wait for her to release me? Is it rude if I pull away? She smells like jasmine or lavender, something icky-sweet, mixed with coffee and cigarette.

When she finally releases me, I don't know what to do or where to look. I do know I now have another reason for people to stare at me, but Ms. Gillis just goes on with class like she hasn't just emotionally scarred the kid in class already loaded down with enough emotional baggage to need multiple therapists.

"Okay y'all, I made the final changes to the back-to-school PTA newsletter we were working on last week, so time for story pitches for our first issue. Colin and Kelly, get up there and do your thing."

The two editors make their way up to the dry erase board, where they write "news," "editorials," "features," "sports" and "center spread" across the top of the board. Students in class begin calling out suggestions that Colin and Kelly write under the appropriate categories. Most of the suggestions have some new-school-year angle to them: new teachers to campus, new school rules, new gadgets and tech. There's a lot of buzz about the new district we're in for football and what that means for post season play. Someone suggests a feature story about interviewing students who graduated last year about their first few days of college. Another student suggests a center spread on this year's best-dressed freshmen that morphs into best dress from each class that morphs into this year's hottest fashion trends, which makes me wonder how they'll determine this, because, for a school with no uniforms or set dress code, everyone practically dresses alike.

Someone wants to write an editorial on adding an extra minute to the passing periods, while another student wants an editorial on preventing teachers from assigning homework on weekends. There will be a news story on the new testing schedule and procedures explaining how academic departments will have assigned days when they can give tests, so that students won't have multiple tests on the same day, which seems like academic coddling to me. There will be a point-counter-point on whether students should work and a sports feature on the quarterback because, well, he's the quarterback.

Story ideas flow back and forth and make their way to the appropriate column on the board. I suggest a sports feature on Victoria Pusateri from cross country, but the idea goes nowhere. Colin says they'll run a sports box with meet results, but that's all there'll be room for. The board is packed with ideas, and the pitch meeting begins winding to an end, when Ms. Gillis chimes in from the back of the room.

"Don't forget the feature on Ethan."

Ethan-Matthew, I think before the full significance of the moment sinks in.

"Colin and Kelly, y'all can work on that together. You're gonna want to interview Grandma Honey and Mr. Huck and probably talk to some kind of doctor or psychiatrist about trauma. Oh, and you can probably talk to someone in ROTC about terrorist stuff."

"My dad's a hospital administrator," Colin says. "I can probably get him to recommend a shrink I can talk to."

Another voice shoots up from the middle of the room. "My mom is friends with the chancellor at Ol' Miss. I bet they have like a Middle East expert or someone we can call."

"Okay, everybody knows what they have to do, so you guys try to get something done before we leave today. Colin and Kelly, y'all make sure to get a picture of Ethan's parents when you interview him.

Ugh, it's Ethan-Matthew.

Beads of sweat begin to collect on my upper lip, and I feel my heart racing, thumping, pounding the way it did when I tried to catch Wiley and Reid on the final stretch this morning. My hands feel tingly, and I can feel my lungs constricting. After two panic attacks earlier this summer, I thought I had become fairly astute at feeling them come on, but not this time.

"Ms. Gillis, I need to pee."

Not my most decorous moment, but I need to get out of the room with as little teacher inquiry as possible. Dad's satchel, the leather one Mom and I got him for his birthday when we were on vacation in Italy, the one he forgot at home that morning, hangs from my shoulder as I dart out of the room before Ms. Gillis can ask any questions or try and tell me to wait until the end of class.

Speed dial. Please be home. Please pick up.

"Gramps, please come get me. Please. Can you hurry? Please come get me."

"Front of the school. I'll be right there."

Four minutes. I hide in the bathroom for the entire four minutes it takes Gramps to pull up to the front of the school and text me, "Here."

Blinds closed, curtains drawn, I crawl into a ball on the bed in my dad's old room, while Gramps runs his fingers through my hair repeating, "You're okay. You're okay. You're okay."

14

When I return to practice on Wednesday, I realize Reid is exactly the kind of person you need in your life when no one else in your circle knows what to say to you after you think everyone has heard about your freak out.

"Ethan-Matthew Cruz Canton Chadwick von Bartleby the Scrivener, welcome back. If you need to pee there's a perfect shrub for that on today's route, but fear not, we, in solidarity, will pee with you." And then he gives me one of those bro headlock hugs that says, "Dude, it's all good."

And then we run.

How she does it, I still haven't figured out, but CC is waiting for me when I come out of the gym after cross country.

"Hey, Einstein. I have something for you," she says, handing me a box of Hot Tamales.

"I love these."

"I know."

"Hey, no Han Soloing the Hot Tamales."

"That's not all I have for you, my young padawan."

"Is it Christmas? My birthday?"

"You're funny. No. It's a pass from my mom. She said you can use it any time you need to."

At this point, I don't know if this is going to get really awkward or if I'm supposed to be all blasé about it or whether I should express big time thankfulness, when Reid jumps in.

"Hey, babe. You waiting for me?" Reid asks as he emerges from the gym.

"I came to get you boys to walk me to class."

Which we do, the faintest hint of jealousy for Reid accompanying us.

I purposely go to advanced journalism late by stopping in to see Ms. DeSoto. We talk about what happened in class. She rolls her eyes and says, "*Sinvergüenza*," enough times for me to have no doubt about how she feels about Ms. Gillis.

I don't know why I always assumed all teachers got along and liked each other, but when I tell Ms. DeSoto that Gramps had to talk Grams down from skipping over the principal and calling the superintendent, she tells me how much she loves Grandma Honey and wishes she would have called. She reminds me that I can come by her office anytime I need something. She adds that if I need to, I can leave class and come chill in her office.

When I get to journalism class, everyone is busy in their routine while Ms. Gillis sits at her desk editing yearbook pages. Looking over to the board, I see the names of the students assigned to each story. There is no assignment for me. I do find my name under the new column for copyediting. I feel a few sets of eyes lingering on me as I hand Ms. Gillis the pass from Ms. DeSoto. Barely glancing up, she takes the pass from me and points me to a basket labeled "Copy" that has two editorials and some news briefs in it for me to edit. What's that cliché about cutting the tension with a knife? I could have done it with a spork.

As I work through an editorial espousing the benefits of working while in school, someone in a rolling-chair ambles up next to me. It's Kelly Pfeiffer, co-editor of the paper.

"How's it going?"

I'm wondering who wrote this mess, but I decide to say something far more diplomatic. "Pretty good. Although I think my grandparents might insist I get a job if they read this," I say, hoping I sound the slightest bit convincing.

"Oh, that's good. You doin' okay?"

"I'm good," I answer, and I actually am.

A couple of sleeping pills, a phone appointment with Dr. Robles, Gramps rubbing my back and Grams offering to call her friends on the school board helped bring me back to something close to normal.

"I just wanted you to know I'm sorry about Monday. I didn't know you weren't cool with the whole feature about you."

"It just kind of caught me by surprise."

"I honestly thought you knew about it. When Ms. Gillis texted me about it on Saturday, it just seemed like everything was set."

"Don't worry about it. It's not your fault. I just freaked out a little bit."

"It's okay. I don't really talk about it much except to my grandparents and my therapist."

"You're in therapy? Of course, you're in therapy. I mean it makes sense."

I get the feeling that Kelly could have this conversation without me, but I like that someone in this room is finally talking to me.

"Grief counseling," I say. "It's been good. I mean, the whole things suck balls... sorry, that's highly inappropriate and very disparaging to balls."

"Well, it doesn't seem like your sense of humor has been affected."

"How do you know I have a sense of humor?"

"I can just tell. I'm very perceptive. Anyway, I really am sorry about how this all went down. I told Ms. Gillis that we should drop the story, but she was like 'he'll come around.' But I kind of put my foot down about it, so don't worry, she's kind of pissed at me too right now, but she'll get over it. Glad you're back," she says and then rolls away.

I eat lunch with Reid and CC. Wiley and Micah join us, which makes me feel less like a third wheel. Last Friday, it was just Reid and me while CC tended to some cheerleader functions before that night's away game. Reid calls himself a football season bachelor and says it's just something you got used to with cheerleaders and football players. I feel a little bad for wishing I were the one dating a cheerleader, one cheerleader in particular.

While we grab lunch from a little hole in the wall *taquería*, where the aroma of *comino* and anise whisks me to the kitchens on Mom's side of the family, Reid asks if I'm ready for the meet tomorrow morning. At the risk of sounding like a major nut job, I confess I'm kind of nervous about the starting gun. I explain how hearing it last week really triggered me. I don't want to be known as the meltdown kid who freaks out in class and who has to keep hiding in the bathroom until his grandfather can come rescue him.

Reid is true to form. "Dude, if you're gonna hide out in bathrooms, you gotta stop using the main hall bathrooms… those are fucking disgusting. Use the ones in the science wing because they are quality."

"Thanks. I'll keep that in mind for my next freakathon."

"Dude, all you did was say you had to pee and ran out of class. The sheer number of kids running out of class at this place on a regular basis would astound you. Hell, I ran out my English class last year because my car was getting towed."

"Your car got towed?"

"Hell, no. I wasn't gonna let that happen…. But if you're ever coming back late from lunch and your teacher tells you that if you get one more tardy, you'll have to come to Saturday school to make up the time, don't park at the church across the street from the English wing. Those suckers will tow your ass."

"I'll make sure to remember that if I ever get a car."

"And, seriously, nobody knows you hid in the bathroom. Hell, I know everything that happens at this school, and I didn't know until you texted me. I don't know what your therapist is telling you, but all I can tell you is, I got your back."

I believed he does have my back, even if he gets us back late from lunch. And, damn sure, we don't park at the church across from the English wing, because those suckers will tow your ass.

15

The temperature has already climbed to 90° for the boys' varsity heat, and I can feel drops of sweat sliding down my face. My heart beats with rapid force, and tension grows inside me. But also, I feel something different, something almost soothing. Something like family.

Before the race, Grams and Gramps meet me under the canopy wearing matching Blue Lacy cross-country shirts and photo buttons of me pinned to their shirts. I met Reid's parents who were cutting bananas and slicing bagels as the assigned parent volunteers for the meet. Mr. Tibbits notices my Tardis phone case and asks the standard Whovian discussion starter: "Who's your favorite companion." Mr. Tibbits is a Donna fan, typical, but at least he doesn't pick Rose, while I favor Martha. Mrs. Tibbits arranges bananas and bagels like we were honorary Junior League members and not a bunch of teenagers who inhale food regardless of presentation. She emanates kindness and kisses me on the cheek for good luck before the race.

From my point on the starting line, I can see Grams and Gramps there to cheer me on. CC stands a few feet to the left of them with Victoria Pusateri, who, once again, has easily won her race. Reid lines up next to me. Wiley stands on the opposite side of Reid, and Malibu and Gage are next to me.

In the corner of my eye, I see the race official raise his arm in the air. I swallow. I know the shot is coming. Racers lean forward in anticipation. Our arms drop to our sides ready to spring forward.

Reid turns his face to me, a wry grin etched on his face.

It's coming. I sense it.

Reid reaches down. He interlocks his fingers between mine. My attention shifts.

The gun fires.

He squeezes my hand. Lets it go. And we run.

Wiley finishes fourth, Reid seventh, and I come in fifteenth.

Everyone is coming up to congratulate us as we walk in circles, cooling down and catching our breath. Coach B offers his congratulations and then goes back to cheer on the rest of the Blue Lacy runners. We follow after him to support our teammates.

Reid stands next to me, yelling out the names of our team members as they cross the finish line. Maybe I'm making too much of it. So what if Reid squeezed my hand in a way that felt oddly intimate and was something that had never happened before? Reid also makes a joke out of everything and is unflinchingly spontaneous and has been the epitome of kindness. He knows when to ask if I'm okay without it feeling like he's just randomly checking in out of obligation. And he is dating CC. Damn, Ethan-Matthew, you are such a tool. You told him you freaked out at the last race when the gun went off, and this week you don't ever remember hearing it.

Reid is the biggest goof I have ever met. At the moment, he's standing next to me, waving his cross-country jersey over his head like a lasso and woof woofing at each Lacy runner who goes by. Yep, definitely making something out of nothing because now Reid is spinning CC around singing, "Tale as Old as Time" from *Beauty and the Beast*.

"Reid, you're definitely the Beast, right?"

"I'm clearly the Beauty, right CC?"

"Um, you two are a couple of LeFous, but I am definitely the Beauty," CC says.

"Oh, heeellll no, I'm at least Gaston," Reid counters and then releases CC as he loudly continues singing his "B&B" repertoire, not caring who hears him, "...and every last inch of me's covered in h-a-a-a-a-i-i-i-r!"

"You have just as much chest hair now as you did when you were eight... and you shave your legs," CC reminds him. "I'm going to say bye to Victoria, and I'll see you later this afternoon." Then, she turns to me, "Einstein, great race. You were awesome," and she pep-steps off.

"You were almost awesome. I was awesome," Reid quips.

"I was pretty awesome, too."

"You, Mr. Cruz Canton Benedict Cumberbatch Winthrop Haliwell," Reid says as he puts his arm around my shoulder and guides me toward our canopy, "were two places away from awesome, close to awesome, but not quite. Again, I *was* awesome."

Of course, I had only one retaliatory option. I pulled away from Reid, took the banana peel in my hand and threw it with a significant amount of force square at his chest. Not hard enough to get him angry, but hard enough so he has to think, "I better not rub it but I kind of want to." And then, I run toward our canopy with Reid chasing behind me.

Coach B looks like he's won the lottery. Both varsity teams finished first, and both JV teams finished second. On the bus drive back to campus, he has me sitting next to him to talk race and training strategy. From the conversation, I get the distinct feeling that he thinks he can take at least four kids to state this year and that he wants me to know that even if he hasn't talked to me directly about everything going on in my life, he is there for me, too. Of course, I already know this, but it's nice to have another shoulder to lean on.

When we get back to the school, I ask if Reid wants to come hang again. He reminds me that he and CC have a thing planned, which seems vague to me, but who am I to pry into people's dating relationships, especially when I'm secretly crushing on one of the people in said dating relationship.

"Have fun at your 'thing.'"

"I'll text you later."

"Cool," I say and turn to walk home.

I turn back around because of the whole budding journalist thing and because I really want to know. "Hey, Reid."

"Yeah?"

"Um, why did you squeeze my hand earlier today?"

"Because I wanted to... and because you needed it."

I watch as he walks to his truck, gets in, and drives away.

Just before midnight my phone chirps.

Reid: Wyd

EM: Utube

Reid: dude, lame

EM: that's my middle name

Reid: not matthew

EM: fu

Reid: too tired ha!

EM: how was your thing

Reid: meh

EM: uh, oh

Reid: ????

EM: idk, just wondering if you broke up or something

Oh, shit. I hope I'm not projecting too much wishful thinking.

Reid: wtf

EM: you said meh I'm confused

Reid: i'm confused
EM: so you didn't break up
Reid: we aren't dating
EM: stfu, what?
Reid: who told u we were dating
EM: no one, i just figured
Reid: ur crazy
EM: what, i'm confused idk whats meh ????
Reid: long story, 2 tired
EM: k hang tomorrow?
Reid: can't, got a family thing and homework... tons
EM: yikes
Reid: dude, that's old people talk
EM: my dad used to say it
Reid: yikes sorry
EM: jk
Reid: u suck
EM: meh lol
Reid: jr year sucks ass
EM: sucks 2b u
Reid: im fucked c u @ practice
EM: nite
Reid: toodles
EM: old people talk
Reid: my dad says it
EM: lol
Reid: nite

16

It takes a little bit before I figure out it's my phone buzzing on the nightstand that wakes me. Why the hell is Reid calling me so damn early in the morning? Rubbing the sleep from my eyes, I see that the call is from CC. *Hurry up and answer before she hangs up*, runs through my head.

"Hey, hello. What's up?"

"Good morning, Einstein. Did I wake you?"

"Nah, no, I was just..." *Don't say in the bathroom, say something normal*. "...hanging in my room."

"You had breakfast yet?"

"Nope, not yet."

"Wanna go with me?"

Don't sound too eager, don't sound too eager.... "Yeah, sounds cool."

"Pick you up in 30."

"Okay, bye."

Holy shitbombs. What the hell is going on? Reid had a meh thing with her last night, I found out they aren't dating and now she's on her way to pick me up for breakfast.

Shower. Fast. Dress. Quickly. Shorts—khaki. Shirt—Doctor Who T-shirt or standard Pearl Heights uni of untucked oxford with sleeves rolled into cuffs. Doctor Who it is. Wait, no—oxford. No, it's hot, so T-shirt. Wait, does she like Doctor

Who? Oxford it is. Twenty-two minutes, dude. Pick a damn shirt. "Doctor Who" it is.

Shoes? Sneakers, no Vans. Yeah, definitely Vans. Wait, maybe go back to Pearl Heights uni of the oxford with leather driving loafers. No, T-shirt and Tom's—very caszh. No, no, I got it, Chacos. Reid said I definitely needed Chacos and took me to get some after school one day, so definitely the Chacos, plus it will show off my white feet and cross-country tan lines, which actually look pretty cool. Okay, decision made. Got it all together: khaki shorts, Doctor Who tee and Chacos.

Teeth brushed, check. Deodorant, check. Hair, combed, light product. Looks good, though not cool like Reid's.

8:22. Now what? Wait outside? Does she honk? Do I invite her in? You're overthinking, Ethan-Matthew. It's breakfast, not a date, just friends hanging. Wait, is this a date? But she asked me. That's okay, I'm cool with that. I don't care about that kind of thing, not that I know. I've never had a girlfriend. I'm a seventeen-year-old virgin, unless three times in the shower yesterday changes that. I don't know these things. Did I put on deodorant? Sniff pits. Oh yeah, I did. Did I brush my teeth? Dude, snap out of it!

Two quick taps on the horn. I tell Grams and Gramps I'll be back later and bound out the door for whatever we're calling what we're doing. Oh, yeah... breakfast. It's just breakfast, Ethan-Matthew. Chill, dude, chill.

"Hey, Einstein," she says as I hop into the front seat, "cool shirt."

"Oh, yeah, I just pulled something out of the drawer."

Most of the time when I see CC, her hair is pulled back in a ponytail, but today she has on one of those thin hair band things, so her hair is loose and tucked behind her ears. Her small gold loop earrings shimmer in the morning sunlight every time she moves her head. She's wearing a white blouse off her shoulders with little eyelet holes that form into flowers. Her shorts are those short-cut girl khakis, and she's wearing Chacos. Good advice, Reid, good advice.

"You feeling brave, Einstein?"

"About your driving or breakfast?"

"Breakfast, silly. I'm an excellent driver."

"Okay, let's get breakfast brave. But I'm warning you, I've had authentic *arroz brut* in Mallorca."

"Not that brave, I think. We're just getting out of the Pearl Heights bubble."

"We going to the hood?" I tease.

"To these kids, that IHOP we just passed is the hood. No *arroz brut* though, whatever that is."

"It's delicious. Not scary at all. It used to be made, a long time ago, with blood and internal organs, and the locals used to say you have to wash your feet into it, but it's basically meat broth and vegetables these days."

"My mom makes *arroz con pollo*—so good. When the Pearlies come over, they eat that shit up."

CC maneuvers us out of Pearl Heights, through downtown and into a part of town mixed with tire shops, tattoo parlors and homes where the esperanza and bougainvillea spill unabashedly into each other in front yards and where decorative iron bars cover the windows. CC suddenly pulls into a parking lot that makes my heart swoon almost as much as it did when she honked the horn for me earlier this morning. Walking into Panífico gives me an immediate flashback to the *panaderías* we visited during my childhood visits to South Texas, the Rio Grande Valley where my mom grew up. All around the shop there are glass cases bursting with the bright colors of shell-shaped *conchas* in pink, yellow and white. There are *marranitos* lined up in neat rows, *empanadas de camote, calabaza, manzana, piña* and *cajeta* along with *cuernitos*, jelly tacos and Mexican wedding cookies. *Semitas de anís, campechanas* and the pink *piedras* that Mom and Dad both loved to dip into their coffee. The aroma of bread, sugar, cinnamon and brewing coffee floods over me. Every part of me screams, yassss!

We each grab an aluminum serving tray and tongs and meander from case to case considering our selections. CC picks a pink *concha* and a jelly taco. I pick out a *marranito*, basically gingerbread in the shape of a pig, and a pumpkin-filled *empanada*. Next, CC takes a carton of milk from the refrigerator case and a ceramic coffee cup from the coffee station as I pour a cup of rich, aromatic coffee, perfect accompaniment for the *pan dulce*. We choose a table by the window that looks out onto the neighborhood, a neighborhood so vastly different from the streets of Pearl Heights. It's hard to believe we're only a ten-minute drive away.

Graffiti peppers the building across the street. There's so much concrete. The only hints of nature are the weeds fighting through cracks in the sidewalk, but the next block over across the intersection at the stop light is another Catholic university. It is a testament to the architectural majesty of gothic steeples and towers that contrast starkly to the neighborhood around it. We're definitely out of the Pearl Heights bubble, but I feel nothing but comfort and contentment sitting here.

Of course, it doesn't hurt that I have CC plopped in front of me, smiling and doing that thing where her hair cascades to her face each time she leans forward, followed by the effortless tucking of strands of hair behind her ears. Causal effervescence. The hair, the smile, the almost perceptible sparkle in her eyes. Maybe she kind of knows what she's doing, maybe it's intentional flirting, harmless teasing, but I don't care. I've already ascribed to her a level of above-it-ness. Tearing her pink *concha* into pieces and dipping it into her milk, CC, in that moment, is pure friendship, the kind of girl you would want as your girlfriend, if you could ever get over the fact that she is hopelessly and forever out of your league.

"Hey, nice Chacos, Einstein," CC says, looking down at my feet.

"Reid helped me pick them out. I think they're pretty cool."

"Yeah, and nice feet. You've been getting some San Antonio sun. Well, except for your feet."

"It's my half-Mexicano guy badge of honor. I tan nicely."

"The Cruz of your Cruz Canton."

"Damn right, baby." Holy shitbombs! Did I just say that? Play it off, play it off. Recant. Follow up. Quickly. But then, no need.

"Cruz, that was your mom's side?"

"Marisol Greer Kennedy Cruz."

"That's a fabulous name."

"Yeah, my Tita Cruz loved those old black and white movies... *Goodbye, Mr. Chips* and *Mrs. Miniver* that Greer Garson starred in. She was nominated for best actress in *Goodbye, Mr. Chips* and won it for *Mrs. Miniver*. So, when she had my mom, that's one of the names she picked."

"And Kennedy?"

"Oh my God, Lito Cruz was a huge JFK buff. He had a huge Kennedy memorabilia collection. So, with their last child, they put together their favorites. And they were like mondo Catholic. Hence, the Kennedy love. That's why Marisol and all the Virgin Mary stuff had to come in somewhere."

"Do you see them often?"

"Oh, they passed away years ago. They were like really old when they had my mom. My aunts and uncles on my mom's side are all in Mexico, so it just made the most sense for me to come live here. You've got the whole name thing going on too, Carmelita. I, like, have seriously never heard that as anyone's name in real life."

"Came from my mom. She grew up in El Paso, and there is like this little-known folk hero she learned about in a Mexican studies class. Carmelita Torres...they called her the Auburn Warrior. She led these women in riots that shut down the border between the United States and Mexico."

"Whoa, seriously?"

"Yeah, so she was like this radical chick who fought against all this crazy shit that Mexicans were unclean and inferior.... When the Mexicans would cross the border for work or whatever, they would make them strip down and force delousing and spray them with chemicals before they could enter the country. It was like all kinds of eugenics bullshit that was going on way before the Nazis and World War II. Hell, they gave the Nazis the idea."

"I've never heard this before."

"Hardly anybody has. It was like Jim Crow for Mexicans. If you were Mexican and trying to cross the border, they would like strip-search you and check you for lice. Mexicans had to basically take IQ tests to determine whether they were fit to come into the country. It was like really awful, so Carmelita Torres led this spontaneous revolt and got all these women to refuse the body checks at the border. Anyway, my mom found her really inspiring and named me after her."

"So... you're like a radical Latina chick out leading protests and shit?"

"Hardly. I barely even speak Spanish. I mean, I love all the heritage stuff like this, *pan dulce*, the *arroz con pollo* and *tortillas* I make with Mom, really all of it. I even did *folklórico* dancing as a little girl. I just never picked up the language."

"Your mom speaks Spanish."

"Yeah, she kind of says it's her fault I don't."

"Why's that?"

"She didn't speak English until like third grade and has really bad memories of feeling dumb and teachers making her feel dumb because she couldn't speak English, even though lots of kids around her didn't speak English either. She just wanted to make sure I didn't struggle in school, so she made sure she spoke English to me at home."

"Is that weird being around all this Mexican culture and not really speaking Spanish?"

"Kinda. I'm used to all the haters about it. I've heard it all— Diet Mexican, Mexican light, coconut, *pocha*, *trigueña*. I just ignore it. And like my other namesake, Selena Quintanilla... God, my mom loved her. She didn't really speak Spanish either. She was always messing up speaking Spanish in interviews and would just laugh it off. So I don't think it makes me any less of a Latina because I don't speak Spanish."

"I don't think it does either. And my mom loved Selena, too. You know what? I got some of the criticism, too, from family on my mom's side, although none of it was mean-spirited. I got called *güero*, *güerito*, *blanquillo*, *bolillo*, *el medio medio*. But really, no one was ever mean to me. Sometimes it felt like I wasn't white enough for white people and not brown enough for brown people."

"Did your mom grow up here, too?"

"No, in La Joya, in the Valley."

"What's your dad's name?"

"Sawyer Tripp Canton III."

"So that's where the Mr. Huck comes from."

"Yeah."

"Don't take this the wrong way, Einstein, but your mom has Kennedy and Greer, and your dad Sawyer and Tripp.... Then, what's up with Ethan-Matthew?"

"Not the first time I've heard that. When you grow up with an unusual name, you get a little tired of always having to explain it. And I think my dad thought it was kind of pretentious for me to be the fourth Tripp. The Ethan-Matthew thing is hard enough. You know what it's like, Carmelita."

"Hell yeah, but I've been CC so long, most of my friends probably can't remember what my actual name is. As for you, Ethan-Matthew, your parents sound awesome."

"They were. Hey, you didn't call me Einstein."

"Yes, I know."

Maybe she's just having a little fun with the new guy, or maybe she's just really this sweet. Either way, for the first time in a long time, staring at this girl with a twinkle in her eye and the tiniest crumb of pink *concha* kissing her utterly perfect cheek, I feel I can have a chance with her. Also, that is one lucky *concha* crumb.

17

By the time CC gets me home, I know her and her mom's story. Ms. DeSoto met CC's dad when they were here for college at Trinity University. He left them when CC was four, and she basically sees him at Thanksgiving, unless Heights is in the playoffs, and for two weeks in the summer. They've drifted farther apart as she's gotten older. Ms. DeSoto started off as a chemistry teacher in the district before getting her counseling certification, and she's been passed over twice for the head counselor position but has stayed because, despite the district's affluent makeup, there are still kids in the district who aren't affluent—"apartment kids," they call them. They're kids who live in the tiny portion of the district that is Section Eight housing. She stays for those kids. I meant to ask about CC and Reid's "meh thing," but I forgot.

Over the next few weeks some things are a pretty cool and some are just, you know, shit happens. Cross country is definitely in the cool column. Varsity boys have won two more meets, finished second in another and third at a huge invitational with lots of much bigger schools. We've also had an off week, and I've been getting progressively faster. I'm nowhere close to making Wiley nervous, and I probably can't catch up to Reid either, but I've also noticed that he has had to step up his game a little. We both know I'm not going to match his times. I like that he knows he can't take me for granted and that he pretends we're in an epic clash for cross-country superiority and world peace.

Dr. Robles likes the progress I'm making, despite a couple incidents of losing it with Grams and Gramps over really minor things, like forgetting to close the garage door and aggressively insisting they don't have to actually put my laundry in the drawers for me. He's having me track my highs and lows and he has me doing a lot of journaling. It's not the writing I'm used to doing—slices of life, social commentary, reporting of events and activities—but journaling about those highs and lows, sorting them out, explaining them, questioning them, reacting to them. And honestly, it hurts to do it. Some of the things I end up writing about are things I'd like to ignore, like why people can hate others so much, and a lot of "why me," but I'm guessing that's the whole point of the exercise.

CC's schedule is jammed. Every time I turn around, she's off with the cheerleaders at some event or another. Sometimes they are doing presentations at the elementary schools or standing behind school officials at some event or another. Like the rest of us, she's taking about a hundred AP classes. So basically, Reid, CC and I are almost never all together. I see Reid every morning at practice, we walk to most of our classes together, and he hangs with me at home after school fairly regularly. Sometimes for lunch, it's me and the other cross-country guys, and sometimes it's just me and Reid.

Advanced journalism class is definitely in the that's "just life" or worse column. I'm still relegated to spreadsheeting and editing. I've edited every story for the first issue of the newspaper as well as the yearbook spreads. Kelly is the only person in class who legitimately talks to me and actually lets me do a couple of fairly major revisions to copy, but way on the down-low. We did story pitches for the second issue yesterday in class, and, once again, I had no stories assigned to me. And today, copies of the first issue have arrived from the printer, and I've been given the actually enviable, because it gets me out of class, task of delivering papers to the various newspaper stands around campus.

Unfortunately, it doesn't take the entire class period to deliver papers to the newspaper stands, and I have to head back to class to sit around and do nothing of consequence. On the way back to class, I stop at the wall of panoramic pictures and find my dad again. That smile permanently etched on his face looks just like mine when I can muster one. Whoa, major serotonin drop. I can feel it like one of those Harry Potter dementor things just flew by me on its way to the restroom or detention. I give Dad a parting glance and head back to class. Maybe I should journal about avoiding this hallway because that seems like a completely reasonable option: avoid the school's main thoroughfare.

When I get back to class, people are on their feet and fervently gesticulating over something called "senior side-parking." Elmsmere Drive runs right through the campus on the far side of the school. On one side of Elmsmere are the back fences of homes that abut Pearl Heights High School. On the other side of Elmsmere are the arteries leading to the most popular campus activities and organizations. The band hall sits at the entrance of Elmsmere, a behemoth of practice rooms and garage doors in the back that roll up to reveal storage for timpani, tubas, marimbas and marching uniforms. There is a dance studio behind the band hall, where the cheerleaders and dance teams practice. Next to that is the computer tech building filled with computer labs for programming classes and also home to JROTC. There is a small faculty parking lot behind the computer tech building that also opens to the practice gym, which opens on the opposite end to the entrance for the football stadium. Essentially, if you are involved with any activity at school, you are funneled into that corner of campus.

Student parking on campus is restricted to juniors and seniors, and there are limited spaces available for on-campus parking to begin with. The school actually issues more parking permits than there are spaces, and you can't park on campus without a permit. The permit is nothing more than a fundraising lottery ticket for the opportunity to possibly park on campus, if the stars align and you also have a stash of four-leaf clovers and fairy dust at your disposal. Most students end up parking on the streets in the surrounding neighborhoods and walking to campus. Along the length of Elmsmere, from the band hall to the football stadium where the fences of the homes separate them from the campus, a curb runs the entire length of the road. This curb is known affectionately and traditionally as "senior side-parking." Parking is still first-come, first-serve, but senior side-parking is, apparently, sacrosanct parking for seniors *only*. The ultimate transgression is to not be a senior and park along senior side-parking.

Seems pretty simple. Not so. The seniors on the newspaper staff, *The Blue Review*, are riled up in a way that seems disproportionate for a parking space. But according to the raised voices in the room, too many juniors are parking in senior side-parking, and to hear the talk, one junior parking there is one too many. Listening to an abnormally passionate defense of seniors-only parking, I can't help but sit down in my corner of the ostracized and internally chuckle and become annoyed at how bothered they are over parking spaces.

When I look at the assignments board, I notice multiple senior side-parking stories have been added into the mix. They want an editorial extoling the virtue of parking spaces for seniors only, an editorial on respecting tradition, a news story on the rules and regulations of campus parking. They even want a photo exposé on juniors, or at least their cars, that park "illegally"—their word for it. It all seems like pretty one-sided coverage, not really the idea behind journalism, so I choose this moment to join the conversation.

"Why don't we write an editorial from the perspective of juniors that they should be able to park there, too?" I say.

The blowback is immediate.

"Uhh, you don't really know the situation, new guy" a senior girl, I think her name is Torrie, counters in a tone that stings like fire ants (also a thing in Texas—trust me, you want no part of them). "Parking there has always been just for seniors." And then, she picks up her phone and begins texting away while announcing, "I just sent a message in the senior girls' group chat to turn in every junior they see parking there."

"Damn," I say, and go on about how wackadoodle they're being. "Wackadoodle," that's a word Dad would say. I wonder what my hardcore journalist dad would think of his son, the copy assistant and paper boy.

"A junior perspective editorial is not necessary, Ethan," Ms. Gillis says.

WTF, it's Ethan-Matthew. And did she just get after me when these dumb shits are getting all worked up over parking spaces?

"That Owen kid parks there a lot," someone offers.

"So does Jake Foley and Scott Hamby," adds Torrie, "and I just got a picture that Reid Tibbitts is parked there right now."

Obviously, I know Reid, but I also know the other guys they're complaining about. They're all band kids. One is the drum major, and the others are some kind of band officers who get to school really early for band stuff. It makes complete sense for them to park there. Reid gets to school before 6 in the morning for cross country. Why would he park blocks away or in a farther parking lot when he can park right next to where we practice.

They're still bitching about it when the bell rings, the girls in the class holding up their phones to show messages in the senior girls group chat to others in the class. I can't wait to get out of that room. Thankfully, it'll be just be me and Reid for lunch today.

I make my way to Reid's truck that's parked in senior side-parking. Reid starts his car by remote and beeps me in as he walks to his parking spot. As Reid gets into his truck, he tosses me his phone.

"Look at that. Punk-ass Kathy Rhodes turned me in to the senior girls' group chat for parking here. Said someone should 'slash my tires—lol, jk guys,'" Reid blurts out in a mockingly shrill voice, "and then the bitch just smiled and waved at me in the breezeway."

"How'd you get that group chat message?"

"CC sent it to me."

"How did..."

"CC gets everything."

Then Reid spills the tea. Tells me about how Torrie, the girl from journalism class, has first period off and by the time she gets to school, all the on-campus parking is gone. She wants to park in senior-side parking because her first two classes are right by it, and she hates that she has to end up parking so far away. She was like extra late one day and took a reserved spot in faculty parking and got towed, so she was pissed. They told her if it happened again, they would revoke her parking permit.

"So, she's, like, all these juniors need to learn their place, and if they can't park where they're supposed to park, then they shouldn't be able to park on campus at all. Stupid, scrunch bag. I guess she forgets she parked there all the time last year and nobody complained then. This senior class is a bunch of whiny-ass punks always complaining about..."

As Reid pulls away from the parking spot and from the school, he continues to rant. I feel the annoyance that started in class growing, my chest tightening.

"Stupid shit. So what, you have to walk an extra block or something? Get your ass to school early if you want a good spot," he continues, eyes on the road and gesticulating with one hand.

I realize what's happening. Dr. Reyes had talked to me about the multiple manifestations of grief. Disproportional anger is one of them. Been there, done that multiple times. My heart rate quickens. I clench my teeth tightly together. I can feel my right foot tapping aggressively on the floorboard. My hands are on my lap squeezing and releasing my quads, my breathing labored, my complexion pallid. I'm probably moments away from rocking in my seat, when Reid looks over and does his Reid thing.

Crossing an open lane, Reid whips a turn onto the next residential street and pulls over."

"Dude, are you all right?"

God, I'm embarrassed because as much as I want to hold my shit together, I can't, and tears force themselves out of my eyes, like they've been fighting to escape my entire life. It's a snot soaked, blubbering cry with rambling eruptions of "What the fuck is wrong with these people" and "It's a fucking parking spot" and "There are real fucking problems in this world.... People lose their fucking lives because of screwed up religious shit, and you're complaining because you have to walk" and "Oh yeah, Ethan, that's not necessary." "It's Ethan-Matthew, for fuck's sake."

I'm rubbing my forearm back and forth across and under my nose, spreading snot and blubbering tears across my face and down my shirt, apologizing for the scene and the mess I've made.

"Hey, it's okay. Seriously, dude. If I had all the fucked-up shit that's happened to you happen to me, I'd be having ugly cries every damn day, probably almost as ugly as the one you're having. Seriously, dude, you should see your face."

Maybe it's intentional, or maybe it's just a gut response to a really awkward situation, but Reid shakes me from crying to a laugh-cry combination that ushers me back to the moment. In one of those spontaneous Reid moments, he next reaches for the quarter cup of left-over iced Frappuccino sitting in the cup holder and throws it on me.

"What the hell, Reid?"

"You can't go back to school looking like that. You have to go home and clean up."

Reid drives me home, and as I rush upstairs to shower, I hear Reid telling Grams and Gramps, "The dufus spilled Frappuccino all over himself."

After coming upstairs to wait for me, he shouts outside my bathroom, "Dude, your Grams is awesome. She has acai bowls for us."

"Yeah, she's great," I call from the shower, cold water rushing over me and hopefully washing away the puffiness from my eyes.

Of course, San Antonio is so damn hot that a mid-day shower isn't a bad idea on the regular, but when you start off your lunch period blubbering like a big ol' baby in front of your new best friend, a shower seems the best option to wash away snots and the taint of feeling stupid that often accompanies vulnerability. Dr. Robles often reminds me that emotions are nothing to be ashamed of, but that doesn't mean I'm down with emotionally barfing in front of other people. Reid, however, has quickly rocketed past the designation "other people."

"E-M, I'm as big a fan as any other red-blooded American boy of the long shower," he calls, "but leave junior alone for now. We have to get back to school sometime today."

"Whatever, dude. I'm done," I say turning off the water. "And his name is Rufus."

"Cool. I call mine Alphonso."

18

Reid and I are late getting back to class, but he texted CC, CC texted her mom and Ms. DeSoto wrote us passes for class. Damn, the girl may really run the school.

In journalism class the next day, Torrie is still leading the rant on senior-side parking. She's already written her editorial calling for detention, loss of campus parking privileges and towing for anyone who violates the tradition. She's also working on a news story about the student code of conduct and how students who willfully do things as heinous as parking on the senior side as juniors violate the conduct contract all students sign at registration. Basically, she's writing a second editorial couched as a news story by including quotations from girls in the senior girls' group chat.

A few months ago, I was set to be the editor of my school newspaper, and now I'm stuck in a corner fixing commas in copy. "Just until June," becomes my new mantra. Once June comes, I can wash the dust of this closed-off community from my feet and get the hell out of here, just like my dad did.

Sometimes I don't even know how Dad and Mom ever came together. Sure, they met as Texas kids going to college in Chicago, but their world experiences were so different. Mom grew up in the Rio Grande Valley of South Texas in the little town of La Joya, and before Tita and Lito passed away, I used to love visiting them. It was almost like living in two worlds at the same time: Mexico and the United States. Mom did the whole assimilation thing into the American way of life while still holding on to her Mexican culture. When she spoke Spanish, there was an underlying passion to it that reminded me of the Mexican soap operas Tita would watch. And when she spoke English, there was the trace of her Mexican accent. Dad called it the *salsita* in her voice, said that when she spoke you couldn't help but drink it in. And sometimes, at dinner parties or holiday gatherings, long after Mom had left the Valley, she would, at the behest and beckoning of the crowd, break into singing *Y Volveré* from here mariachi days. Here voice would soar as she sang:

No sufras más, quizás mañana
Nuestro llanto quede atrás
Y si me dices que tu amor me esperará
Tendré la luz que mi sendero alumbrará

And if the room didn't love her before, they adored her after that. She tried to pass it on to me, but Dad said I inherited his inability to carry a tune, which didn't stop either of us from belting out tunes in the shower. Mom was unabashedly *Mexicana*. She may have left the Valley, but the Valley never left her. And Dad loved that about her.

I loved both halves of me and every day I missed the people who created the me that I am. But I don't even recognize myself anymore. It's not the life they would have wanted for me, but I don't know what I can do about it except wait for the next stage to hurry up and arrive.

CC meets up with me after school. She wants to hang, says it has been too long since we spent any time together. So, she's come over, and we dangle our feet in the pool at the house and drink the sweet tea we picked up after school.

"I am starting to get a little jealous of all the time you're spending with Reid. I thought he was my bff," CC says, stirring her tea with a straw.

"Well, if you haven't noticed, he's kind of needy, and I'm a stabilizing force in his life."

"Yeah, that's what I hear," CC replies, the slightest hint of a question or possibly envy in her voice.

"I guess you talked to him about yesterday?"

"Yeah, we talked. I mean, don't feel bad, but it freaked him out a little, but nothing major. He's cool with everything."

"He was pretty great. I don't know what I would have done without him. I really didn't want Gramps to have to come get me from another meltdown."

"Do you want to talk about it? I mean, you don't have to if you don't want to."

"No, it's cool. I just got so frustrated about that whole stupid parking thing, you know, compared to real tragedies."

"Yeah, I saw Torrie's text in the group chat. She's just pissed because she petitioned student council for assigned parking, and they voted against it. She's like super toxic when she doesn't get her way. She's always been that way."

"I know I shouldn't have gotten so worked up about it, but... I don't know, it's more than that, I guess. That whole journalism class is shitbombs crazy. I should have gotten out when I had the chance."

"Weird, people usually love that class."

"Probably because they actually get to do something, and Gillis doesn't hate them."

"Yeah, she does play major favorites, but what do mean you don't get to do anything in class?"

"They won't assign me any stories to write for their precious *Blue Review*. I just sit in there and do busy work every day."

"That's so messed up."

"I know, right?"

"So what are you gonna do about it?"

"I guess, I'll just try writing stuff on my own and hope they'll eventually use some of it."

"Stop talking," CC says, holding her arm outstretched, her palm practically in my face. "You are not waiting around for permission from them. Hell, the first time I met you, you were writing. No one had to give you permission for that."

"Well, what am I supposed to do?"

"I don't know. Start your own paper."

"Start my own paper?"

"Yeah, why not? Write what you want."

"I don't know. I mean, I don't even know what I..."

"Ethan-Matthew Cruz Canton..."

Damn, she sounds scary. She has that same tone my mom had when I would put my socks on the kitchen table or take her phone charger.

"You have to do this. Nobody puts Baby in a corner."

We laugh at that, and she splashes water at me. We laugh some more. I really have missed hanging out with CC. I don't know, it feels rewarding, I guess, having someone who thinks you're capable of doing something you hadn't even considered.

I think about what she said the rest of the evening. Am I really going to start my own newspaper? Am I really going to take on an endeavor like that just because CC splashed water at me and giggled? Or am I going to do this because she believes I can? Or can it be that I think this might be the thing to get her to really notice me?

I tell Reid about it after practice the next morning as we head back into the locker room in the gym. He's almost more excited about it than I am.

"E-M, that is so awesome. You should totally do it. Screw Gillis trying to keep you down! Dude, I'll help you set up your underground press, get scoops, go all muckraker crazy and shit."

"How do you know about muckraking?"

"I've seen *Newsies,* c'mon, dude."

"Movie or musical?"

"Both. Batman singing in the movie... Oh my God, he was awful."

"He was awful, but no muckraking necessary. I'm thinking something more traditional, less *National Enquirer.*"

"That's cool. I'm just impressed that someone with such small *cojones* is going to buck the Pearly Heights system."

"Whatever, I have perfectly lovely *cojones.*"

"I didn't say they weren't perfectly lovely. I've seen them. Hey, eyes front, freshman," Reid barked at the eavesdropping kid in the locker room with us. "I'm saying, unless you're a fifth grader, they're on the small side."

"Whatever," I said wrapping my towel around my waist and heading to the shower. "I'm taking my balls and going home."

"That's the shower, dufus."

"It's a figure of speech."

"Use hot water. It might make 'em grow."

After the meet on Saturday, Reid, Gage, Malibu, Carlisle and CC come over to help me put my not-underground but alternative, though not alternative in a pejorative sense, newspaper plan into action. We settle on an online format, the same route so many other high schools have gone to for their school paper. We have decided to keep the whole thing to ourselves until we're ready to, as they say, go live with the site. Reid suggests blood oaths, but the rest of us assure him we can keep a secret without the need to shed bodily fluids.

We conduct our own mini-pitch meeting, dole out assignments, cover some journalism basics and essentially get to work. Wiley is a computer genius who makes extra money building gaming computers for other students and has been coding for years. And Reid, who struck me as the kid you picked to do group projects with because he was super cool and then regretted it because he did absolutely nothing and left you to do all the work, has proved to be the biggest ally to have on this project. He's motivated, enthusiastic and an organizational flow chart guru. Also a damn good writer.

When Gramps pops in to let us know pizza has arrived, I catch the look of joy and relief on his face, as if he can finally relax a bit because maybe, just maybe, his grandson will be okay. I understand what he must have been feeling. Looking around the room, I'm starting to feel, for the first time, like I want to be here, like I belong. When the first person you meet at your new school is a big-time, hard-core cheerleader, who you are also crushing on, you learn a little something about celebrating things. In this moment when my favorite things have coalesced, camaraderie and journalism, I feel a Blue Lacy cheer stir inside me, the chant reserved for trying to convert on fourth down, for goal line defense, the one I first heard at the pep rally, the one used for the things in life that make you feel young and alive.

In this moment as we set aside our labors to go downstairs and scarf pizza, I feel young and alive. My eyes linger on CC, and I can feel that chant inside me:

Woof, woof, rah!
Woof, woof, rah!
Rah, rah, rah, rah!
Woof, woof, rah!
Woof!

In my reverie, I completely miss someone else's eyes lingering on me.

19

Perhaps we're throwing a little shade at Ms. Gillis and being slightly immature. We are teenagers after all, but we're going live with *Blue Dawg Alt* the day before the second issue of *The Blue Review* comes out. We don't know it now, but we're in the calm before the shit storm.

Everybody—Reid, CC, Malibu, Wiley, Gage, Carlisle—have status updates ready for their social media, ready to post the link to our digital newspaper. All that is left is to get the news out to campus. We have it all worked out. Right before taking off on our run for practice, Reid will post a Snapchat story to announce our presence and, we hope, momentum will follow.

Reid stands next to me breathing in and out like he's in one of the classes where you learn how to birth a baby. He's flapping his hands the way the does before a race and psyching himself up to record a Snapchat story to announce us to his followers, which includes most of the school.

"Okay, okay, I'm ready," he says to Malibu, who is recording the whole thing.

"Go for it," Malibu says.

"What's up, what's up, Big Blue Lacy Dawgs. Reid Tibbitts here, but you already know that, and if you don't, why not? Hey, I'm just kidding, but you might not know this guy," he says as he reaches over and pulls me into a bro side hug and noogies my head like I'm eight years old or something. "The is Ethan-Matthew Middlemarch DeMarco Von Doodlesbury the seventh, but some people just call him Einstein...."

"Not anymore," I pipe in.

"Like I said, some people call him Einstein, or you can call him E-M, or what I call him, Matty-C."

"You never call me that."

"I do now. Anyway, Mattie C comes to us from España as a senior newbie, and he's going to be the next whatever famous journalist you've never heard of, and he's starting a whole new digital newspaper with all kinds of cool shit you won't find anywhere else. So go to the link here and on my Insta bio to see what my boy Matty-C is bringing. Woof, woof, rah! Peace out!"

"Dude, that was awesome," I congratulate Reid. "Did you just now think that all up?"

"You like, Matty-C? I'm hella extemporaneous."

"Not sure about the Matty-C, though."

"Okay, so no disrespect or anything, but maybe you can let people slide on the Ethan-Matthew thing. It's kind of a lot to get out, and maybe, like this is a fresh-start kinda thing for you... save the Ethan-Matthew for, you know, formal stuff. Just saying."

"Um, yeah... I guess that can probably work."

"Hey, you two gonna chew the fat all morning or you coming to practice?" Coach B bellows at us from the gym.

Since Coach B doesn't allow phones during practice, we have to wait until after practice to find out how our project has gone over at a place that is all about its traditions. Even though today's practice is hills, I go into it pleased with what we have put together.

Our lead off story in the *Blue Dawg Alt* is a video vignette that runs under the headline, "Zach in hats creates worlds of his own." It starts with a video of a group of students eating lunch in the quad and a voice over Gage recorded.

VO: "Even when Zach Stone sits with his friends at lunch, he's really not with them. Sure, he is there. Sure, his friends pay attention to him and include him in the group, but most of the time he's in a world of his own making. A world he is creating in the comic book script he is working on—all the time."

Video cut to Gage doing a stand up at the front of the school.

Gage Standup: "But even if you don't know Zach Stone, who is often called Zach in Hats because of the fedoras, pork pies and bowlers he wears every day, from the original comic he writes, illustrates and posts online, you've probably seen him in the halls."

Student interview: "Zach in Hats is awesome. Like he holds the doors open during passing periods until everyone goes through. It's like he puts other people ahead of himself."

Gage Standup: "But it wasn't always so. Sometimes kids just didn't get him."

Student Interview: "Back in middle school, kids weren't always very nice to him. I don't know... they thought he was kind of weird. Nobody but him was wearing hats like that, and he was always walking around just like talking to himself and stuff. Lots of people were jerks to him."

And the video package goes on. It explains how by talking to himself Zach is working out his comic book scripts. We show images of his comics and share how so many students have come to appreciate Zach.

Zach in Hats isn't the kind of kid to have his story told to others. He's just one of the kids going about living his life. One of the kids who, aside from a few idiosyncrasies, is just another kid in the crowd. His story is exactly the kind of story

I want to tell, and now, I'm finally getting to, even if it isn't me doing all the telling.

Our first issue contains point and counterpoint editorials on senior side-parking, highlights from cross country, swimming, band and the gaming club. We hit the constituencies so often overlooked and give them a moment to shine. Because I know in the absence of information, people will make things up for themselves, I tell my story complete with pictures from throughout my parent's and my life together.

Just Another Wednesday

Hints of cinnamon and caramel danced in the air as I rubbed sleep and a longing for summer from my eyes. Only two weeks of school remained, but my heart and mind had already jumped ahead to summer.

It was just another Wednesday.

My mother, Marisol Cruz Canton and my father Sawyer Tripp Canton leisurely sat in our kitchen drinking their café cortado.

Her hair was up in a cross between bun and ponytail that looked effortless and coiffed at the same time. She wore a pink silk floral blouse, white capris, and heels. Always the heels.

Dad wore his designer jeans rolled at the cuffs, his Chelsea boots and multi-color striped socks casually exposed. His shirt white, chambray, fitted under a classic navy blazer. Classic, always classic.

It was just another Wednesday.

Maybe if we had argued about something. Maybe if I would have sat down for one of those family bonding moments you see in movies. Maybe.

But it was just another Wednesday.

The Closest Thing to a Normal Life 115

I grabbed a piece of toast, kissed them both on the cheek, and waved good-bye like always.
It was just another Wednesday, except it wasn't. It was the last Wednesday I would ever see my parents alive.
It was the worst fucking Wednesday of my life.

    I explain how I heard the news. I explain how two Spanish Muslim brothers and their cousin, enraged over stories the Foreign Press Service had run on moderate and progressive Muslims denouncing extremists and radicals in Islam, had posed as custodians. They planted IEDs throughout the building and burst into the newsroom, shooting indiscriminately before setting off the bombs. I explained how my parents wrote some of those stories and how my parents, thirteen other journalists and the three terrorists all died that Wednesday. I recount the days that followed, the funeral and my move to Texas. I tell my story the way I want it told. It hurts. It evokes a flood of memories, but it also frees me. For the first time since school started, I walk down the halls unencumbered by the burden of hiding my pain.

    By the time I check my phone after practice, I have 203 new followers on Instagram and more likes than on any single thing I have ever posted. As I walk through the hallways, it feels as if I've grown up in Pearl Heights. People smile at me, wave to me, thumbs-up me. I get head nods, "Hey, dude" and even a couple of "Yo, Mattie-C." In class, kids who had ignored me before, notice me. Some of it has a pitying vibe to it, but most of it feels like genuine acknowledgement and understanding.

    This day feels like one of those movie scenes where someone is walking along, peppy music plays in the background, the sun is shining, cartoon birds chirp and swirl about and everyone throws you love along the way. And everyone knows it can't last. The abrupt record scratch stop is coming. In teen movie parlance, it's the scene where the skinny, geeky kid is lured to the hot chick's place for the night of his life and, only after having stripped down to his tighty-whities with his hands cupped over his eagerness, the hot chick emerges with her pack of mean girls loaded with cameras and unlimited data plans to blast his embarrassment and eagerness all across the web.

My tighty-whitie moment comes when I receive a slight ego boost from the complimentary comments of my AP literature teacher as he prepares to begin class, and a hand-delivered summons arrives requesting my immediate presence in the principal's office. In my twelve years of school, thirteen counting kindergarten, I have never been called into the principal's office, not even over my little shoving match with Robby Márquez. In a way, I kind of like the thrill it gives me, but like every other good kid summoned to the overlord of the school's lair, my mind also races with visions of torture, harsh interrogation and a complete loss for any reason why the principal would need to summon me.

The secretary I hand the summons to calls me sweetie and tells me to go on back. I'm expected, she says. A woman in a powdery blue pant suit stands up to greet me.

"Ethan, come on in. We haven't met. I'm Dr. Caldwell. I'm the principal here."

Reid said I should save my name corrections for formal moments. Summoned to the principal's office feels like the ultimate formal situation.

"It's Ethan-Matthew."

"Excuse me?"

"My first name is Ethan-Matthew. It's all one name. It's just this crazy thing my parents did because they couldn't decide between the two, and they didn't want a name people would automatically shorten, which is kind of funny because

The Closest Thing to a Normal Life

by giving a me a two-name first name, people automatically shorten it to just the first name, but it's just one name run together, so it's Ethan-Matthew."

Yes, I'm rambling, but I've never been called to the principal's office before.

"Thank you for letting me know, Ethan-Matthew. I'm sorry about what happened to your parents and that I haven't spoken to you about it before now, especially now that we have an important issue to discuss, Mr. Canton."

Okay, I know I've never been to the principal's office before, but I know when they switch from calling you by your first name to calling you Mister, shit is about to go down.

"Yes?" I ask, feigning any knowledge of whatever she can possibly mean.

"This website you've put up..."

"Yes, ma'am?"

"This *Blue Dog Alt*...It's not a school sanctioned publication?"

I know she means that as a statement and not a question. I lived with two top-class journalists for too long not to know when someone is trying to intimidate you under the guise of kindness and faux questions.

"No, ma'am, it's not, but that's kind of the whole point of it being something alternative."

"Mr. Canton..." There's that mister thing again. "We have school publications, which, if I'm not mistaken, you are a part of."

If I'm not mistaken—this is one of those things adults say to try to make you think they are having a genuine, impromptu conversation with you, when they really have an agenda and aren't really much concerned about your part in the conversation. It's a fake way of them trying to sound fallible, genuine, like there is the slightest possibility they might be, even though they know they're not, mistaken. I know she wants a reaction, that she is waiting for the angsty and impulsive teen to surface, so I merely answer.

"I am."

"Well, Mr. Canton?"

That's another thing adults do. They try and give you the impression that they respect you as an equal, that they value your input. They continue with the honorifics, the misters and sirs to show respect, but it's really designed to let you know your place. It's a false respect rooted in the contrast of an adult bestowing pretention. She's waiting for an answer, for me to finish her thought, but it's a ruse, a ploy to get me to say something she can use against me for my own best interest, or—cue the mantra of every superhero movie conflict in the world—"the greater good."

But I wait. I say nothing. People, I have learned, don't like awkward silence.

Silence.

More silence.

Continued silence.

Success.

"Well, Mr. Canton, perhaps we will have to look into some video broadcasting news production classes for the future."

Another adult ploy: the olive branch. Let me offer you something I think you want but still keeps me in control because in reality I'm offering you what I want but want you to think it's what you want.

"But for now, since we don't currently have those classes, it would be best if you confine your efforts to the sanctioned school publications we do have."

Here is where she is either expecting argument or acquiescence, protestations of how this isn't fair. But that's not my plan.

"Why?"

I can see she hasn't expected anything so direct or succinct.

"Excuse me?" Another adult tactic to make you question yourself. A chance for you to realize you've stepped too far over the proverbial line.

"Why, and I'm not meaning to be disrespectful—*a common kid tactic that lets adults know you kind of know what the hell you're doing*—do I need to 'confine my efforts to the sanctioned school publications' we have?"

"Mr. Canton, you are new here, so you probably don't really understand this..."

Try not to roll your eyes. Try not to roll your eyes. Try not to roll your eyes.

"...but we are very much about our traditions at Pearl Heights, and our publications are a part of those traditions. They are also supervised by an adult, a certified teacher. I'm sure you were just trying to be edgy by using profanity, but that really isn't appropriate for school. An adult sponsor would not have let that slip by, and even at that, the adviser is not the final authority on that. You probably aren't familiar with prior review...."

Is she kidding me? Does she really think I don't know Tinker v. Des Moines, Hazelwood v. Kuhlmeier, Dean v. Utica Community Schools? This is the stuff we study in journalism classes with certified journalism teachers.

"...but school administration ultimately decides what goes into publications. Besides, you all will be applying to colleges, and may come to regret being recorded or in print using such inappropriate language."

At this point, my internal dialogue is now having to scream, *Don't roll your eyes.* We used "dick," "shit" and the big f-bomb, but only once each. Hell, I've heard Grams say worse, except for "fuck," but that so isn't the point. We aren't creating a school disruption, we aren't being lewd or vulgar, we aren't advocating drug use and, most importantly, which is where school law on publications lands, we aren't a school-sponsored publication.

"Well," I say standing up to leave, "thank you for your concerns. I'll certainly keep that in mind for future stories."

My grip on composure and maturity is fading and my annoyance is growing. Annoyance at the attempt to get me to cease and desist the first thing that made me feel connected to the community I now find myself in and annoyance that I'm missing my English class for this lame discussion. Sure, my teacher's fascination with Thomas Hardy confounds us all, but his jokes are the worst in the best way. He's passionate about writing and British literature, and Michigan football, but he can also dish on Big Foot, *The Walking Dead* and *Phineas and Ferb*. I'm missing all of that for this.

"Mr. Canton, you don't seem to understand what I'm saying. I'm afraid..."

She's afraid? This is another adult tactic. But I learned from my parents not to fall for bullshit. "I'm afraid" is meant to sound intimidating and altruistic at the same time.

"...you're not going to be able to go forward with future issues. This just..."

"Dr. Caldwell," I say still standing and working my way to exit, "I know we used some colorful language, but we're kids telling real kids' stories to other kids. Sometimes that gets gritty and colorful. We're not trying to be edgy, we're just being real, and..." I haven't played the dead parents card yet, so this seems like as good a point as any to. "...this is something that my parents would be really proud of me for doing. I haven't been able to find my place at this school, I haven't found my place on *The Blue Review*... so this is what's helping me get through everything going on in my life."

I have looked at this year as something to just get through, survive until June, but in the moment, I realize I have nothing to lose. I'm out of here in June, I'm not tied to this school or its traditions. I literally have nothing to lose, so I become even more emboldened.

"Thanks for your concerns, but I really need to get back to class. If you'd like to discuss this again, I'm sure my grandparents will be happy for us all to sit down together and talk."

I turn and walk out, heart pumping, knees knocking. I pull my phone out and text Reid.

EM: Dude, just left principal's office
Reid: No shit. For what?
EM: Blue Dawg Alt
Reid: No shit? crazy gtg teacher looking at me
EM: k

Later that day, as I walk into journalism class, I can feel the chill emanating from the room. There's a combination of people looking at me like I've stepped in dog shit, and the rest look at me like I was dog shit. It's that wonderful experience of walking into a room and everyone stops talking, which lets you know they were talking about you before you walked in.

Of course, I'm used to that in this class. Ms. Gillis glares at me a little longer than usual, but I've known from the moment this idea popped into existence that she would take *Blue Dawg Alt* as a personal attack, and in a way, it is. It is an attack on the complacency of tradition, an attack on the hierarchy of high school and an attack on the selfishness of trying to regain faded high school glory at the expense of students.

The Blue Dawg Alt seeks out the ignored, the overlooked, the unsung and the derivative. Zach in Hats will never make the pages of *The Blue Review*. Dalton Birdwell, the koosh ball kid who walks throughout the hallways during passing periods tossing a koosh ball to himself. No one on *The Blue Review* staff is talking to him, trying to find out his story. No one is talking to Bernadette "Birdy" Whitley, the clerk at the Pic & Pac convenience store across the street from Pearl Heights Middle School who has worked there for 38 years and who follows the lives of Pearl Heights kids when they start coming into the store on their own, once they hit middle school. Birdy, who told me the first time I walked into the store, "You're the spitting image of your daddy," and said how she broke down in tears when she read about what happened to him.

My parents taught me to observe the world around me. To take it all in, to zoom out for the big picture and microscope in for the details, and then ask so what? They taught me to look for connections, to think of the fragments of life as pieces of a puzzle to try and fit together. Mom and Dad would love *Blue Dawg Alt*. Mom would love that CC pushed me to do it, that CC looked like she wanted to kick my ass for initially waffling on the idea. Dad would have loved Reid and his *esprit de corps*, his effortless coolness while also not giving a shit about being cool.

They would have loved that I have these people in my life. They would want them for me. They would want someone who would call me out for even thinking about backing down from the hard things. They would want me to have someone I could completely let go and ugly cry in front of and who also calls me out on my shit. I hate that my parents will never know these people. So, screw Ms. Gillis sitting at her desk furtively and randomly staring daggers at me. Screw Dr. Caldwell for trying to manipulate me with delayed sympathy and for trying to intimidate me with faux administrative concerns over content. My parents died because somebody didn't like what they as journalists had to say, so the petty-ass concerns of two grown-ass adults looking to safeguard their status quo means shit to me.

Plus, people are reacting to what we're doing. Seniors comment on how stupid they think the controversy over senior side-parking is. The consensus of the buzz around campus in the days after we publish is for juniors and seniors with permits to park wherever they can find a spot and for sophomores to not even try. We write an editorial encouraging the football team to stay through to the entire school song when the band plays it after games instead of running off to the locker room before it ends. We encourage the team to support the band who supports by performing before the game starts to well after it ends.

No way in hell am I going to stop.

20

So, I don't.

By the first week in November, my life feels almost—sorry Dr. Robles—normal. In class, it becomes like I've always been around with only the slightest scent of new kid still clinging to me. Even the kids in journalism class almost accept me—almost. I'm still not doing anything other than copy-editing, but most of the staff has started to recognize that I know what I'm doing. I may not have had editor behind my name, but kids on staff are coming to me as if I do. Often it happens outside of class to avoid the ire of Ms. Gillis, but it is happening. Torrie and the football guys never warm up to me, but Kelly takes to asking my opinion on all manner of *Blue Review* matters.

Life is good.

Mostly.

Reid is right. I get faster over the cross-country season. Good thing. Coach is right. He qualifies seven runners for the regional meet. Good thing. This bodes well for qualifying at least four runners for the state meet. Good thing... mostly.

As I'm going into the fourth mile at the regional cross-country meet, a runner from another school has moved to pass me on a curve, and our ankles cross. We tumble to the ground on top of each other. I don't pop up as quickly as I expect to and, while I'm able to run without limping, my season ends at the regional meet. I've gone a pretty good while without a major emotional freak out, but when I see Gramps waiting for me at the end of the course, I fall into his hug and sob and sob. The physical pain subsides about the time the blood running down my leg dries. Only then do I realize how much I wanted to qualify for the state meet. In my mind, I had imagined my parents there to greet me and celebrate advancing to state, but both were figments of my imagination and a reminder that I'll never have Mom and Dad there to celebrate my accomplishments or hug me when I hurt. Reid, who has pushed me all season in an unrealistic belief that I can catch him, qualifies. Wiley qualifies and Victoria, of course, wins the regional meet. The one time I thought Reid would know what I needed, he didn't. I wish he would have grabbed my hand and squeezed it at my last ever varsity meet the way he did at my first, but the pure elation on his face at qualifying for state jolts me into the realization that this is his time, not mine. Our friendship can't always be about what I need. This time, Reid needs to see me being happy for him, which I am.

I do get to go to the state meet. Reid's parents have insisted that his *Dawg* crew be there to cheer him on at state, so when the time for the meet comes around, they load up their Escalade with snacks, me, Malibu, Gage and Carlisle and drive us up to Round Rock, Texas for the state meet.

Our next issue of *Blue Dawg Alt* is loaded with cross country coverage—a slight conflict of interest for us, but who cares. Victoria became 5A girls' state champion, Wiley finished 12th, Reid 27th and Coach B was named cross country coach of the year. With our season officially over, I worry a bit about what will occupy my time now that I am no longer desperate to survive until June.

Seasons in high school are marked by sports. When the football team, in a shocking upset, loses in the first round of the playoffs, the school's collective attention and interest shifts to basketball season. And though I don't know a give-and-go from a pick-and-roll, I sit with Reid in the stands of every game, home and away, to cheer on the cheerleaders. There is less spectacle with basketball but also less formality. During football season, cheerleader watching—wow, does that sound creepy—is impeded by railings and a track, barriers that reinforce the spectator aspect of the game. But with basketball, it feels like we're on the court with the team and the cheerleaders. Reid and I always sit in the lower-level stands, which allow us to have actual eye contact and conversation with CC during the games.

Reid and I have become each other's shadows. Reid has eaten so many dinners with us and spent so many nights over at the house that Grams and Gramps offer him his own key. We're always together, anyway, so it doesn't make much sense. Reid takes it anyway. He loves it and insists on unlocking the front door even when it isn't locked.

The change in sports seasons isn't the only change sweeping the campus. There's a tension, a dividing of camps, an uneasiness hanging over the school like a fog. I see the first evidence of tension during homecoming week. At the time, I'm annoyed by it, but write it off as little more than immature teen behavior that comes from being spoiled and living in a bubble. Spirit days are part of the homecoming week tradition. There's a different theme for each day during homecoming that students dress up for. There's "80s Day," "Twin Day" and, in an homage to one of San Antonio's biggest traditions, "Fiesta Day." CC tries to explain the hullabaloo surrounding Fiesta. "Hullabaloo" was definitely a Dad word. If Mom and I were ever squabbling, he would come in and say, "What's all this hullabaloo, boo-boos," and we would laugh at the ridiculous voice he would use and usually forget why we were squabbling.

CC promised we would "hit Fiesta hard" when it came around, and Reid said he would fight her over taking me to King William's Fair, but that we would definitely watch her in the Battle of Flowers Parade. Apparently, there would be plenty of events for us to split or that the three of us could attend together in the ten-day event that started as a parade back in 1891 to commemorate the heroes of the Battle of the Alamo and the Battle of San Jacinto. But Fiesta Day during homecoming is the first taste of an even bigger ugliness to come and a peek at the underlying hate festering across the country.

I had no idea what to wear for Fiesta Day, but Reid said he had me covered. When the day finally arrives, he brings me one of his guayaberas and a sash covered in medals. Every ounce of teen inside me tells me I'm not supposed to like this shirt, but I can't not fall in love with it. It's decidedly ethnic: white fitted linen with the most intricate and colorful stitching of red and navy-blue thread embroidered in a panel down each front side of the shirt. The navy-blue stitches zig zag around a diamond shape stitched in red with a blue cross stitched inside the red diamond. The pattern of a half red diamond with a half navy-blue cross repeats on each side of the center design as if it's part of a bigger tapestry. The embroidered pattern rests over panels of the most elaborate and tightly stacked pleats. The guayabera is simple, elegant and stunning all at once.

"Reid, this is fucking awesome."
"Yeah, it's pretty bad-ass."
"Like I could wear these every day."
"Well, that one cost $250, so maybe not every day."
"Holy shitbombs. Seriously?"
"It's cool, don't worry about it. You can have it."
"I can't..."
"Shut up and take the damn shirt."

I decline the sash of Fiesta medals, because as cool as they are—different groups, organizations and businesses designed and sold medals to raise funds for different charitable organizations and it's a thing to collect them—I don't want anything covering up my new favorite shirt.

Fiesta is a celebration of the rich Mexican heritage that imbues every part of San Antonio, and Fiesta Day at school reflects it. Girls across campus sport the most brightly colored Mexican dresses with ornate floral patterns embroidered from top to bottom, while others parade around in *coronas de flores*. Guys either wear guayaberas, though none as gorgeous as mine, or sombreros. It's a glorious celebration of Mexican culture. Mom would have loved this.

I am loving this day until I start to notice the kids not dressed in Fiesta gear. Sure, there are the kids who just don't participate and wear their everyday clothes, their regular jeans and T-shirts, their oxford shirts and khaki shorts, their baby doll dresses and shorty shorts. But there are also those who are making other, obvious statements with what they wear. Hats are not allowed in the building except during these-dress up days, so with the sombreros pulling my attention, I initially miss the dots of red baseball caps bobbing indiscriminately down the halls. On this day celebrating Mexican heritage, a crop of privileged White kids has decided to wear their Make America Great Again hats. I have put the budding journalist inside me aside to appreciate the beauty of the Mexican side of me, but now I can't help but see the conscious choice too many students have made. Mixed in with the red MAGA hats are a spattering of green T-shirts with the words "Border Patrol" in large white print on the front. What a bunch of assholes. I think of my Lito and Tita, both born in Mexico, of my *tías* and *tíos* who all moved back to Mexico, who were all educated, intelligent, kind, loving and proud of their Mexican heritage. How can people be so stupid, disrespectful and ignorant of the struggles and reasons people choose to cross the border. I try to ignore them, roll my eyes every time I pass one of them and find it pretty disgusting. I chalk it up to stupid bravado and election enthusiasm. I hoped it isn't a true reflection of how they really feel. By pajama day, as hard as it is to believe, the sartorial stupidity escalates.

For a population where most aren't even eligible to vote, the students have divided into definite camps, sides and factions. It shouldn't surprise me that the student body, made up mostly of affluent White kids, is pretty conservative. But I am surprised at the level of vitriol you can hear around the school. There are students who are clearly just following the leanings of their parents, and then there are also students who are social justice dilettantes. There is a minority, however, that's clearly passionate about their political affiliations. What is unfortunate is that one side feels emboldened to revert to the basest disdain for decorum and civility. The MAGA hats are everywhere, especially on the heads of guys who keep them on until the last possible moment they walk into the building. I have to say, when you see what they wear and listen to them, patriotism seems more like White nationalism and a new red scare.

November sucks because the side that got three million more votes lost the election. For the other side, November marks the launching of a new level of drunken power that gives permission to a host of deplorable behaviors. Trouble is on a slow boil.

A week off for Thanksgiving can't have come at a better time. After watching a few post-election pundit debates in English class, the tension between the debaters is reflective of the tension festering on campus. *The Blue Review* doesn't help matters much by devoting the center spread of the issue before Thanksgiving break to the presidential election results. Because

I've spent the last four months culling through past issues of the paper, I know that this is the first center spread ever devoted to a presidential election. Yes, a Thanksgiving vacation is definitely needed.

The week off is also the hardest week of the year for me. Dr. Reyes and I have talked about what to expect, how the most insignificant thing can trigger a response from me. We even talk about how trying to avoid triggers can elicit the types of responses I'm trying to avoid. It's not like we celebrated a traditional American Thanksgiving living abroad anyway, especially because my journalist parents had spent years enlightening me on the myths perpetuated about Thanksgiving. Dr. Reyes is helping me deal with the holiday season in general.

The week starts off as a bummer. I knew it was coming because Reid told me about it. He has left for the week to visit family in Dallas before going to New York for the Macy's Thanksgiving Day Parade. I feel a little silly missing him. College applications, admissions essays, Netflix and YouTube take up a good chunk of my time, but I've really gotten used to Reid just always being around. With Reid away and a week off from school, time with CC suddenly becomes the thing I look forward to.

I intended to sleep in on my first day of Thanksgiving break, but no, it's 6:30 in the morning, and I'm sitting on the curb outside the house waiting for CC to pick me up and take me to a *tamalada con las señoritas de la iglesia*. I may have pretended I didn't know anything about a *tamalada*, but I've been making tamales with my *tita* since I was a little boy. From the early days of meeting CC, I've told her I'm working on becoming a southern charmer, but if there is something I don't need any help with, it's charming *las señoritas*. I've been doing that my whole life. *Las señoritas* see the light-skinned guy come in to help with the *tamalada*—which already impresses them because guys like to eat the tamales, but they never want to help make them. And then when I hit them with *"Buenos días ¿En qué les puedo ayudar?"* I'm no longer just the *güerito*, I'm *el güerito guapo*. And if speaking to *las señoritas* in Spanish isn't enough, when I start spreading *masa* on corn husks with the artistry of Diego Rivera, it's all *"Ay, m'ijo, mira qué suave hace los tamales."* They love me. Across the table, CC rolls her eyes at me.

I definitely hear about it from her when she takes me home.

"Um, excuse me, but those ladies are supposed to love me, and now it's all '*Ay*, Mateo' and *m'ijo* this and *m'ijo* that."

"Um, you forgot '*güerito guapo*.'"

"Well, you are kind of cute."

Holy shitbombs, she just called me cute. But cute like a puppy or cute like I wouldn't make the worst boyfriend? Damn, I've been spending so much time with Reid that I just figured I had settled into the friend zone with CC before even attempting to be more than friends. Play it cool. Exude confidence. Be more like Reid.

"I'm way more than kind of cute."

"You actually are. And you make tamales and speak Spanish. You're the child my mother wishes she had."

"Whatever."

"I know, I know. But my mom does think you're pretty *guapo*."

Even if I hadn't spent the last few months in therapy and been hearing the voice of Dr. Robles in my head on a loop, learning to know what people are and aren't saying when they talk, I still would have known that, yes, Ms. DeSoto probably does think I'm pretty *guapo*, but so does her daughter. She's just not ready to admit it... yet.

CC lets me sleep in a bit today, but not by much. San Antonio in November is an odd and wondrous mix of temperatures. When CC picks me up at 9 in the morning to walk the trails at Brackenridge Park, temperatures are in the low 60s and only rise into the mid 70s by the afternoon. It's perfect weather for a walk through the park. Though I had never considered myself the kind of person to get freaked out by birds. As soon as we park and get out of her car, we're practically surrounded by flocks of birds: big-ass black vultures wandering about, hanging out on picnic tables and chilling on the outdoor grills. It makes me think about all the people who've had cookouts here and whether they cleaned those things or used foil or something, because everywhere I look, those big-ass vultures are perched on every grill in the park. They're cool and creepy at the same time. Nope, definitely more on the creepy side.

There are more than just black vultures. The park is a rookery. Egrets and herons rest high in the trees. They also cover the surrounding area in bird shit, and the place definitely stinks where the egrets congregate. It is a stunning sight to see the trees packed with hundreds of birds. CC has a bird pamphlet that she keeps from an elementary school field trip to the park, so we go about attempting to identifying as many birds on the pamphlet as we can find. We're able to easily identify the black-bellied whistling ducks, mallards and wood ducks, which are kind of meh, because, well, they're ducks. But there are so many types of birds, the challenge is actually kind of fun.

The list of birds is exhaustive, with species as basic as sparrows and field birds, but it also includes Carolina Chickadees, red-shouldered hawks and golden-fronted woodpeckers. We aren't hard core bird watchers—no binoculars or pith helmets—but we get giddy when we spot a black-crested titmouse. If I wasn't intrigued enough by CC before, this morning is opening a new level of admiration. She isn't interested in sitting around in a Starbucks drinking iced coffees or binging on Netflix, not that I hate any of that. Instead, she's drawn to the same dorky shit I've been drawn to as the kid who actually likes school field trips to the museums for the exhibits and not just to get out of class.

We meander through trails and paths, scoping out the odd assortment of art installments along the way and counting the number of cats who call the park home: 27 at this point. We also wave to dog walkers and observe the variety of humans in the wild. One man, probably in his late twenties, sits shirtless at a picnic table brushing his silky, black hair that flows down to the middle of his back to his waist. At another picnic table, a woman unloads clusters of flowers in cellophane wrapping that she spreads out and makes into arrangements.

We head out of Brackenridge Park and cross the tracks of the zoo train that shuttles kids and families through the park along the banks of the San Antonio River, the Witte Museum and the San Antonio Zoo. We cross over to Davis Park because CC likes to walk by the cottage and craftsman houses that are located in the neighborhood behind Davis Park.

In Davis Park, we find a marker from the Texas Historical Commission that literally takes me home. The huge plaque affixed to a large stone base commemorates the Acequia de Arriba, an irrigation ditch that the people who lived in the area petitioned the King of Spain for in the late 1700s. The missionaries in the area opposed the acequia, but the king relented in 1778 and the flow of water from the acequia helped the area flourish. Seven ditches were irrigated and the limestone from the excavation was used in the development of the city of San Antonio, and water from the acequias was channeled to neighborhoods, gardens and the five missions in San Antonio. CC is as fascinated by it as I am, and then she practically skips through the neighborhood garden across from the historical marker. Damn this girl, this cheerleader who can cover herself in glittery makeup, throw round-off backhand springs, follow vultures in a park and get absorbed in dorky history stuff. I love that we're spending so much time together.

But nothing can prepare me for the CC I see on Thanksgiving Day.

Another early morning. It's literally the crack of dawn when CC shows up to get me. Without my knowledge, she has registered me to volunteer with her at The Raúl Jiménez Thanksgiving Dinner, which I find out is a pretty huge deal. Raúl Jiménez started the dinner in 1979 with the goal of feeding 100 of the city's elderly and less fortunate. The Thanksgiving dinner now feeds 25,000 of the city's hungry and in-need citizens. Jiménez was a restaurant owner who had a heart for the needy and believed no one should be alone on Thanksgiving. He passed away in 1998, and his family has continued the tradition.

It is the most amazing thing I have ever done. There are 5,000 people volunteering: men, women, children, college kids, young and old. It's heartwarming, just overwhelmingly heartwarming. And the meal is open to everyone. There are tourists visiting the city who wander in and get fed. There are people who have no one to spend Thanksgiving with, people who have no home and people who have no way to provide this kind of meal for their families. The sounds of trumpets and *gritos* from Mariachis echo around the convention center, along with the unmistakable laughter that emanates from joy. The smile never leaves CC's face the entire time we're there.

Lots of high school kids volunteer at events like this. Some are clearly here to add a line to their resumes, some are here fulfilling mandatory volunteer hours (a contradiction I have never understood) and some are here by force, coercion or parental threat. Not CC. CC has so many volunteers from cheerleading that she doesn't have to run around trying to finesse and fudge the required number of volunteer hours needed for National Honor Society membership. She doesn't need anything extra to pad her resume in an effort to impress colleges and scholarship committees. No, this she does because she loves it, and I feel honored that she shares it with me. I feel like nothing and no one else matters but CC.

After a while, my phone starts vibrating in my pocket. My phone vibrates and vibrates, but I don't want to be the stereotypical teenager constantly checking his phone at an event of this magnitude. I turn it off. I mean, I'm here to volunteer. CC and I have the task of handing out plates of food. Person after person files by for food, so I don't have a moment to check my phone, even if I want to. By the time we leave, I'm exhausted in the very best of ways.

When I wave goodbye to CC and walk into the house, another sea of activity greets me. Grams' two sisters and their children, their children's spouses and their grandchildren are in various stages of Thanksgiving Day activity. The aromas swirl around me, and I suddenly realize I'm famished. Cursory greetings are exchanged, introductions and re-introductions for family members not seen in years and some extra-long hugs communicating condolences for unimaginable loss. Grams tells me to run up and shower, relax for a bit, and she'll call me down when dinner is ready. I love her for this, for giving me permission to not have to perform or answer the dizzying array of questions to come. I bound up the stairs and suddenly remember, shitbombs, I forgot to turn my phone back on. As my phone glows to life, I immediately go to my texts.

Reid: Hey
Reid: Hey
Reid: u there?
Reid: ????????

Reid: Ethan-Matthew Pocahontas der Cranberry Burberry von Butterball?????
Reid: WTF
Reid: ??????WTF???????????
EM: sorry sorry sorry sorry sorry—really, really sooo-oooooory
EM: phone off all day
Reid: you suck
EM: I know sorry sorry sorry
Reid: why no fone
EM: volunteering
Reid: RJ dinner?
EM: Yah
Reid: CC?
EM: yah
Reid: k
Wait, what? What's with "k"? That felt kind of abrupt. "K" is rarely good. Is he annoyed I took so long to respond? Just ignore it. Don't make it a thing.
EM: hows nyc
Reid: fucking freezing!!!!
EM: how was parade
Reid: fucking freezing
EM: so it was cold
Reid: dude, my balls are now small as yours
EM: mine are perfectly lovely
Reid: saw your bird pics
EM: vultures r fucking creepy
Reid: hate them
EM: back tomorrow night?
Reid: yah
EM: cool
Reid: can I ask you something

EM: duh, of course
Reid: u miss me
EM: duh, of course
Reid: cool, miss u 2
EM: hang saturday?
Reid: duh, of course
EM: gtg grams calling for dinner soon
Reid: later
EM: peace

I knew when my phone was vibrating earlier it had to be Reid. I also didn't want to chat with him when I was with CC. That was my and CC's time, but I kind of regret doing that now because I really do miss Reid, and I can't wait for him to come home. But for now, shower and Thanksgiving dinner.

21

The week off from school seemed to have been just what everyone needed to diffuse the tension.

Pearl Heights has a stellar academic reputation, and semester exams are a prime example of how that reputation perpetuates itself. The week after Thanksgiving is set aside for exam reviews because each teacher is required to give a comprehensive final. The rationale of preparing us for college accounts for us having to review every infinitesimal detail from day one of class and then spit it all back on exams that feel intentionally designed to wreck GPAs.

Just like in college, Pearl Heights has a dead week after review week. School activities grind to a halt. No sports, no practice, no extracurricular activities—just studying, non-stop studying. Most of the teachers hand out study packets, which CC and Reid tell me end up mirroring the exams they give, but there's still lots of material to cover. On top of the regurgitation element of the exams, they all must include essay questions, so you really have to know your shit if you hope to keep your GPA above water. It's intense, but it also keeps most of us focused on school rather than the post-political tension waiting to punk us all.

Dead week aside, other traditions are also going on, which I discover when CC asks me to be her date to *Faux For*, which rhymes with gopher, and is, as best I can describe, a prom alternative. Most Pearl Heights traditions have been around for ages. *Faux For*, however, has only been around since the late 1980s and has pretty progressive roots. What was explained to me is in the late 1980s someone circulated a petition around campus to allow students to bring a same gender date to prom, which is pretty damn progressive for that time. But a school so set in tradition isn't going to allow anything so scandalous to happen, and Pearl Heights imposed prom restrictions that continue to this day. Students have to submit the name of their prom date when tickets are purchased, students must arrive with the date they purchased a ticket for and present school IDs. Any student who changes a date must purchase a new ticket, and no single sales of tickets are allowed.

Like students from all generations, when authorities apply onerous restrictions on students, they tend to rebel. The difference with the *Faux For* rebellion is that it grew into a tradition. Although no one ever took a same gender date, it was more about the principle, and students began holding *Faux Prom for Everyone* that morphed into *Faux For* and much more. Junior and senior girls now pay $500 to be on the *Faux For* committee and organize the entirely non-school sponsored or sanctioned event. It is hosted off-campus during winter break, and only juniors and seniors are allowed to attend. The girls ask the guys to be their dates for the night. The committee picks the theme, arranges the venue and menu, and gets to attend the exclusive after party that is only for committee members and their dates This seems contradictory to the origins of the event, but I've decided to pick my battles, as the end of senior year feels within actual reach.

This year's theme is "The Mod Squad," which means hitting Goodwill in search of '70s attire. At first, I'm slightly confused when CC tells me she and Reid were originally going as friends but is sure someone else will ask him. Therefore, she has asked me, and now, I wonder if I'm going as a friend. I certainly hope she's thinks of me as more than a friend. Maybe CC got tired of waiting for me to ask her out and took matters into her own hands. It's not like I haven't thought about asking her out because I have... a lot. How would I do it? Where would we go? What would we go in? Gramps' Mercedes? Grams' Volvo? The Vespa? I don't even have a license to drive. Believe me, the thought of kissing a girl in any of my grandparent's vehicles is a major buzz kill. Besides, what if I'm wrong about everything? I seriously have no game. I don't know if she's just super nice and mega cool or if she's even remotely into me. If she is into me, then I have a whole new set of issues to figure out. If she's not, then I've possibly screwed up the best thing I have going at this point in my life. The bottom line is, I choose the path of safe resistance: I pine for her in secret.

Final exams week is hell. Everyone takes two finals a day. They're scheduled for ninety minutes each in the morning with Friday reserved for make-up testing... if you're crazy enough to miss an exam. Teachers have the rest of the day for grading exams, and students have the afternoon to continue studying. Over the review week and dead week, I find myself resenting all the pressure put on us for finals. Then again, when I turn in my last exam, I actually feel proud of myself, accomplished. I mean, I'm not going to say any of that to my teachers, but damn, I hate admitting that I kind of appreciate them for the challenge.

After surviving finals and no longer having to dwell on leitmotifs, units of atomic mass, neutrinos, conquistadors and the "Columbian exchange," my mind has time to dwell on heavier matters. My life has reached the moment we have all been tiptoeing up to: Christmas. Previously, the Christmas break was when I would spend time with Grams and Gramps in San Antonio, and they would dote over me and catch up on all the happenings in my life. It was a time for laughing and lemon ricotta cookies and 1000-piece jigsaw puzzles. A time for popcorn and pajamas while watching Christmas classics: *It's a Wonderful Life, Jingle All the Way, The Ref* and *Die Hard*.

Grams would put up four Christmas trees around the house but wait until I arrived to decorate the last one. We would go shopping for new ornaments each year that happened to be my current obsession. We would decorate the tree with everything from sports to superheroes, my cartoon and television favorites: Superman, Spider-man, Snoopy, Woodstock, Doctor Who, Transformers, Meeko, Lilo, Flik, Elmo, Walking Dead, Frosty, Rudolph and Jack Skellington. She never cared that it didn't match the Martha Stewart standards of her other trees. It wasn't until I was older that the tree would get decorated all the way to the top because we would only put up ornaments as far as I could reach. So many of my mornings were spent lying on the floor and looking up at the tree, imagining conversations between Rudolph and Spidey, between The Doctor and Optimus Prime.

Grams would make brown sugar cookies that I looked forward to all year. Just like I learned the techniques of making tamales from Tita Cruz, I learned the craft of decorating cookies from Grams. Her brown sugar cookies were the canvases for her elaborate cookie art. She showed me how to mix, color and pipe the royal icing, how to sift, zest and crack eggs with one hand. As a child, my cookies were messy explosions of color, sprinkles and pearls, but Grams set them out with her creations as if they were of equal majesty.

Christmas used to be, as cliché as it sounds, the most wonderful time of the year. Now, as strong as Grams and Gramps are for me, a palpable miasma has surrounded us. Nothing overtly obvious but traces of memory haunt us in still whispers. Of course, they love me and don't regret bringing me to live with them, but I'm also a constant reminder of what they've lost. Still, I've learned some things about grief along the way. Along with it flat-out being okay to grieve, it's also okay to be happy along the way, too. Aside from Grams and Gramps, the thing that has made me happiest is my friendship with CC and Reid. I figure it can't hurt to add them to our family traditions. Reid does have his own key to the house, but most of the time when he's over, we're either in the pool or hanging in my room, so his contact with Grams and Gramps is pretty limited. Not anymore.

The best thing about our cookie decorating tradition is that we all used to join in: Mom, Dad, Gramps, Grams and me. This year CC and Reid join my grandparents and me. And just as I expected, Reid has everyone laughing so much, we worry we'll pee in our pants. He jokes about how three weeks into school I was still walking into the wrong classroom in the science building, "like he would actually sit down, start unloading his backpack and then look around and realize he was in the wrong class." He also tells them about the cat that attacked me on one of our morning runs.

"I would hardly call it an attack."

"Dude, it jumped off at fence at your head."

"Well, thanks to my cat-like reflexes, it didn't lay a paw on me," I say, and the room groans, literally groans and Grams squeezes icing at me from a piping bag. "Really, Grams? At least I didn't get pooped on by a bird."

"Stupid bird. Hit me right on the nipple," Reid says.

"Oh my God, how did you guys win any meets at all this year between pooping birds and attacking cats?" CC chimes in to say.

"No, no, no, no, no," Reid objects, "You can't say anything. You're not the one to talk, when one of your cheer moves ended up kicking that freshman girl in the face. Bam, blood everywhere."

"Oh, my God, she walked right into it. It's not my fault she doesn't know where to stand on the line."

"Um, you're the *head* cheerleader, right? Or are you the kick 'em in the *head* cheerleader?" Reid quips, and we all laugh.

"Reid, excellent job on the cookies. They like look the ones I used to make... when I was seven," I tease Reid.

"Oh, leave him alone," Grams says, grabbing his face that way old people do, and kisses his cheek. "These look more like the ones you did when you were five."

"Grandma Honey, ouch," Reid says and hugs Grams with one arm.

Neither Reid nor CC had ever seen *Jingle All the Way*, the best-worst Christmas movie ever. Watching it, we have a "grand ol' time," something Dad used to say. We munch on the cereal mix Grams made and eat the cookies we decorated as we nestle on the couch. Reid sits on one side of me, resting his head on my shoulder, and CC on the other side, her head resting on my other shoulder. I'm genuinely happy. Grams and Gramps sit on the love seat across from us. They have watched this movie with me every year, even though, I know, they hate it, but you endure for those you love. It's as perfectly normal as we can hope for, and I kind of think of it as my Christmas gift to them.

The next morning, we get up early, dress nicely and go to church. Is it because Christmas falls on a Sunday this year or that Grams and Gramps are ready to let go of something? For the first time since the funeral, we're going to church, the same church where we had the service for Mom and Dad. My breath draws short with my first step inside. The day of the funeral rushes back to me. I can smell the flowers, the lily and eucalyptus saturating the air, see the framed portraits of my parents standing guard in the foyer, hear the whispers of grief and murmurs of loss, feel the trembling of my knees and the quivering of my hands. Every part of me wants to race from the church and run for my life the way I did at my first cross country meet, almost as much as every part of me also wants to embrace the memory of my parents in this sanctuary.

We find seats near the back. Some friends of theirs come for hugs and handshakes. There are smiles, wishes of Merry Christmas and the lingering grasps of hands that communicate the depth of emotion words fail to express. The service is an expression of joy and gratitude for the gifts we have received—gifts of family and friends. And then the sermon turns to the gift of sacrifice, about how the entire Christmas story is based on a gift of sacrifice, how a father sacrificed his child to be raised by someone else, and the incredible trust it must have taken to trust your only child to someone else. I'm not sure whether I believe in fate, but, sitting in between Grams and Gramps this morning, I understand a little more about just how much my parents loved me.

After church, we drive to the cemetery. Grams has two wreaths made of magnolia leaves with red Christmas berries and pinecones that we place at each of their graves along with two poinsettia plants. Grams tells them I'm doing really well and that they would be really proud of me. She says this year's Christmas tree was especially lovely and that lots of Mom and Dad's friends wish them well and ask if there's anything they can do for them. Gramps tells them how much he loves and misses them and how they really would be impressed by all I have accomplished. Then, they say their goodbyes and say they'll wait for me in the car.

Standing there, I take it all in the wreaths, the flowers, the granite headstone. A light breeze agitates the leaves of a nearby tree, and I just start talking to them the way Dr. Robles said I should try.

"Hey, Mom, Dad. I miss you guys. Grams and Gramps are great. They've been so awesome to me, really. It's just, I don't know... I'm kinda getting used to it here. Sorry if that bothers you, Dad. I mean, I get why you had to get outta here. There are things about this place I really hate. Lots of guys at school are racist dicks. Sorry, Mom, but they are. They have no idea how stupid they look and sound because they have no idea what real problems feel like. I didn't make it to state in cross country, like I had hoped, but I started my own underground newspaper. It's not really underground, but we're—me and some kids I've met—telling really good stories and, you know, pushing back against the man," I say, chuckling a bit to myself as I kick the ground with the point of my shoe.

"I have made two really good friends, CC and Reid. You'd really like them. CC is all fiery Latina, even though she doesn't speak Spanish very much. She's all about culture and heritage, diversity and equal representation. She does all kinds of volunteering and is like into all kinds of social justice causes. And Reid... he's so awesome. He's super funny and like the most confident person I've ever met and doesn't care what anyone thinks. He's always teasing me about everything from my balls to my name. And the dude threw coffee at me—it wasn't hot or anything. I was just kind of having a freak-out moment. Anyway, they've been great. You'd really like them. You know, they are actually a lot like you guys. That's kind of funny."

I reach into the pocket of my sport coat and pull out my photo button from cross country. "Grams and Gramps ordered these during cross country season. It's a pretty good picture. They keep telling me how much we look alike, Dad. You should have seen them wearing these at every meet. We're trying to figure out where to take my senior pictures. CC took me to the Japanese Tea Gardens—that's a possibility. I applied to Northwestern... a couple of other schools, too: USC, NYU and Boston University. I also applied to UT. Gramps was pretty stoked about that. I hope to hear something before too long. Anyway, I really miss you guys. I wish so bad you were here, but you know what, I'm eventually gonna be okay. *Soy fuerte por su ejemplo. Ustedes son mi corazón, y en todo lo que hago estoy viviendo el cuento de su amor. Gracias por todo. Los amo mucho.*"

22

Plans for *Faux For* are set. CC will come to my house, where Reid, who's going with Victoria, will meet us. We'll take the obligatory pictures, and then all four of us will ride in Reid's truck to the shopping center where the charter buses will take us downtown to the hotel the committee booked to host the event. The whole thing is an organizational juggernaut. Waivers and agreements are signed and filed so everyone knows there's no departing from the event. Every appearance of propriety and good ol' fashioned fun is the way the event is billed, but from what every student attending knows, there's little in the way of adult supervision, just a few moms and dads of committee members and, unless it's something extremely egregious, the few chaperones there will ignore most of what they see. Still, tradition.

Our photo session is a hoot, as we say in Texas. The 70s don't get near enough fashion props. We look good. Reid sports a pair of lime green polyester pants, and I wear a pair of white ones. We both wear white platform shoes and long-sleeved ultra-clingy silk shirts that, despite winter weather finally arriving in San Antonio, we have unbuttoned almost down to our navels. Aviator sunglasses and a couple of gold chains complete our ensembles. Victoria has on a fringe vest over a white peasant blouse with puffy sleeves and a flowy floor-length flower-print skirt. But CC, and maybe I'm biased here, has rocked the mod-squad theme harder than any of us. She has on a gold lamé mini-dress with knee-high white go-go boots. She has a wide hair band over her hair, straight with the ends flipping out in a big curl. She looks like she stepped right out a James Bond movie. Our pictures are a collection of every disco-movie, exaggerated pose we can concoct. We laugh so hard and even talk about skipping the whole thing just to hang out together instead, but we can't let CC's organizational prowess as one of the planning committee members go unnoticed, so we load ourselves into Reid's truck and take off for a wild night.

Ten minutes into *Faux For*, I think I'll never have to attend another event in my life because this one has everything. The organizers have arranged for a casino night as a "Mod Squad" activity. There are blackjack, roulette, and craps tables. On entering, everyone is handed a stack of chips, and their winnings are good for raffle tickets and prizes. There's an open buffet, a magician who goes around the room doing close-up magic and a DJ selecting numbers for the dance floor. It is a sight to behold. Between the food, games, music, magic and dizzying array of 70s attire, I'm having the best high school experience ever. We dance, take photos in a booth and hit the gambling tables. I prove to be a terrible gambler and lose all but two of my chips, which I exchange for a raffle ticket.

Two hours have flown by before we realize we haven't eaten a thing. We sit at a table with the cohort of friends I've amassed over my first semester of senior year: Reid, Victoria, CC, Wiley, Malibu, Gage and their dates. While eating, we all laugh at the dance moves Reid displayed for us a few moments ago. I haven't laughed or been this carefree in months. We start pointing out the people in the room we who are already drunk, including Reid who claims only a slight buzz from the whiskey someone snuck into the party.

That's when Kelly, from *The Blue Review*, comes over to our table and says, "Hey, guys. Love the outfits. And Ethan-Matthew, I just wanted to say your last *Blue Dawg* was really good. I loved that story about Mrs. Patterson, the special ed teacher. I had no idea she used to work as an undercover cop in Hawaii or even that she had been in the military. That story was so fun, and then to pair it with the editorials on the lack of diversity in the teaching staff," she says, pulling up a chair to sit down without missing a step. "It was pure genius. I had never considered that in my entire time in this district that I've never had a Black teacher."

"Thanks, I appreciate that. We have some really cool stories we're working on for our next one. Are you guys doing something on *Faux For*?"

"Oh, hell no. It's not a school event, and it's just safer to pretend this thing doesn't actually happen. It's good clean fun and all, but someone's gonna throw up in the parking lot for sure, someone is breaking up with someone and someone's not going home a virgin anymore. So, yeah, we just don't touch it."

"You hear that, Reid," CC says. "You better not throw up in the parking lot."

"I'm not going to throw up in the parking lot. Besides, I'm in complete control of my *flaculties*," Reid jokes as he exaggerates slurring his words—at least I think he's exaggerating.

"Hey, we told you to stop hitting on the *flaculty*, you big flirt," Malibu says.

"How do you think he has straight *A's*?" Gage adds.

"I *earned* all those *A's*, except maybe physics."

"Don't you have Mr. Sutton for physics?" Wiley asks.

"I hear he has a cute ass," CC says.

Reid throws both hands in the air and shrugs, and the table laughs and issues utterances of mock contempt and shock.

A new voice enters the conversation, a voice harsh with biting contempt. "Why are you sitting with traitor boy, Kelly?" Torrie asks, shooting a cold stare at me as she walks up with Connor McCade, one of the football guys from journalism class.

"What are you talking about?" Kelly hits back.

"Seriously, Kelly? This guy..." she says, not even attempting to use my name. "First, he pity-parties his way onto staff and then stabs us in the back with his stupid online thing that nobody reads."

I'm literally speechless, a deer in headlights. The "nobody reads" stings, even though I know it isn't true because of the assortment of people stopping me in the hallways at school and giving me story suggestions.

I'm at a loss for words, but CC isn't. "Oh my God, Torrie, could you be more of a bitch? Go be bitter somewhere else."

This moment can't get worse, but it does.

"You're the one who's gonna be bitter somewhere else, when they build the wall and deport you," Connor snarls, the smirk on his face revealing how clever he considers his barb.

"What the fuck, asshole?" Reid blurts out, jumps to his feet and pushes his way from behind the table toward Connor.

Unphased, Connor hurls the egg roll in his hand at Reid and lurches forward himself.

Chaos ensues.

Wiley and Malibu jump up to put themselves between Connor and Reid. Gage puts himself in front of Reid while I try to hold him from behind. Glasses spill over, chairs fall backwards, "fuck you" is repeated, someone screams. Other guys in the vicinity join in the separating and holding back efforts before two dads and a mom make their way over to find out what's going on and calm things down.

The moment, as brief as it was, lingers in the air and ripples throughout the room, gossip spreading through the cliques and clusters interspersed around us. My heart is still pounding. I can feel Reid's heart pounding, my arm wrapped around him. I appreciate his instant chivalry but am thankful for everyone who stepped in as human obstacles, because they would have fought with each other for sure. I'm mostly glad that it did not come to that, because Reid is like a skinny waif, and Connor looks like he regularly appears shirtless on the cover of *I'll Kick Your Skinny Ass* magazine.

There are several minutes of *oh, my gosh, can you believe that, what the fuck* and *seriously, what's their dysfunction*, along with numerous recaps of what transpired. I just want to get back to the best night of my life.

"Wait, wait, wait.... I need to know something," I say.

The chatter at the table stops and everyone gives me their attention.

"Reid, how do you have an A in physics?"

Hoots, hollers and ooohs return to our group as all eyes turn to Reid.

Never one to miss an opportunity to remain in the spotlight, Reid stands up very dramatically and says, "Because..." He pauses, making sure all eyes are on him and begins singing, "My milkshake brings all the boys to the yard," then turns and twerks at us.

A few balled-up napkins fly in Reid's direction as laughter returns.

"Oh, my God, please stop," Victoria says pulling Reid back down to his seat.

Reid sits down basking in attention as our table and the tables around us applaud his performance.

Malibu leans forward, rests his elbow on the table, points a finger directly at Reid and in deep, direct tones, says, "Young man, if you are going to become a male gigolo slash pool boy, all you need is a C in physics."

The entire table breaks out in laughter, tuning out the lingering negativity. We bail on the after party because nobody in the group except me and CC can go, so we board the bus with the rest of the plebeians and ride back to the parking lot. I decide that I have the clearest head and drive us in Reid's truck to the twenty-four-hour Whataburger we end up at after any sports game because Reid likes to see how many special-order stickers he can get. He also always snags a Whataburger number tent for me because he says every true Texas kid has a collection of them.

After rounds of fries and onion rings with the spicy ketchup, our evening winds down as extended curfews reach their limits. We drop Victoria home first and then CC because we don't want her driving home alone so late. We'll figure out the situation of her car at my place later. Reid's in the back seat as I pull the truck up in front of her house, keep it running and walk her to her door. The bite of cold air stings our faces as we pull our coats tight to our bodies in a futile effort to keep warm.

"Thanks for tonight. It was the most fun I've had in a really long time... minus the racist insults," I say.

"Oh my God, Einstein. You're probably the only person who could make me laugh about tonight."

"Hey, you called me Einstein."

"I know. I think you're always going to be Einstein to me."

"I think I'm pretty lucky you're the first person I met here."

"I think I'm pretty lucky, too."

"I'm sorry that asshole was so awful to you tonight."

"He's always been an asshole, but I don't even want to waste any time thinking about someone that small-minded. I'm just glad you were with me," she says just before reaching up and pulling me into a kiss.

Her lips are soft and warm, and I instantly forget the cold biting through my small coat and ridiculously thin silk shirt. She pulls away, squeezes my hand, turns to unlock the door and says good night. As she disappears into the warm shelter of home, I'm bathed in the residual warmth of my first kiss while the cold methodically returns, and I'm reminded that all kisses, first kisses and last kisses, fade no matter how desperately you try to hold on to them.

23

We had texted Reid's parents earlier in the evening to let them know he would be spending the night with me. His buzz is wearing off, but, again, we're not stupid. Well, we are about some things, but drinking and driving isn't one of them. It really doesn't matter to Reid's parents that he's spending the night again. Up in my room, I grab a towel and a pair of boxers to shower away the effects of a night of dancing, while Reid plops down on my bed.

"I don't have any extra clothes here."

I reach into my drawer and throw a pair of boxers at Reid.

"Uuuggghhh, not Star Wars."

"Hey, not my fault Trekies are merchandising amateurs."

While Reid showers, I crawl into bed and stare at the ceiling thinking about the kiss, thinking about how to tell this story for the rest of our lives. It will be that she kissed me first. Aside from Reid in the back seat of his truck, the moment couldn't have gotten any more perfect for me to kiss her—moonlit night, cold weather encouraging physical proximity and a bonding experience after an encounter with bully. The stars were probably aligned in the sky above us, and I stood there literally and figuratively frozen until she made the first move. But I liked that. It was so CC—self-assured, spontaneous, sweet, and absolutely perfect.

As Reid flips off the lights and crawls into bed, we both lie still and stare at the ceiling, lost in thought until I have to ask the question that has lingered with me most of the evening.

"Reid, can I ask you something?"

"Shoot," he says rolling onto his side to face me.

"Are you like a closet MMA fighter or like secretly know judo?"

"No," Reid chuckles, "I've never been in a fight in my life. I've never even seen a real fight. Pearlies don't fight."

"Are you serious?"

"There hasn't been a school fight in the three years I've been in high school and long before that, too."

"You weren't worried that walking pile of muscles would kick your ass?"

"I didn't really think about it."

"He could have really..."

"Yeah, I know, but," he says adjusting his position and moving closer to me as I turn to face him, "guys have been joking about this border wall shit for a while now. It's stupid, and I'm just sick of hearing it, and CC's been my friend forever. I love her..."

My heart sinks a little and a bit of foreboding begins to churn inside me, wondering if I'm going to ruin something between them.

"She knows me better than anyone, and I wouldn't let anyone hurt her, except I think I'm going to hurt her more than anyone else possibly could."

"What are you talking about?"

"I know you like her. I think the whole world knows you like her, and she likes you, too. She's liked you for a while, but she didn't want to do anything to take advantage of all the emotional shit going on in your life, none of us did."

"What does that mean, none of us did?"

Reid lets out an audible sigh. "You remember the *thing* me and CC had a while back that you asked how it went, and I was like, 'meh.'"

"I remember."

"It was about you. She told me she liked you, told me all about meeting you in the stands of the stadium, but I told her I liked you, too, that I noticed you that first day of practice and that I couldn't take my eyes of you that first time we all went to lunch and when we met to plan for *Blue Dawg*."

Then, for the second time in the same night, someone reaches for my face and kisses me.

When I wake up, Reid is gone. I look out of my window, and CC's car is also gone. Maybe I dreamed everything from last night. Maybe it was all an elaborate ruse painstakingly executed over many months by the popular kid illuminati, and, before long, I'm going to end up tied to a flagpole in my underwear.

I text CC. No response.

I text Reid. No response.

Definitely getting tied to a flagpole in my underwear.

So many questions run through my head. What is going on here? Why am I not hearing from either of them? Are they playing me? Do I have a girlfriend now? A boyfriend? Holy shitbombs, what was that? I mean sure, I let CC kiss me, but I also let Reid kiss me. Of course, I've never kissed anyone before. I've always just assumed I'd have a girlfriend, do the traditional thing. I'd never considered a boyfriend. What if you just love who you love? It's funny that I felt the same thing when each of them kissed me—startled. I hadn't expected it from either of them. I'd thought about kissing CC on her porch, but I knew I wasn't going to go through with it. I'd never thought about kissing Reid, but I remember wanting him to hold my hand when I fell at the regional meet and didn't qualify for state. Neither kiss would have happened had it been left to me. CC's kiss was soft and delicate. Reid's strong but gentle. CC kissed me and walked away into her house. Reid kissed me, said good night, rolled over and went to sleep.

And now, I can't stop thinking about each kiss and about how their "thing" was about me. What was that about? Did they get together and lay out ground rules? Did they wager on whether they could both kiss me, on who could win me? Am I joke to them? Is CC really the awesome girl I think she is? Is Reid too good to be true with all his emotional support? Surely, I'm reading too much into all of this. Real people aren't this devious. They're just busy. Maybe they're embarrassed and trying to process it all. Maybe each is afraid I've picked the other.

Oh, my God. Who would I pick? CC, of course. I've been puppy-dogging after her from the moment she first walked up to me. This is the way it's supposed to be, right? But I've never had a Reid in my life before. This is a guy I've ugly cried in front of, a guy who helped me create the thing in my life that has given me purpose, a guy who I have no inhibitions with, and a guy I love. Is it really all that different?

If this were happening with any other person, Reid and CC are the ones I'd talk to about it. What do I do now, if they ever respond to me? Do I only talk to CC about me and her, only talk to Reid about him and me? Do they know that they've each kissed me? Shit, Reid has seen me naked, teased me about my balls so often I don't even notice it anymore. Is that fair? Did he have an unfair advantage that CC didn't? Wait, wait, wait? Has he had boyfriends before? Is he out? It's never come up. No one has ever said anything. Is everyone just that evolved, or does no one know? Well, CC knows. Do his parents know? Is this one of those our-name-is-a-really-big-deal-in-this-community-so-don't-bring-shame-on-the-house-of-Tibbitt's thing? What would Grams and Gramps say? What would my parents think about this? Sure, they wouldn't care, and they'd say, "We love you no matter what."

When I finally make it downstairs, Grams and Gramps want to hear all about *Faux For*, so I tell them all about how terrible I am at gambling, about the close-up magician pulling cards and trinkets out of places that had to verge on physical assault and how the editor of the school paper complimented me on my online paper. I conveniently left out anything about racist comments, nearly coming to blows and kissing a boy and a girl in the same night who are currently not communicating with me. Thankfully, I don't have time to dwell on all of this because I spend the rest of the day helping Grams and Gramps take down Christmas decorations and put them away.

At seven that evening, I send the same text to Reid and CC.

EM: Hey—everything ok? Just wondering

And then I open YouTube on my laptop to watch my new obsession, close-up magicians, and I try not to obsess on whether they will eventually answer. I watch about twenty minutes of videos when I see the floating ellipses that someone is responding.

CC: ...

CC: ...

And then another interminable pause.

CC: Hey, crazy day. Text u tmrrw?

EM: Hey, sure cool. You good?

Pause.

Pause.

Pause. Pause.

No response.

Okay, well at least she responded. That's a good thing. Maybe she's still upset about the shit Connor said. It was pretty awful, but tomorrow.... Yes, tomorrow all will be good again.

More magician videos. More text ellipses.
Reid: can u come outside
Holy shitbombs. Was not expecting this... at all.
EM: Be right out.

I throw on a hoodie, socks and my Adidas shower slides and bound downstairs and out the front door. *Shit, it's cold out here. I should have put sweats on, too.*

"Hey," Reid says, leaning against his truck parked at the curb in front of the house.

"Hey."

"Dude, you aren't cold?"

"A little. I'm good."

"Hey, so sorry about today. Things got a little weird last night, and I just thought maybe you needed some time."

"You could have said that to me."

"Yeah, sorry."

"You and CC decide this together?"

"We talked this morning."

"And?"

"You're freezing, so I don't want to keep you. I'm really not supposed to be here. We kind of agreed to that, but I couldn't just leave you hanging. Me and CC are cool, and we want us to all be cool, but we both really like you, and we like us all being friends more, so we decided we'd just back off a little and see where things go. Anyway, please go back inside, you're gonna freeze your tiny balls off."

"They're perfectly lovely balls."

"See you."

"Later," I say, turning to go.

"Hey," Reid calls out to me.

"Yeah," I say, turning back to face him.

"It's okay if you don't pick me."

And then he gets in his truck and drives away.

24

After three weeks off from school, it's actually nice to get back to a normal schedule. CC and I have the same basic conversation Reid had, minus the "It's okay if you don't pick me." She also replays what Connor said to her and says, it doesn't bother her. Her plan is to avoid Connor and Torrie and take the high road if their paths cross. She wants to grab lunch together our first day back at school, but I have some *Blue Dawg* business to take care of: interviewing the school librarian.

The library has been a refuge, a place for me and so many students needing a place where they can belong. Our library has all the typical high school library resources: reading areas with comfy chairs and bean bags, posters of celebrities celebrating reading, rows of computers with printer access, displays of new book releases and racks of publications, besides the aisles and aisles of bookshelves. The library is a hot spot for Pokémon GO. Nowadays, no one has to whisper or tiptoe around. People use their regular voices in the library that Mr. Ruddell runs. He has sectioned off an area with board games and decks of playing cards and tables where kids can spread out with their Yu-Gi-Oh! decks.

Mr. Ruddell also set up a cafe section where students can eat their lunch and a coffee station for students where they can get a cup of coffee for a quarter, a dollar or nothing, if that's all they have. Mr. Ruddell hosts a huge book fair each Spring for the campus and community as a fund raiser that he matches with grant money he's received to purchase a 3D printer and create a Makerspace in the library. His library is a melting pot of Pearl Heights, a place that welcomes the poor, the rich, the jocks, the geeks and the lonely outcasts yearning to feel connected to some place. There are kids from every demographic in Pearl Heights, and many of them claim this library as a sanctuary.

During my interview, Mr. Ruddell says he opens the library early and keeps it open late for those kids who don't have the resources to be successful in school, which was the way he grew up. He recounts how as a kid he would walk to the public library after school and wait there until his dad got out of work to drive them home. The librarians took care of him, helped with his homework, showed him how to use the microfiche (I had to Google that) and taught him how the library was organized. They also slipped him snacks. Now, he wants to do for other kids what the library did for him.

For me, Mr. Ruddell is a lifesaver. He doesn't care whether I use the library for studying or checking out a book or for escape, and he has always been helpful with the *Blue Dawg*. He's helped me research schools that have really successful online publications and has kept his ears open for story ideas. He never imagined he would become the subject of a profile for *Blue Dawg*.

After my interview of Mr. Ruddell, I spend two hours following around one of the profile subjects I came across through Mr. Ruddell: Aaron Cerrillo. I met him one day when Mr. Ruddell's car had a low tire. Aaron came into the library and said Mr. Ruddell could follow him to his dad's shop and he would fix it for him. Fix it for him? Who would fix it for him? His dad? Him? I was definitely intrigued.

I've since found out that Aaron, at fifteen, works at the tire shop his dad owns. So, I decide to find the shop and see what Aaron's up to. The shop is about a mile outside of Pearl Heights, in an industrial area. The shop is in a cinder block building painted mustard yellow with the name Cerrillo's Tire Shop sketched in large red block letters. It has three garage bays, and there's a rack of individual tires for sale out front. As I walk up to the shop, a car comes rolling in on a tire desperately in need of inflation. Aaron soon appears and asks the driver how he can help. The man gets out of the car and explains he noticed his low tire when he left work. Aaron looks the tire over and asks if the man has the tire lock and promises to have it fixed in just a bit.

It's impressive. I didn't even know what a tire lock is. Aaron snatches a tire jack in a second-nature move, flips it around, maneuvers it under the car and jacks it up effortlessly. Then he unscrews the lug nuts with an impact wrench and has the tire off before I can write it all down, trying to describe the work. Just then, Aaron takes off his flannel shirt and casts it aside. He has a ribbed tank-top on underneath. He's as skinny as me but his arms are sinewy and cut. He pulls the tire off its rim, marks a spot with a yellow grease pencil and swirls it in a tub of water. In fifteen minutes, he's handing the man his tire lock back and showing him the roofing nail that flattened his tire. The finale is when the guy follows Aaron into the office and pays him $10.

Aaron's story is super impressive. When he was in third grade, I find out, he moved with his family from Hidalgo County, where one in three people lives in poverty. He spoke only Spanish then. By fourth grade, he took the state standardized tests completely in English. His parents still speak only Spanish, but they own the tire shop and help Aaron's older brothers run a restaurant they opened. I look at Aaron's hands. He has grease under his nails, and his knuckles bear the remnants of knicks and cuts. He has textbooks stacked in the shop's office, where he studies when he's not fixing flats. On weekends, Aaron often runs the shop on his own. The family rents a duplex just inside the Pearl Heights boundaries, where he shares a room with his two younger brothers. His story has impressed and inspired me so much, I feel honored to tell it.

Telling people's stories makes me feel alive. After all I've been through, half-living, going through the motions, feeling like life will never be good again, nothing feels better than feeling alive, than telling other people's stories so they stay alive. I don't want to feel any other way, which is why I settle into a place with Reid and CC where I can continue to feel alive by simply living. Tita Cruz used to say, "*A fuerza, ni los zapatos entran.*" In other words, you can't force shoes to fit. Things will happen or they won't, you can't force them. We will continue as we are. No changes. We'll be friends who may or may not become something more, because I've already lost too much in my life to risk losing anything else that matters to me.

Although I'm getting to tell stories and I'm halfway to graduation, I can't help but feel the tension building around the country. Comments like Connor's at *Faux For* are finding support and festering around us. No one says anything to me directly, but throughout the day walking the halls, I hear little comments, snide remarks whispered loud enough to hear but not loud enough to trace. Fake news is the favorite epithet or lame stream media. How can people make these awful comments about someone whose journalist parents were killed for doing their job for legitimate news outlets, not fake media. I'm learning that mean is the default for too many people out there, and people are growing bolder. Students still aren't allowed to wear hats in the building, but it doesn't keep guys from hanging MAGA hats from their backpacks or sporting them in their back pockets.

"Build the wall" has become a refrain batted and bantered about along with more students wearing border patrol T-shirts. Aaron tells me when I interview him at the tire shop that he's heard "build-the-wall" comments directed at him and that, for the first time in his life, someone yelled "beaner" at him from a passing car as he walked into school. Other Latino students say they've also heard such comments as "Go back where you came from" and "Speak American" when they're talking in Spanish.

Tensions are definitely building.

25

A look of incredulity overcomes Reid when he finds out I have never shot a gun. So now, he has a new obsession: to take me hunting. I explain, argue and register my objections about guns, but he ignores them all. I protest. He persists. I complain. He persists. I'm really getting annoyed that he won't let it go and that he can't understand why he should. Just when I think I've finally got him to drop the subject, he actually uses a tone with me that I didn't think him capable of: indignation.

"For fuck's sake, Ethan. We aren't poaching ivory or robbing liquor stores. Hell, we're not even killing Bambi. Stop being such a little shit and try something new, dammit. I've been doing this my whole life, and I'm not some backwoods bubba going all second-amendment bat-shit crazy. It's just something fun. Holy shitbombs, dude."

"That's my thing," I say with a little more bite in my voice than I expect to come out.

"Well, I'm taking it because you're being a dumb ass," Reid says with even more bite than I've used.

It feels like we're fighting. I don't like the feeling. I want to bring down the temperature, but I don't want to hunt. I'm not judging what he does, but it's not for me. So, I construct a litany of excuses, hoping he'll get frustrated, dissuaded or finally understand that I really don't want to do this.

"I don't have a shot gun."

"We have plenty."

"I don't know how to shoot."

"I'll teach you."

"I don't even..."

"I've got it all covered. This isn't my first rodeo. Have you ever been to a rodeo? Scratch that, we'll get back to that another time. Don't worry about anything. I'll take care of everything. All you have to do is show up. Seriously, it's not a big deal."

Dr. Robles has worked with me on ways to avoid angry outbursts. Reflecting, counting, breathing, visualizing, thinking through outcomes. Clearly, we still have work to do because none of it is working. I snap.

"No big deal? Oh my God... How can someone so smart be so fucking stupid. God! Can't you get it. I don't want to do this. I don't want to hunt or shoot anything or even touch a goddamn gun!"

"Whoa," Reid says, holding up his hands in an epic fail of an attempt to diffuse my outburst, his eyes wide with the unmistakable traces of panic.

"Fuck whoa. Goddammit, Reid. I thought you'd get it, that you wouldn't be like everyone else, thinking I should get over it already and move on. I don't care if I sound like some whiny, psycho, anti-gun nut job. Reid... some assholes stormed into the room where my parents worked and shot up the place. They killed fifteen people, including my parents. So no, I don't want to go hunting with you. I don't want to shoot anything. I don't want to kill anything. I don't want..."

I don't get to finish. Reid pulls me into his arms and hugs me harder than I've ever been hugged.

"Okay, okay, okay. I'm sorry, so, so sorry. You're good, you're right. Really, I'm so sorry for not getting it. It's okay.

We're okay. I'm so stupid," Reid keeps repeating in a stream of repetitive remorse. "We'll go camping, rucking. No hunting, no guns. Just you and me."

I hear nothing, I only feel the hug, strong and comforting. I don't want it to end.

We pick a weekend to go, clear it with Grams and Gramps and get ready to add camping as a notch to my belt of new experiences. I hadn't really thought of Reid as the stereotypical Texan before. He is, and I guess I'm being stereotypical, pretty progressive about social issues, doesn't have a hint of Texas drawl, and dresses like he stepped out of a Tommy Hilfiger ad.

When the day of our excursion finally arrives, and we get to his house to load up and leave, Reid's Texas roots are on full display. He says he doesn't drive a truck just for show, which becomes abundantly clear. We load up a tent, outdoor chairs, sleeping bags, an air mattress, a generator, knives, grill plates and two large ice chests. We load orange safety vests (in case others are out hunting), a first aid kit and our duffle bags. Mrs. Tibbitts has packed up plastic bags of onions, bell peppers, tomatoes and seasoned cubes of beef for us to use for shish kabobs. She's also included brownies and crispy cereal treats. Reid really did take care of everything, and all I did was pack a few things and show up.

Reid's family owns property in Live Oak County, Texas, about an hour and a half south of San Antonio. They lease the land out for hunting during deer season and use it throughout the year for fishing, riding ATVs and just getting away. They have a ranch house on the property, but Reid says we aren't having a spa weekend, so that I can have an authentic Texas camping experience.

We arrive at our camp site, a vast, open tribute to Texas brush and bramble, as dusk settles around us. After unloading the truck and setting up the tent, I plop myself in one of the folding chairs, pull out my journal and begin to describe the live oaks buttressing the perimeter, "sentinels guarding us from the clamor, contention and perpetual assaults of uncivilized civilization, their gnarled branches craning to the deepening darkness in reverent benediction." I feel a connection to camping awakening in me as we build a fire and cook the smoked sausage we brought. I don't want to give Reid the pleasure of throwing it in my face that I initially bitched about even coming on this trip, but I am blown away by the experience already. Granted, all we've done is set up a tent and built a fire, but so far, he's proving me wrong. I can feel Reid basking in my camping exuberance. Reid, in such a Reid move, because he surprises me and then I realize I shouldn't be surprised by him, goes to the backseat of his truck and pulls out a guitar. For a few minutes he strums and finesses his fingers around the strings, playing cords, while I watch with growing awe. Then, he begins to sing:

Oh where you lay
Your head tonight
I'll roll away alone
And close on down

Take up your wings
And fly back out
And we'll pretend
Forget we're dead

When he stops, I think I've made him uncomfortable, staring at him so long before I find words to say. "Oh, my God, Reid, did you write that?"

"Nah, it's called 'Ariel Ramirez' by this singer I like."

"How did I not know you could do this?"

"I don't know. It's just something I do for me."

"You're amazing. Really, I mean it."

"Thanks."

He continues strumming as the fire crackles in the background, a slight breeze rustling the trees around us. Stars pepper the night sky, the waning crescent moon glows on us and the wisp of an approaching chill nestles into the air around us.

"Reid?"

"Yeah."

"Why me?"

"Because you've never been camping before."

"You know what I mean."

"Because I like you."

"Did you think I was..."

"We didn't know. Me and CC. You were new and we didn't know anything about you and then we found out... you know, stuff.... So, we didn't know if you were gay or just European. Either way, we both liked you."

"Are you..." I pause not because I'm trying to be politically correct but because I don't want to be intrusive, but I also want to know.

"Out?" he says, asking the question for me.

"Yeah."

"Just to CC. She's known for a long time. It's never been a big deal. We figured it out way back in sixth grade, but dating in middle school is stupid, so it just didn't go anywhere other than 'That guy is cute' and 'Who do we like this week?' Until you came along. That first day at practice, I was like, 'Whoa, who is this cutie?' And then, you came to lunch with us. God, we couldn't believe it when we both admitted that we liked you. I mean we figured the odds were on CC's side."

"Why did you wait so long before talking to me?"

"Have you ever tried hiding a boner in running shorts? Not happening. I didn't want to be popping wood in front of everyone."

"And none of the guys, like know or suspects anything?"

"I don't know what people know. I don't really care. It's really nobody's business. I figure why does it matter, since I haven't really been interested in anyone? Have you never dated or liked anyone?"

"Not really. We traveled a lot, and I knew I was going to college in the States, so I don't know, I just always did the friends thing."

"You know the friends thing isn't the worst thing."

"Yeah, I know."

Sometime later, we put out the fire and crawl into the tent.

After the initial shock of not remembering where I am when I wake up, I realize Reid is already up and out of the tent. When I step out of the zippered opening, I see that Reid has what looks like backpacks resting near our chairs and has water boiling over the fire.

"It's not your Frappuccino, but we have instant coffee."

"Damn, dude, I thought you liked me. Black coffee, that's what dictators and despots drink."

"I grabbed a bunch of those flavored creamers from the convenience store we stopped at and a ton of sugar packets. You'll survive."

"And breakfast?"

"Pop Tarts on the grill, a true camping delicacy."

We clear the campsite and then Reid hands me some very unfashionable brown coveralls and an orange vest with more pockets than those cargo shorts uncool dads wear.

"What's all this for?" I ask stepping into the coveralls.

"Rucking."

"Wait, what the heck is rucking?"

"Think hiking on steroids. We wear weighted rucksacks and run the hills and trails out here."

"When did I agree to this?"

"I told you about it. Quit your whining."

"Whining? Um, I'm not whining, I'm fact-checking."

"Whatever. There's lots of thorny brush and dry branches around, so you need the coveralls to keep your pretty boy skin all pretty boy."

"I don't have pretty boy..."

"Unh-unh-uh, don't interrupt. You need the coveralls in case you fall or something. They'll keep you from getting all scuffed up. There shouldn't be anyone out hunting here because we haven't leased the land to anyone, but you never know if someone might be here without permission. So, keep the safety vest on. The rucksacks..."

"Those ugly-ass backpack things?"

"You're interrupting again. Yes, those ugly-ass backpack things. They have extra padding on the shoulders.... You'll thank me for that later. Oh, and they have 40 lbs. of weight in them."

"Forty? Why not a hundred?"

"Silly rabbit, that comes later. Anyway, there's 40 lbs. in each sack, and there will be a little extra weight from the water in the Camelbak.... You'll thank me for that, too."

"I think you're overreaching on what I'll be thankful for."

"Interrupting again," he says, putting a shush finger on my lips. "We'll set out on the trails for an hour, possibly two, and see how we, and by we I mean you, feel after that. Now we are not going to stop and chronicle every time you see a jackrabbit or feel the need to wax poetically on the bucolic splendor of the Texas landscape."

"SAT prep class kicking in there, I see."

"Quite the concomitant effect. Anyway, we aren't stopping every time you want to write something in your journal, so I brought my GoPro that you can strap on and document the experience to your little journalist heart's content."

Damn this Reid guy.

By the time we get back to the campsite, we're a filthy mess. Sweaty, dirty, grimy, just all-around pretty disgusting. Any delusions of the superiority of my fitness level evaporates when Reid straps my ruck sack to the front of his chest for the last half hour of our two-hour trek. We wash our hands and cool off with the jugs of water we have in the coolers. Having spent most of the morning running through open fields in thick boots and coveralls has worn out our good humor.

"Let's go," Reid says, grabbing one of the gallon jugs of water and motioning for me to grab one as well.

"Where?"

"The river. You stink."

"Not as much as you do."

"Debatable."

The temperature is in the low seventies, but I know the river is going to be a lot colder.

"Are you kidding? That water has to be freezing," I protest. "You're not going to be taking one of your long-ass showers. You're just gonna rinse off some of that stench. Think of it as a polar-bear swim."

Never in my life have I been more right and more wrong about the same thing. Right that the water temperature nearly sends me into shock from the cold and wrong that I would eventually acclimate to it. While I stand there in my boxers, going in only up to my ankles, Reid wades right in, submerges to his neck, rubs his armpits clean and wades right back out to dry off.

"Quit being such a pussy and get in."

"That is derogatory and anti-woman."

"Okay, quit being such a person who will not endure a little cold water to stop smelling like a stank-ass little punk."

"That is much more politically correct, although..."

"I am fixin' to get in there and dunk your ass."

"Okay, okay," I say as I begin inching farther into the water. "Cold, cold, cold, cold."

"Get in, you big baby!" Reid encourages as I slowly wade in up to my neck and follow Reid's example.

"Holy shitbombs, it's so fucking cold. I don't think my balls are ever going to crawl out from inside me again."

"How could we tell if they did?"

"You're not funny," I say to him, even though it actually is funny, and I just don't want to admit he's right again.

After getting out of the river, we wash our hair with the water from the gallon jugs and the shampoo Reid had in his shave kit. We put on dry clothes and head back to the campsite.

We grill the steak cubes with the vegetables on the skewers Mrs. Tibbitts sent and make Reid's caramel-apple-in-a-cup dessert. We unwrap caramels from a bag, drop them into the cast iron skillet on the fire, cut up apples into cubes and sprinkle cinnamon and pecans on top, then mix it all together and scoop it into cups. As we sit around the campfire, Reid strums his guitar again. I feel almost overwhelmed by the day, but in a rewarding way. I have rucked for the first time in my life, grilled a Pop Tart over an open fire and came the closest I will ever come to actual polar-bear swimming. The shitbombs of my life seem worlds away from me out here under the Texas sky with my best friend strumming his guitar.

Sitting by the fire as night creeps in, I get lost in Reid's guitar strumming and singing a Damien Rice song:

Cold, cold water surrounds me now
And all I've got is your hand
Lord, can you hear me now?
Lord, can you hear me now?
Lord, can you hear me now?
Or am I lost?

Three weeks ago, I worried that I had once again lost the two most important friends in my life. Two weeks ago, I yelled at Reid about coming on this trip, and now I lament we'll leave in the morning. Maybe it's the tension building back at school. Maybe it's worrying about college acceptance. Maybe it's the wariness that nothing will ever be this perfect again.

Reid sings.

My mind races.

It races to the day I met CC. The day she marched right up to me and announced her presence in my life. The day she picked me up for *pan dulce*, and I saw the CC separate from the way everyone expected her to be. My mind races back to the day that Reid bear-hugged me and spun me around before we even knew each other. Races to the day he grabbed my hand and calmed my anxiety, to the day he doused me in coffee as an alibi my senior side-parking meltdown. And it races to when these two powerful forces in my life kissed me on the same night. Reid who unselfishly gave me permission not to choose him. CC who said she would always love me regardless of what I did in my life or whom I did it with. How is one guy so unlucky and so fortunate at the same time?

Every time I see CC, my pulse quickens, my goofiness level elevates and my ability to converse coherently abandons me. She is gorgeous. She is bold. She is kind. She is what I picture a high school girlfriend to be. But is this what I want, or is it what I think I'm supposed to want? Even Reid thinks so.

Why think the odds are in her favor? As I think about it, the odds really aren't in her favor. By virtue of cross country and our parallel school schedules juxtaposed to the frenetic nature of her schedule, I see him way more than I see her. Grams and Gramps are pretty laid back about things, but no way is CC spending the night, but none of us thought anything untoward about Reid becoming my de facto roommate with his own key to the house. Even before I knew he liked me, our bond was intimate—the ugly-cry thing, conversations about hopes, dreams, fears and nightmares long into the night. There are the inside jokes, the banter and the complete lack of modesty between us. Someone more jaded might find that dubious on his part, but Reid doesn't do dubious.

Staring into the night sky, thoughts race through my mind. I love being with CC when I'm with her. I love seeing CC when I see her. I love the idea of CC, but I look forward to Reid. When we are not together, I look forward to when we will be. When I have something to say or share, I seek him out first. And when I need my hand held, I want him to hold it.

With the fire dying down, we put it out, secure our site and crawl into the tent. I've heard people complain about camping, about roughing it, and I secretly had wished we could stay at the ranch house, but an insulated tent and air mattress have made what might have been the most uncomfortable element of the trip almost enjoyable. Sometimes, you don't realize how tired you really are until you lie down, but I fight sleep because I don't want any of this to end. I want to lie here and continue bandying about the grand debates of the cosmos: crunchy or creamy peanut butter (crunchy, and Reid is wrong), vanilla or chocolate (vanilla, and we're both right), Dr. Pepper or Coke (damn, these Texas boys really like their Dr. Pepper), beach or mountains (he's mountains, and I am beach, but no wrong answers). I'm not going to bring up the

Star Wars v. *Star Trek* because I don't want to hear him yell "Jar Jar Binks" ad nauseam, although I have to admit it's a strong argument.

I can hear his breathing slip into sleep. I want to hang on to this moment until my courage catches up to my qualms. How would things change? Who would I hurt? What all would this mean? Is this even really what I want?

Qualms be damned.

Reid is turned away from me. I loosen my legs from the sleeping bag and inch deftly, silently toward Reid's sleeping bag. My breath, short and sharp, brushes past my lips as I finesse myself into his sleeping bag and press my body to his. His body releases itself into mine, the disquiet of doubt drifting away like the embers of a fading fire.

26

My eyes blink open to Reid looking into them. He smiles at me. My ebullient response betrays any attempt at being casual.

"Ethan," he says, the grin on his face widening, "you're in my sleeping bag."

"I can go back to mine," I tease as I mock-turn to leave.

"You're good," he says, pulling me closer to him.

I can feel every part of his body pressed against mine, the sinewy tautness of his runner's physique, the angles of knees and ankles intertwined, our chests rising and falling in a synchronized symphony. He touches his nose to mine as his hands travel south along the map of my body until I feel them harbor in ports hitherto uncharted.

"Ethan-Matthew," he says in the most mischievous tone I have ever heard from him, "you're right, they are quite lovely."

I thought the drive home might be awkward, both of us thinking about what we have done, giving each other side-glances, but we're the same Ethan-Matthew and Reid we've been since the day he randomly showed up at my house. We do discuss our relationship. We agree that we aren't boyfriends. We're the same friends we've been. We aren't friends with benefits but rather friends with mutually beneficial interests that sometimes will manifest in various stages of undress. We aren't having sex, but we also aren't pretending anything platonic either. We also aren't telling anyone. It's not that we're embarrassed or feel the need to hide, we just don't think it's anybody's business but ours.

Reid pulls his truck into the driveway of my house. I grab my duffle bag while Reid grabs the ruck sack that he's gifting me. We put bags of tamales we bought from a family selling them on the side of the road in the garage refrigerator and then, for the first time, we have an awkward moment. I don't want him to go. He doesn't want to go, but we have school in the morning, Grams and Gramps are waiting inside, and we need real showers. Just when the awkwardness is almost unbearable, Reid becomes so Reid and punches the crap out of my shoulder.

"Dude, I'll see you tomorrow," he says, chuckling as he walks toward his truck.

"That was so first-grade of you," I shout at him.

"Your balls are so first-grade," he shoots back.

"You said they were lovely."

"I meant that. See you tomorrow," he shouts back and hops into his truck, double-taps the horn and drives away.

I could definitely see myself camping again, especially if they're all like my first camping trip, but I'll definitely take a hot shower with my multi-function showerhead over a Texas polar-bear swim anytime. So, after the most glorious and loooongest of showers, I have coffee and crumb cake with Grams and Gramps and tell them everything, well, almost everything, about the weekend.

"Your dad used to love to go camping with his buddies," Gramps says.

"I didn't know that."

"Oh, yeah, he and his buddies went all the time back in high school."

"What about you, Gramps? Did you ever go camping with Dad?"

"I went a couple of times when he was younger, but when the boys got older, they went on their own. Besides, camping was never my thing. I'd rather spend that time on the golf course."

"I wonder why he never told me that he loved camping?"

"It was a long time ago. After you came along, everything became about you. It was like his life before you didn't exist or matter anymore," Grams says. "When he held you for the first time, he just cried and cried. He didn't think he could love anyone or anything as much as he loved you."

"He used to make up songs to sing to you as a baby. I used to tease that his singing voice was so bad that it made you cry," Gramps jokes.

I told them all about Dad's singing in the shower, how Mom and I would beg him to stop and how he would then break into "Let it Go" over and over and over, which was actually pretty entertaining. Then I tell them about Reid's singing, about how his voice, rich and sweet, floats out of him as effortlessly as smiles come to his face.

"We're glad you've made such good friends, Ethan-Matthew," Grams says. "And that CC is very pretty."

"She's pretty awesome. But you guys already knew her long before cross country or when she came over to decorate cookies with us, right?"

"We saw her at the games and knew who she was, but we never really knew her until she started coming around to see you," Grams says, a definite hint in her tone.

"The Canton men have always had pretty girls chasing after them. Your Grams pursued me relentlessly."

"Oh, Huck. Don't make me show the boy the notes you used to leave in my locker."

"I'm safe. Kids these days can't read cursive."

"Sorry, Gramps, I'm fluent in cuneiform, hieroglyphics, ancient runes, Sanskrit, emoji, along with cursive, and I speak three dialects of bullshit."

27

Prospects have looked good for the Blue Lacy baseball team, and baseball is the most important sport after football and basketball. From all the enthusiasm around the school, I've become excited for the upcoming pre-season game with the newest rival for Pearl Heights, Los Toros from César Estrada Chávez High School, a school in a smaller division down from us. According to Reid, they are complete bad asses. They were one out, one base hit and only one inch away from a state championship last year. Unlike our well provisioned team, Los Toros are a rag tag team of kids from a poor school whose hard-working blue-collar parents hold barbeque plate sales to raise money to buy the team uniforms, bats, balls, and bus rentals. Thes Chávez kids don't have the benefits our players have: private coaches, batting cages in their backyards, the best equipment money can buy.... Nevertheless, Los Toros have accomplished quite a bit despite their impoverished, circumstances. I looked up information on Chávez High School. Their student body is 94% Hispanic, 3 percent Black, 2 percent White and 1 percent other. The school is located on the far South side of San Antonio, and 86% of the students are on free or reduced lunch, which classifies them as an economically disadvantaged school.

Today, the stage is set for a battle between the new rivals: the privileged Big Blue Lacy team versus the rag tag Los Toros from a school named after a former farmworker and civil rights leader. Although I'm not a sportswriter, the budding journalist in me knows a good story in the making.

Reid and I drive the five minutes over to the baseball stadium right after school and get there about four o'clock, well before the 5:30 gametime. I have never been to our baseball stadium, and when we arrive, I take in the sight of what looks like a rather ordinary baseball field. We walk through the chain link gate, show our student IDs to a parent sitting at the ticket table and head for one of the two sets of bleachers. There's a press box, and behind it there is a gaggle of dads working the concessions stand. They're pouring ice over canned drinks, unloading snacks and sweets purchased from a bulk store, melting cheese for nachos and, outside the concession stand, searing meat on a grill the size of a small sedan.

On the field, the Blue Lacy baseball guys are throwing balls back and forth while the cheerleaders hang painted paper banners along the fence line that runs along the Blue Lacy dugout. The scoreboard behind center field is basic, with markings for innings, balls, strikes and outs. Advertisements for local businesses cover the back wall, and country music blares from large speakers.

After finding seats on bleachers with a good view, Reid and I sit down, and I start taking pictures and jotting down notes and snippets of ideas in my journal. I describe the "squeak of brakes as the yellow busses modern-day stagecoaches pull into Dodge for a high noon showdown..." Oh no, too corny. "...between the biggest bats in the state"—ooh, no—maybe "showdown between the toughest ten-gallon bats in Texas." Again, too corny. I take another tact and describe "the clicking of cleats on concrete as the, pick your poison, heroes or villains from César Chávez High School stride into town ready to see who will emerge as the new sheriff in town." Hmm, maybe stretching this extended metaphor a bit far.

As it gets closer to game time, the stands on both sides of the press box fill up. I look over at the Toro's side and I feel a kind of kinship with them. They remind me of the neighborhood kids and cousins I would play with when we visited Tita Cruz and Lito. The women and men in the stands remind me of my *tías* and *tíos*, their laughter spirited and unabashed. Naturally, there's also a sizeable group of Toro students. The sense of brotherhood coming from the Toro fans keeps stealing my attention as I want so desperately to eavesdrop and here their Spanish.

The atmosphere in the Pearl Heights bleachers, across from the Toros' is different, less familial, more individual. Because the Blue Lacy parents run the concession stands and man the grill while other dads cluster in groups of three or four observing the goings-on from various perimeter positions, our bleachers are dominated by students. I look over our bleachers and notice something odd, almost ominous. Starting from the top row and going down about four more rows, the stands are packed with upperclassmen all wearing untucked long-sleeved white button-downed oxford shirts. There's some weird shuffling as a kid moves from the top row of the group to the bottom row, or the second row to one of the other rows. I draw Reid's attention to it, but he doesn't think anything of it, just that those guys are being the assholes they usually are. Naturally, Connor McCade is in the group.

After a sophomore girl sings the national anthem, the teams are introduced, and it's time to play ball. Of course, there's an altogether different game going on as well that only some of us know anything about.

28

The words "play ball" usher the two teams into action. As the Blue Lacy team takes the field, the three rows of upperclassmen pull out and doff their red Make America Great Again baseball caps. What a bunch of tools. Our pitcher launches his first pitch of the season—strike one. The MAGA hat guys roar loudly. On strike three for the first batter, the MAGA hat crowd erupts from their seats. Among their whistles and whoops, the word *bueno* also can be heard. Two more players, two more strikeouts and two more things are abundantly clear—our pitcher is a stud, and the MAGA guys aren't going to get any less obnoxious. They utter stereotypical Mexican *gritos* any time something good happens for the Blue Lacy team and any time something doesn't go well for the Toros. They break into chants of "Taco Bell" from time to time and just generally do everything they can to insult the Toros. I can see that CC, down on the sidelines, is turning to look up at them and definitely wants to say something to them, but in her cheerleader uniform she represents the school and has to be on her best and most PC behavior—even if the jerks in the stands deserve nothing but contempt. The MAGA crowd isn't exactly alone for long. Soon, the Toro fans strike back, sounding like they aren't going to take it quietly.

As disturbing as the MAGA crowd is, it's equally disturbing that no one has objected to them or even seem fazed by their antics, on this side of the stadium anyway. The Toros crowd has taken special interest in them and has even been recording them off and on throughout the game.

Despite all of this, my first high school baseball game is a blast. Three innings into the game neither team has scored, and it seems like something is always going on. The Toros definitely have their troubles connecting bat to ball, and the umpires are having a hard time, too. I learn that it's fairly safe to yell, "C'mon on, Blue" and "You're killing me, Blue." "Open your eyes" is also fairly common. Reid is a hit in the stands as he repeatedly heckles the umpires: "Hey ump, is this your phone? You missed another call!" "Hey ump, if you're just gonna watch the game, come sit over here." "That was almost the right call. Better luck next time." "Hey ump, how can you sleep with all these lights on?" "If you had one more eye, you could be a cyclops."

And Reid doesn't stop with the umpires. The Toro players hear from him as well. "Don't worry, your mom still loves you. Wait, no she doesn't." "My porch has a better swing than that." "Is your dad the coach?"

Maybe because we're so caught up in the game and having so much fun, we also take some playful risks. Sometimes, after standing up to cheer a play, when we sit back down, we accidentally on purpose have our hands touch and linger together. Sometimes we pretend we're so engrossed in the game that we don't notice that our knees are touching. When our pitcher strikes out another batter to end an inning and everyone is standing up to cheer and hug, we get to stand up and hug each other, as well. It's innocent fun, no big deal and, we think, unnoticed.

By the fourth inning, there's still no score, but we have come awfully close. We left runners on base in the second inning, and there was a questionable out called when our player slid into home in the third that really got the MAGA crowd riled up. But the Toros are now dishing out their own level of obnoxiousness, too. When one of our more pale-skinned players—okay, he looks like he needs sunscreen in fluorescent light—comes up to bat, the Toro students pull out their sunglasses and hold their hands out to shield their eyes. Throughout the game they yell things like "Casper," "cracker," "blowfish" and "8-Mile." When CC and the other cheerleaders chant, "Let's go, Heights," the Toros join in with "Let's go, Whites." Tensions roll in like the dusk pushing out the bright light of day. The lights of the stadium create dark shadows to match the dark feelings pushing to burst out.

While we wait for the fifth inning to start, CC and I go to the concession stand for snacks and burgers hot off the grill. We stand in line, waiting our turn, when we hear comments from behind us.

"*Oyes, coco, ¿por qué vas a la escuela con esos pendejos?*"

We know they're students from Chávez calling CC a coconut. They're two guys around our age, just kids like us. I start turning to respond to their derogatory comment, when I feel the just-ignore-it tug on my arm from CC. But they continue provoking us, this time in an exaggerated Mexican accent.

"Coconut *sheerleader*, no speeeka da Spanish?"

This time, I don't let her stop me. "*Oyes, pinche cabrón, ¡cállate! Vale más que no hables así con ella otra vez.*"

"Chill, Ricky Martin. We're just messin' wit chall."

"Well, try doing it without being assholes," I say, and we turn forward, willing the line to move faster so we can just get back to our seats.

After a couple minutes of really uncomfortable silence, we order our food, pay and start making our way back to the bleachers, when our new friends offer a parting comment.

"Your friends are dicks," one of them says as we walk away.

"They're not my friends," CC shoots back at them, "and they're not the only ones who are dicks."

We finally score in the sixth inning. I would have never imagined I could get so excited about the game, but when our player rounds second and gets the go-ahead signal to take home, I'm standing and cheering, "Go, go, go, go," like everyone else in the stands. Elation fills our side of the stands, and the Blue Lacy dugout erupts. The MAGA hats respond, as well. The entire group hoops, hollers and bellows louder than before, and the top row of guys, in a move that feels coordinated, pulls off their white button-downs to reveal identical red T-shirts underneath. They spin their white shirts like rally flags above their heads, raising the school chant, deep and ominous:

Woof, woof, rah!
Woof, woof, rah!
Rah, rah, rah, rah!
Woof, woof, rah!
Woof!

With a run on the scoreboard, a sense of relief and ease seems to wash over our team, while the Toros radiate tension and frustration. With one out, one run and a man on second, the Blue Lacy crowd is enlivened again. Everything suddenly matters more than before. Every moment, every motion is calculated and second-guessed. Every twitch and turn is magnified and multiplied in significance. No Blue Lacy player wants to be the one to throw away the lead. No Toro player wants to do anything to seal their fate.

No one is sitting down in any of the stands. Our second base runner, leading off, is checked by the pitcher. A brief collision occurs. Words are exchanged. Momentary shoving ensues. There are "heys" from both sets of fans. Coaches leave the dugout, and an umpire positions himself between the two rivals who feel the weight of winning and losing choking out their better judgment. There are stare downs and bowing up between the two rivals, but order is quickly restored, and the game continues.

Two pitches into the next batter, a wild throw gets away from the catcher and our player advances to third base. The Toro fans look as if their world has come to an end. There are hands held up to faces in concern and disbelief. Riotous cheers ripple through our section of the bleachers.

Things get worse with the next pitch.

A sacrifice fly to deep center field sends the base runner tagging up and sprinting for home. A precise throw to the cut-off man and a relay throw home makes for a valiant but unsuccessful Toro effort. Two outs but two runs have scored. Elation contrasts with agony. The inning ends with the next batter, but the bravado the Toros marched in with has all but boarded the bus going into the last inning.

The Toro's coach is pep-talking the hell out of his players. "*Vamos, vamos, vamos,*" I can hear him saying from our seats. The Toro fans are back on their feet, cheering and praying. Whether it's the pep talk, the prayers or our relief pitcher, something has worked for the Toros, when they get their first hit of the game, a single. The Toros have new life breathed into them. A sacrifice fly advances the baserunner to second, and after another base hit, along with an error at third, the Toros are on the scoreboard and down by one. The bravado of the Toros returns while the ebullience bordering on cocky from the Blue Lacy side evaporates into worried optimism.

Our side audibly holds its breath, when the clean-up batter for the Toros strides to the plate. His last name, Rodríguez, is emblazoned across the back of his jersey. The Toros chant his nickname, "Mando! Mando! Mando!" Tall and thin, sweat bulleted on his bronze skin, he lets the first pitch sail by, high and outside. On the second pitch, the thwack of bat to ball stops the hearts of Blue Lacy fans until it rockets foul toward vehicles unwisely parked. The next pitch brushes Mando away from the plate and out of the batter's box, eliciting collective warnings from the Toros' bleachers. Mando mad-dogs the pitcher all the way back to the batter's box.

There are moments in time when you think things slow down enough for you take them all in, muse over them, capture and preserve them to play them back in the theater of the mind, but nothing in life happens that way. The moments happen and then they're gone, leaving little time to ruminate on their deeper meaning in the human experience. This moment calls for that kind of slow-mo preservation, but it doesn't happen. On the fourth pitch, Mando wields the bat like he's Thor whacking a marauding alien out of the sky. No slow motion, no dramatic pauses, just pure power connects the ball with the bat's sweet spot. He basically tears the cover off the ball as four sections of Toros and Blue Lacy fans stand up and fervently petition the gods of baseball.

The ball jettisons past the infield determined to escape the confines of the ballpark. Our centerfielder tucks his arms to his chest, lowers his head and blisters his way toward the outfield wall in a race to become hero or heartbreaker. He becomes both as the ball is about to escape the outfield to become a homerun. The centerfielder, hero and heartbreaker, leaps, extends his arm and glove to the limits of sinew and snatches the ball and the prayers of the Toros right out of the air.

Disappointment ravages the Toros fans—momentarily. In that instant, the Toros' base runner tags up and bullets for home plate as if the collective cheers and hopes of his fans are powering him on. The willpower of *tías* and *tíos*, *padres* and *primos*, *madres* and *mujeres* compel him forward. Muscles throbbing, straining, aching carry the last glimmers of Toros hope in a wide curve around third base and up the chalk line to home plate.

From the instant he stole the Toros' homerun, the center fielder took no moment to bask in his athletic accomplishment and he hurled the ball with precision and power to an awaiting glove. Innings of sweat, grime, frustration, tension, enmity, desire, disappointment and *cariño* all convene in this moment. This is heart. This is passion. This is also the ugly side of sport, because no matter how valiant the effort, not matter how pure the motive, no matter how much your mother loves you, someone loses.

CC, Reid, and I stand huddled together as if we can affect the outcome of the game or lessen the sting should it end unfortunately for us. The MAGA crowd, though somewhat more subdued, continues to draw negative attention from anyone with a sense of decorum and decency. In the time that passes, they have managed to reveal a row of red shirts, a row of white shirts and a row of blue shirts. They wear their subtlety as loudly as their red hats. We wear our disdain almost as loudly. CC has glared daggers at them throughout the game, and Reid has periodically muttered such fine sentiments as "dick wads," "ass hats," "shitheads" louder than just under his breath.

Runner and ball propel toward home plate, locked in an epic race that will decide whether the game ends or proceeds for one more turn at bat. A pause hangs in the air amid the racing hearts and frenetic breathing. The Blue Lacy catcher positions himself in front of home plate, guarding his domain. His body, rigid and ready, crouches for battle. His mitt is projected forward, a beacon illuminating a path for the ball to follow home. Ball hits glove.

Runner dives home. Bodies fall. Dust flies. Hearts pause.

And then a knee rises off the ground, an arm pushes unflinchingly forward and draws back in violent confidence as the umpire bellows in a tone, deep and resonant, "Y-O-O-O-O-U-U-U-U-'R-R-R-E OUT!"

Gloves fly as the Blue Lacy baseball team hurls them into the air with glorious abandon and they collapse into each other in a pile of pure joy, relief and youthful exuberance. Injustice reverberates through the Toros' dugout and through their stands. The Toros' coach gesticulates in righteous irritation. His assistant coach either unsuccessfully or half-heartedly holds him back. The umpire disinterestedly moves away, his job done for the day. Cheers from the Blue Lacy fans rise rapidly into the night air but fall silent just as quickly as they started. Clad in their red, white and blue shirts, the guys festooned in MAGA hats begin chanting, "Build that wall! Build that wall! Build that wall!" Their voices ring above the celebratory cheers, drowning them out. Malice echoes throughout the stadium. And while the rest of us stand by silently, dumbfounded in disbelief at their hate speech, the Blue Lacy's baseball coach aggressively breaks away from his team's celebration and runs toward the stands and the MAGA crowd with his hands held up in the air, yelling, "STOP! STOP! STOP!"

As the "Build that wall" chant dies down, the Toros, stinging from the loss and insulted by the chant, respond in kind. Although measurably less offensive, they respond, "Pearly Whites! Pearly Whites! Pearly Whites."

Both sides lose all measure of composure. Coaches are directing players to stay on their side of the field. Parents are attempting to corral aggrieved high schoolers. Shouts and epithets fly back and forth. Palpable contempt wafts through the park. The basic ingredients of a riot simmer all about us.

Rather than the typical post-game meeting of the teams for the good-game handshakes, the Toros coaches shuffle their players toward their bus. Parents and spectators try to usher students out of the ballpark and defuse tension, but there is only one exit. No one expected the night to end like this, and it shows. Fans, people, bodies, crowd out of the gate and into the parking lot. The MAGA hat guys also have to exit through the same gate, their red hats re-stoking the Toros' furor. Reid and I walk with CC in between us, doing our best to escort her through the crowd and to her car.

Suddenly, someone yells in the general direction of the Blue Lacy players making their way out, "*Pinche gringo* cheaters. Can't win without getting the game fixed."

And then shit gets real.

29

Pushing, shoving, posturing ensues. We find ourselves stuck in the middle of it. There's swearing and finger-pointing. Anger, tension, frustration roil all around us. The game was tense, and it ended with a wisp of uncertainty, but this conflict feels like something more visceral, more dangerous. Then, one of the guys who confronted CC at the concession stand pushes up in front of us and shouts out, "*Órale*, Coconut... you see your friends, bunch of racist cheaters."

"Shut the fuck up, asshole," Reid shouts back as we try to maneuver past the crowd to get the hell out of there.

Whether it is intentional or he's just trying to get her attention again, the guy reaches out for CC and somehow through the confusion and commotion his hand gets tangled in her hair and the straps of her backpack and he pulls her backwards. CC screams, the sound piercing my heart as I turn to see her falling backwards into the crowd.

Punches fly, bodies become entangled, screams and swearing in English and Spanish shoot into the night sky. Reid pushes through the melee and scoops CC into his chest and pulls her up as people crush in all around us. We put our shoulders down and force our way through the madness to get ourselves and CC out of there. The budding journalist in me wants to stay, to observe, to tell this story, but my love for these two people outweighs my instincts and drives me to protect my friends and get away. We force our way through the crowd, finally making it to the outside, only to find that the ugliness of the night has escaped the confines of the baseball park. The Toros players are objecting to being loaded onto their bus. They want to join in the fracas, to support their families and fans pleading their case and defending them against this athletic injustice and the racist jeering. We rush on past them, not wanting to get stuck in their presence should the barricade of coaches fail. When we get to CC's car, we just stand there, trying to take in what we're seeing. CC's front and rear windshields are smashed, and one of her tires is slashed.

My heart begins to race. I can feel my pulse quickening, my breath beginning to shorten. The shouts, the yelling, the fear, mixed with the breeze swirling around us, fuel the panic stirring inside me, even if we have finally made it past the turmoil. The lights and sirens from the two police cars that skid to a stop in front of the field freeze me in a haze of dark memories. I thought the months free from panic attacks and self-wallowing had left the emotional eruption of tears and hyperventilating behind me, until I see the tears tracing their way down CC's cheeks.

How could I be so self-absorbed? This is happening to her. She's spent her evening listening to morons chant racist slogans, had her ethnicity challenged by a different pair of morons, and then was assaulted for nothing more than where she went to school. Now, her car, a car she loves and works to help pay for, sits vandalized for the same reason, for her affiliation to a school. Her car was an obvious and easy target for the unrest of the night. Her rear window, emblazoned with Blue Lacy cheer decals, with blue and silver streamers tied to the mirrors, with all the other windows adorned and painted with spirit messages for the game, was an easy target.

But CC isn't what or who people imagine and expect someone from Pearl Heights is. She isn't the "Pearly Whites" stereotype that the Toros chanted about. She isn't the spoiled, entitled rich kid everyone assumes all kids at Pearl Heights are. She isn't White, isn't privileged, isn't rich. She's the daughter of a single mother who works in a public school. She isn't someone who has extra money just sitting around for deductibles and new tires. She's just CC, someone nice and kind, someone fun and funny, someone who thinks of others before herself. She isn't what whoever trashed her car thought she was.

And, so what if she were that person? Reid is that person. Reid is exactly what people think of when they think of Pearl Heights. He's rich, White, privileged. His $50,000 truck is loaded with every bell and whistle possible. Even if his truck, parked away from the stadium, had been damaged, it would be fixed or replaced without a thought. He lives in an ornately gorgeous and massive house. He and his family travel the world, but that doesn't take away from the person he is. The person who recognizes my emotional triggers and does everything he can to help me get through them, the person who is hell-bent on clearing any obstacle in my path because of all the shit in my past, the person who laughs with unabashed recklessness, the person who doesn't miss a breath throwing himself into a mob to protect his childhood friend. Yes, he is a privileged White boy from a rich family, but it's a family with a frickin' children's cancer ward named for it, a family that donates thousands of dollars in backpacks and school supplies each year for needy kids, a family that funds arts and charitable events across the city. There are plenty of rich privileged assholes at our school, but there are also plenty who are rich and privileged and not assholes.

CC is leaning into Reid, her tears a mixture of anger, disbelief, and pain from having her hair yanked and falling into a mob. More officers arrive and are issuing citations for disorderly conduct. From where we're watching, their enforcement seems focused on the fans from the visiting team. Those who were actually fighting have already disbanded and blended into the crowd. Tension still hangs in the air as people trying to leave the scene behind quickly.

Reid calls a tow truck for CC's car and then drives CC to her house before taking me home. After we pull up in front of my house, Reid turns off the engine, and we sit quietly, the tumult of the night receding into the crisp night air. Flashes of the evening's events return to me in color, sound and scent. The savor of grilled meat and buttery popcorn mixes with shouts of supportive cheers and hostile mantras. It's the juxtaposition of the very best and worst of what people can do. It's a peek at the seedlings of hatred and contempt that spur evil hearts and weak minds to acts of violence, *the kind of violence that cost my parents their lives*. A shiver not connected to the chill of the night runs down my spine.

"You doing okay?" Reid asks, turning from the driver's seat to look at me.

"Yeah, I'm good. Just a crazy night."

"You need to talk about anything, talk to anyone?" Reid offers, a slight hint of caution in his voice, trying not to overstep but also giving me permission to be fragile.

I remember the control slipping away from me earlier in the evening and I wonder how much of a journalist I am if the slightest moment of tension sends me into panic attacks. Yes, I feel a malaise lingering from the chaos of the evening, but I also have a sense of comfort coursing through me. It fills me with warmth, with hope, that Reid could think nothing of putting himself in front of CC for her safety and still have it in him to recognize the triggers that lead me to emotionally implode. Even when a hoard of thoughtless punks put their privilege above even a modicum of decency, there were other people who chose to let the better parts of themselves shine. As I replay the evening, I remember moms and dads on both sides pulling students away and pleading for calm. I see the Toros coach decisively holding his boys back and corralling them to the bus despite their attempts to join the protest. I see the Blue Lacy coach immediately rush to the stands and order the chanting to stop. And I see faces stained with tears and disbelief at what was happening around them, so devastated and crestfallen that we could sink so low. The night's events have poked my panic and grief out of hibernation. But seeing the pain in CC and the love in Reid, I find strength in putting someone else's pain ahead of mine. I think Dr. Robles would be proud of me for this.

Sitting here in this truck that has carted me across city and out to the country, with this boy who only a few months ago was unknown to me, a stranger, a someone who should have never come into my life, I am confronted by this person who knows my hurt and has witnessed my utter grief and, instead of running away from it, has run to it. Nothing can ever replace losing my parents, nothing will ever bring them back, but right here in this moment, I am reminded that no matter how much I have lost, there is always room for more love.

"I'm good. I really am. I don't think I'm normal yet, but I'm getting closer. I don't want to be sad all the time. I don't want to never be able to really enjoy life because I'm too afraid of all the shitty things that happen in life. I don't want to not think of my parents, because it hurts so much to think of them. And, I don't want to feel bad about enjoying my life because I still have one. It's just so fucking unfair that they're gone, but those assholes at the game get to be here, get to have a life no matter how fucking miserable they are as people."

"You know, you've never really talked to me about your parents before," Reid says, reaching over to put his hand on my knee and squeezing it with affection.

"I know. I didn't want to, I didn't, you know, want to bore you or bum you out with stories about them. I really don't know if I can cry in front of you one more time without you deciding I'm just one big-ass crybaby."

"Well, first all, you have no ass, so you can't be a big-ass crybaby. You can be a scrawny-ass crybaby, but that's a definite no on the big ass..."

"I have a perfectly lov..."

"Yes, yes, you have a perfectly lovely ass and balls. So, tell me something about your parents."

30

My face hurts from laughing. After about an hour of telling stories about my parents, the intermittent yawns from a long day and an even more exhausting evening bring the day to a close... with a very romantic kiss. Reid watches from his truck as I make my way inside the house. As he drives away, the tiniest hint of his aroma, a mix of sandalwood and fabric softener, clings to me.

Sleep will feel so good, but the memory of the evening's events keeps me up. Despite my bed beckoning me to surrender to exhaustion, I sit down and attempt to write down everything I can remember. Mom and Dad used to call it writing "contemporaneous notes." I try to describe everything I saw, heard and smelled. I fill pages of my journal with what is part sports-story and part a slice of Americana. It is also an indictment of toxic masculinity and dumbass racism. I spill it all out onto the page and then crawl into bed with only one thought left in my head: Reid's kiss.

When I wake up the next morning, the story of last night wakes up with me. With the events still fresh in my mind and my notes handy, I crawl out of bed, pull out my laptop and begin writing an editorial for a special edition of *The Blue Dawg Alt*. What starts out as a way for me to keep writing has picked up quite a loyal following. People like the stories we tell and the way we tell them. We've even made connections with

student journalists from schools across the state and country who are putting out their newspapers exclusively online.
Something about this piece feels different. I write:

> Last night there was a baseball game. The Toros of Chávez High School played the Blue Lacys of Pearl Heights. It was close, practically epic. Pearl Heights won. The Toros lost. And that was the game.
> That's where it should have ended. That's where the thrill of victory and the agony of defeat should have met midfield in the long held little league tradition of handshakes and the muttering of "good game," "good game," "good game."
> That's not what happened.
> In a clearly coordinated dick move, twenty plus teenage boys didn't just show up wearing red, white and blue T-shirts and seat themselves like the stars and stripes of Ol' Glory by accident. No, this shit was planned.
> When the ump called the Toros' last chance of victory out at home and the Blue Lacy celebration collided with the Toros' disappointment, that moment that epitomizes sport was stolen from both teams. Before the dust from the slide into home could even settle back to earth, the innocence of this kids' game got swept over with the very adult and very real vitriol that has kept the last national election cycle festering throughout society.
> Playing against a team with an all Mexican-American roster, the boorish, entitled MAGA-hat-wearing deplorables from a school known city wide for its reputation as rich, elitist and white began chanting "Build that wall! Build that wall! Build that wall!"

But the opposite happened. Walls came down. Walls of decorum, decency and sportsmanship fell to a racism no longer veiled, no longer disguised by etiquette or embarrassment. Insults, innuendos and invectives flew through the air between the fans of both teams as they tried to exit the baseball stadium, but it was all posturing over punches, bravado over bravery.

Until... hell, as they say, broke loose.

Shouting gave way to shoving as umpires, coaches and some, definitely not all, parents did what they could to halt a melee that grew out of the political tensions spreading to every area of our lives.

Maybe by sheer dumb luck or celestial grace no one ended up hurt, arrested or— as is too often the case when tempers and testosterone clash—dead, but plenty of damage was done. We damaged our sense of civility, our sense of humanity and the simple joy of a game played by children.

That does not have to be the box score of the game. We have a choice. We can choose to say these moments don't define us, decide these moments aren't who we are.

But we can't let these moments go unpunished.

There are always two sides to a story, but this story began when a group of guys who should know better made a choice to display the very worst of what has infected our public psyche by showing up to our American pastime in hats of hate.

It will be up to the administration of Chávez High School to deal with the actions of its students and fans, but the bulk of the responsibility lies with the leaders of Pearl Heights to take swift action. The administration of Pearl Heights must issue an apology to both communities involved. It must come out and strongly rebuke the actions of these Pearl Heights students and immediately suspend them for the near riot they incited with their actions and words.

Baseball may be a kids' game, but it's time for a certain group of childish young men to grow up and face the consequences of their actions.

On deck, the Pearl Heights administration.

Don't strike out.

I upload the picture I took on my phone of the Blue Lacy guys clad in the MAGA hats and wearing American flag apparel. I write a caption, run a quick spell-check and prepare to post the story. My finger hovers over the enter key as I wonder whether I really want to go down this path. Will my words have any real effect in this community so steeped in tradition and so sheltered from the world most people really live in? Do I want any hassle that may come with this? Maybe we should keep to our feel-good stories, our stories of the unsung and the underdogs walking the halls of Pearl Heights unnoticed and unappreciated because they aren't the norm. Still, it's February, college acceptances should arrive soon. I only have a few more months before I'm off to college and can get away from here the way my dad did.

Who needs this trouble? Here I am hoping to hear from Northwestern any day now. Waiting to hear if I will go from budding journalist to journalism major at the school where my parents met and became journalists themselves. How can I not take this risk, when my parents died because telling stories mattered to them, died because someone didn't like that they used words to try and change the world. What those guys did was wrong. So what if kids get dickish in the halls with me over this? So what if people throw shade at me over this?

I can handle the flack.

Enter.

31

My back hurts from where it connected with the lockers behind me. I can still feel the sting on my chest from the two obnoxiously large hands that smacked me square in the sternum and thrust me into rows of combination knobs jutting out to add an extra dash of pain.

"Fuck you, faggot, and your goddamn piece of shit online newspaper."

Holy shitbombs. My head is spinning, and I can't focus on the frenetic chaos zigzagging all around me. I'm dazed. In all my years at school, I have never been physically assaulted, and the "faggot" thing... that's new as well. I don't know this guy, but I recognize him as one of the MAGA hat wearers from the baseball game. This is part of the flack I told myself I could handle.

"Trying to get me *suspended*! I will stomp your faggoty ass," he barks at me with a toxicity I have never encountered before. The veins in his temples literally bulge while the blotchy patches of blood, blush and rosacea in his cheeks make him look like a caged beast.

"Get the fuck off of him," Reid shouts as he comes flying in from the side and shoves raging-rosacea boy.

"Fuck you, Tibbitts, and your faggot boyfriend. I'll kick your ass, too."

The crowd around us grows but dissipates just as quickly as teachers begin converging upon the scene, ordering us to "break it up" and "knock it off." They also make sure to record it all on their phones. This was the most excitement and the closest thing to a school fight any of them had seen in their entire Pearl Heights careers.

My assault ended; however, there is also some other titillating buzz in the school hallways. The "faggot," "faggoty ass" and "your-boyfriend" are echoing. No sooner than I walk into newspaper class, when Kelly grabs my arm and ushers me back into the hallway to show me pictures from the senior girls' group chat. There are pictures from the baseball game of Reid's hand on top of mine, of our knees touching and of the two of us kissing while leaning on his truck in front of my house that night after the game. Someone stalked us after the game to take that picture! I immediately feel angry that my privacy has been violated and then angrier that anybody would think it's okay to out anyone. Then, the real shitbomb explodes inside my head: this is how CC will find out about me and Reid. She'll find out that I've chosen Reid over her. I just begin to consider the hornet's nest I've walked into, when Ms. Gillis pokes her head out into the hallway to inform me that I've been summoned to the principal's office—again.

By the next morning's appointment with Dr. Robles, everything is out in the open and a complete mess. I got assaulted in the hallway and got suspended for it. According to the principal, the piece I posted online disrupted the learning environment. The pictures of me and Reid were passed around campus faster than cooties at a middle school dance. And that opened up a rather awkward conversation with Grams and Gramps. They aren't like omg gross or freaked-out about it as much as they are questioning what is going on under their roof. I explain that nothing happened between me and Reid until the camping trip and that I respect them too much to breech that trust, although we've cuddled and kissed in the house since the trip. I tell them that Reid and I are friends more than anything else and that without them and him, I'm not sure how I would have made it through the year.

Dr. Robles wants to hear all of it. He asks for details of how things are with Grams and Gramps. Do I feel comfortable with the new dynamics of our relationship? Do I feel like I can continue my relationship with Reid around them? He won't just settle for, "Yeah, we talked," as enough of a response. What specifically did we say? What had we come to an agreement on? How did they feel about this side of their grandson?

"Really, it was good. Surprisingly good," I say. "Of course, they wanted to know if I was physically okay, but they mostly wanted to know if I was emotionally okay."

Of course, they assured me, "We love you no matter what." But I also got a little lecture on how hurt they felt that I hadn't told them about how things had changed with me and Reid. That stung a little because of all they have done for me, but they also let me know that nothing has changed, that Reid is still welcome at the house, anytime, that they aren't going to be checking in on us or require doors to stay open.

"But until you've had a condom conversation with your Grams, you don't know awkward," I say.

"Dr. Robles," I say, "I think Grams and Gramps were in cahoots on that conversation, because Gramps was having too good a time watching me squirm. And when Grams said, 'Now I know you kids like using the term 'hard-on' when you talk about your erections, so you tell me, Ethan-Matthew, which term you prefer, hard-on or erection, and that's what I'll use.'"

Dr. Robles almost spits out his coffee on hearing this.

I take a more serious tact with Dr. Robles when I report that CC has gone underground. She hasn't responded to texts from me or Reid. God, what an ass I am. Those two have been friends practically their whole lives and in just a few months, I've broken her heart, driven a wedge between the two of them and made her the butt of hashtags and jokes.

Dr. Robles wants to explore how I came to my decision after pining to him about CC in our previous sessions. We talk about societal expectations and how I was possibly just following the path of expectation set before me until Reid came along and presented another route. He also reminds me that I'm young and will most like journey down multiple paths before choosing which destination to follow. It's the kind of metaphor I appreciate from our sessions.

He also believes the same metaphor would get CC through all of this, too. Her heart will heal, and he feels confident she will welcome both Reid and me back into her life. This isn't much comfort to me. I never wanted to hurt anyone. CC was the first friend I made when I moved here, and I feel like I owe it to her to make her happy and bring her the kind of joy she has brought me. Dr. Robles reminds me that I'm not responsible for anyone else's happiness. I can contribute to it and even take away from it, but I'm responsible for my own happiness. CC, Reid, Grams, Gramps are all responsible to themselves for their happiness. "Give it time," he says to me, and, so far, he's pretty on target about the healing properties of time.

Nothing we talk about in this session will change that I've been suspended from school. Nothing will change that a bunch of racist morons are sitting in class, despite nearly inciting a riot and cyberbullying CC, Reid and me. Never mind that some asshole went all cage-match on me. Now, he's in class, and I'm *suspended*, because I "disrupted the learning environment" by pointing out that guys who behaved really, really shitty deserved to be punished. I can't believe this school that my dad dusted off from his feet, this school that my grandparents have never let go of is driving me away the way it drove away my dad. I can't reconcile these contrasting narratives. How could my dad have run so far from this place while his parents have hung on to it so tightly?

This is what I want to ask Dad. Is he proud of me for wanting to get the hell out of here the way he did? I want to know why he and Mom never wanted me to have the life he had. I want to know if he would be disappointed that for a hot minute I liked it here. I tried to hate it the entire time I've been here because he did, but I couldn't do it. I made friends here. I liked almost all of my teachers and lots of the ones who weren't my teachers. I wanted to rebel against the reputation the school has, but I found myself liking the traditions and liking the people for who they are and not the stereotypes most of them didn't come close to fitting. So really, I feel like I'm being torn away yet again from another world I love.

When I finish the session with Dr. Robles, I feel a mixture of peace and uneasiness. I'm still suspended from school. I still have questions only my dad could answer, but I also feel okay about a lot of other things. It doesn't feel quite like a counseling victory, but in a way, I feel as accomplished about how I'm handling life as I did after my first cross country race. I still have lots to improve on, but I have definitely come a long way. When I stand to leave, Dr. Robles does something he's never done before. He hugs me. Not a bro hug, not a great-aunt-second-cousin-twice-removed hug, but, well... a dad hug.

"Ethan-Matthew," he says to me in a very dad tone as he releases the hug, "You're gonna be just fine. I know it doesn't seem that way right now. I know things seem really awful at the moment, but I'm going to help you get through all of this. You will get through this."

"But how? Everything is so wrong. I've screwed everything up."

"You'll be just fine, and you know I'm here anytime you need me. You know you have lots of people in your corner. We'll talk again next week, but you call me if you need to. And just so you know, I hope my boys grow up to be just as brave as you."

I hug Dr. Robles back, not wanting to let go, even though I know I have to. My tears begin to flow when he says, "Your dad is proud of you. You're a good son."

32

Grams and Gramps normally do dinner up pretty big on the regular, but tonight feels like Thanksgiving dinner has arrived early, although with more of a Tex-Mex flare. Gramps has smoked a brisket and there are baked potatoes large enough to make a watermelon blush. It's all accompanied with sides of charro beans, four-cheese mac & cheese, bacon-wrapped asparagus, Mexican-style corn-on-the-cob and a blueberry-peach cobbler. Could it be an apology meal for the embarrassing condom conversation or a dinner to take my mind off suspension?

Gramps says we're expecting company.

When the doorbell rings, I hope to find CC on the other side and then pray to sweet brown Baby Jesus that Grams and Gramps, more so Grams, will behave themselves, when I see they've invited Reid and his parents for dinner. As I open the door, Reid has a definite wtf look on his face, and neither of us know what to do—hug, handshake, kiss? Definitely not kiss. It doesn't matter. Mrs. Tibbitts moves right past Reid and gives me a momma-bear hug.

"Oh, you darling boy. Are you okay? I'm so sorry you're having to deal with all this... well, shit."

"Mom!" Reid says, blushing at his mother's colorful language.

"Well, that's what it is. Don't be such a..." She doesn't finish her sentence when she sees Grams come into the room. "Honey, thanks so much for having us over. It's been too long."

Off she and Grams go toward the kitchen.

"Hey, bud," Mr. Tibbitts says to me, giving me a combo bro-awkward man hug. "You doin' okay?"

I don't want to sound nervous when I answer him. I hadn't expected to see him so soon after all the hullabaloo. I haven't gotten to talk to Reid about any of this and had no idea how his dad would take it. He is, from everything I know about him, such a traditional man's man. He hunts, fishes, drives a truck, follows sports. If he has any qualms about his son and me, he sure isn't showing it.

"I'm fine, Mr. Tibbitts, sir. Thanks for..."

"Good, good," he says as he moves in between Reid and me, drapes an arm over each of our shoulders and guides us toward the dining room. "Let's get something to drink, boys."

The Tibbitts and my grandparents have known each other for years, so they do a lot of catching up while Reid and I try to hang back all casual-like, as if this kind of stuff happens all the time. Your grandson getting outed via group chat with the boy who's spent so many nights over that you gave him his own key to your house. Oh, and on the same day he gets outed, he also gets suspended for getting his ass kicked by a homophobic bubba with rosacea and an attitude. And if all of this weren't bad enough, CC is still ghosting both of us. I'm pretty bummed she isn't speaking to me, and I have only known her a few months, but Reid is crushed by it. He knew she liked me and thought this whole thing would just work itself out. Sometimes, we guys are stupid like that.

Even though CC is ghosting us, we did hear from our cross-country crew, who were completely ride or die with us. They wanted to know if they could get me an emotional support fish and if I was dating Reid out of pity or because he was slightly goofier looking than me. And when I tell Reid about the text I got from Malibu, he shows me his phone. Malibu sent both of us the exact same text: *wtf dude? you not tryna take dis? im like waaaaaay hotter than that dufus*

We're both laughing when the doorbell rings again. My heart is racing, expecting that my grandparents have reached out to CC and that she'll be joining us. She and probably her mom are going to be on the other side of that door, and we will go back to our perfect little friendship. But when Grams opens the door, it's some dude. He's a little taller than me and Reid but not as tall as Reid's dad. He's like all put together, well-dressed in slacks with narrow cuffs and really expensive looking leather shoes. He's wearing a tailored sport coat, a solid white dress shirt and—how could I not notice?—an Audemars Piguet similar to the one my dad had that is sitting in a box in my closet.

Actually, it's more than similar. It looks exactly the same as the watch my dad had. It's so freakin' expensive that Dad only wore it on special occasions, which is why it was at home the day they were killed. I wore it to the funeral and then put it back in the box, not sure I'd ever wear it again.

Grams hugs him, and they do that stand-back-and-let-me-look-at-you thing adults do, and they hug again before Grams hooks her arm around his and walks him into the living room to introduce him to the rest of us.

"Everyone, our final guest has arrived. This is Ethan-Matthews."

Holy shitbombs.

33

Everyone is standing up, shaking hands and introducing themselves when Grams call us all to the dining room.

Seizing my moment, I call out to her, "You guys start without us. We gotta take care of something real quick." I grab Reid by the sleeve and drag him upstairs to my room before anyone can object to our bizarre and kind of rude departure.

"What's goin' on, dude?" Reid spits out as soon as we get to my room. "Who is that guy and why is his name Ethan Matthews?"

"Hell if I know."

"I thought your parents named you Ethan-Matthew because they liked both names and couldn't decide between them and because they wanted you to have a kinda normal name?"

"That's what I thought, too, but check this out," I say and pull out the watch and show it to Reid.

"No fucking way! That's the same damn watch that dude is wearing."

"I know. This was my dad's watch."

"Dude, put it on."

"You think so?"

"Yeah, I don't know. I mean, I guess..."

"Boys, come on down and join us," Gramps calls from the bottom of the stairs.

213

"Coming, Gramps," I say as I put the watch on my wrist.

At the dinner table, everyone is laughing and passing around dishes, when Reid and I walk in and the conversation stops.

Awkward.

Two chairs are unoccupied. Ethan Matthews is seated at the end of the table, and there are empty chairs on each side of him.

Double awkward.

Grams, the perfect host that she is, steps in and breaks the silence.

"Boys, this is Ethan Matthews. He's a long-time family friend. Ethan, this is our grandson Ethan-Matthew and his special friend Reid Tibbitts."

Seriously, Grams? "Special friend?" Like this isn't awkward enough.

I try to look as if it doesn't faze me, but I'm fairly sure I'm not fooling anyone, until Reid steps in to be exactly who I always need him to be. Thank God.

"Hi, Mr. Matthews. I'm Reid Tibbitts, favorite child of these fine folks," he says and passes his arm in front of his parents like he was presenting fabulous prizes on a game show, "and special friend of Mr. Ethan-Matthew Cruz Canton de los Santa Maria von Schnicklebutt."

Everyone bursts out laughing. I almost pee in my pants.

"Oh, you're such a peach," Grams says to Reid and kisses him on the cheek. "You boys have a seat and serve yourselves some food."

With the awkward and the double awkward mostly behind us, we sit down, and the evening carries on. Mr. Matthews asks us about our activities in school, about our friends and about our future plans. Reid talks about how he hopes to make it to state again in cross country for his senior year and how he wants to get Hermes wings tattooed on both sides of his ankles, but "my boomer parents are super lame and won't let me. Yes, I'm talking about you, Julie and Andrew," he says, casting a mock derisive look at the Tibbitts that he follows with a wink and an air kiss.

I'm so glad that Reid is here to diffuse the weirdness. I honestly would have freaked if Reid weren't here being Reid.

I still have so many questions and don't know how to ask them. This guy, Mr. Matthews, clearly has some kind of connection to me beyond old family friend. And what about the name and the watch?

We dance around these questions for the rest of dinner. Mr. Matthews talks about missing being back in the old neighborhood since his parents moved to Colorado to escape Texas summers. He says that work takes him around the country but never mentions what his work is, and nobody asks. We talk about my college applications, about how I'm hoping to hear from Northwestern and that I've also applied to Princeton, NYU, Creighton, Rhodes College... and, to appease Gramps, The University of Texas. I actually don't have anything against UT. The journalism program there is really strong, and Grams and Gramps are both alums. However, it's just too close to... well, home. At least that's what I used to think before I met Reid and CC. I used to think I wanted to get as far away from here as possible, the way my dad did. I could come back and visit Grams and Gramps on holidays as I had done all my life. That was the plan until I started to entertain the tiniest notion of staying a little closer to the people I love.

By the time we move from the dining room table to the living room for coffee and dessert, I feel like I'm going to lose it if someone doesn't give me some answers. I certainly enjoy the company and have even forgotten how shitty my life is at the moment, but I can't stop staring at the watch and saying his name, Ethan Matthews, over and over in my head. I can feel the chill vibes Reid has been sending me all evening. Never mind, I need some answers.

Then Gramps—God bless that man—stands up to make an announcement before I embarrass myself.

"Everyone, if I could have your attention for a minute. Honey and I are glad you are with us tonight for dinner and to catch up with one another. Reid and Ethan-Matthew, the Tibbitts and the two of us," he says motioning to Grams, "asked Ethan to be here tonight to help us with the situation going on with the school. You know this situation has gotten somewhat serious. The school has contacted us, and they want Ethan-Matthew to finish the school year at the alternative campus...."

My mouth drops and I stand up to protest, but Gramps holds his hand up to calm me down. He continues, "We're sorry that we hadn't mentioned it to you yet, but you already had a lot going on, and we wanted to put a plan together and explore our options before moving forward."

Then, as if they had rehearsed it, Mr. Matthews stands up and takes over.

"This is where I come in," Mr. Matthews announces. "I am a constitutional rights attorney, specializing in first amendment rights, but my firm also does civil rights cases as well representing high school and college students in advocacy and social justice issues."

"Are we suing the school?" I blurt out.

"Well, I've already filed an injunction to keep the school from making any changes to your records or contacting any of the universities you've applied to regarding this discipline issue. I'm hoping we don't have to sue the school, but yes, that's an option we may explore. We are going to look at a number of avenues and approach this from a number of sides, but we are going to be very aggressive in that approach. You all, let me worry about that. In the meantime, I'm going to spend some time talking with just you, Ethan-Matthew, and get some background information and answer a lot of questions you probably have," he says, adjusting the watch on his wrist. "And Reid, I wanted you to meet me too because one of the areas we are hoping to make the school uncomfortable with has to do with some bullying issues and hate crimes based on the assault that happened to the two of you. We've seen the videos of the incident, so I want you to meet with me and one of my associates, if that's okay with you."

"Hell, yeah. I'm ready to kick some legal ass," Reid says as his mom puts her hands to her temples and nods her head in humorous exasperation, and his dad puts his hand on Reid's face and pushes it away.

"Okay, so that's great, Reid. I'll see what we can do about kicking some 'legal ass.' Anyway, that's what brought us all together tonight, plus it's been too long since I've seen Honey and Huck. And, Ethan-Matthew, I'll reach out to you to see when we can find a time to..."

"Can we do it tonight?" I interrupt. I seriously am going to lose my shit if he walks out of this house tonight without giving me any answers.

"Um, yeah. I guess that's fine. Honey, Huck, that okay with the two of you?"

They both agree without hesitation, and after a little more time for pleasantries and some hugs and goodbyes, Mr. Ethan Matthews and I move outside to the back patio.

I'm about to get some answers, whether they are answers I want is something altogether different.

34

For the last three hours I've done nothing but stare at this guy, and now he's sitting right in front of me on a patio chair in our backyard. I can't think of a thing to say to him. Well, that's not completely true. I can think of a million things I want to say to him but in the competition of what to say first, nothing comes out.

"You don't know what to ask do you?" Mr. Matthews says.

"Not really, no. I mean kind of but I, I..."

"Just don't know where to start."

"Yeah... I mean, yes, sir. Sorry."

"It's cool. Don't worry about..."

"You knew my parents, didn't you?" I ask, rubbing the watch that weighs heavy on my wrist.

"I gave that watch to your dad when we both turned forty."

"Oh, okay, that clears up one mystery."

"Why did my parents name me after you?"

With a wide grin on his face, Mr. Matthews says, "Well, that's a long story...."

"I'm not going anywhere. I'd like to hear it."

"Okay, you asked for it," he says and reaches into the cooler Gramps brought out earlier, pops the top off a Prickly Pear Shiner Bock, leans back and launches into a story I didn't know I'd been waiting my entire life to hear.

"I met your dad my freshman year at Pearl Heights. My parents were Blue Lacy alums, too, but they are a couple of years younger than Honey and Huck and didn't really know them when they went to school here. Mom and Dad moved away... college, jobs, started a family and finally moved back here when I started high school. Something I was not happy about at all, and, from what I hear, you know how hard it can be to break into this school where kids have been storming the beaches of Turks and Caicos together on multi-family vacations since they were toddlers."

"Yeah, I definitely get that," I say.

"So, I was kind of an angry kid and didn't care that kids were ostracizing me like I had the plague because I just wanted to be back in school with my friends. I had your dad in three of my classes, and he was nothing if not relentless and a little bit of a diva dude. It didn't matter that everyone else in class was paying attention to him; it mattered that I wasn't, and he just had to win me over, too."

"God, from what I hear, people loved my dad."

"Well, at first, I thought he was an asshole, but the kind of guy you can't help liking. Anyway, we eventually became, I guess, best friends, or best friends at school, anyway. Your dad did all the jock stuff while I was taking choir and theater. For most of those first two years of high school, we didn't have cars and weren't driving, so we pretty much just hung out at school, talked on the phone, stuff like that."

"God, I can't believe you knew my dad back then. What was he like?"

"Oh, Ethan-Matthew... your dad was something else," he said, the confidence in his voice wavering a bit. "I loved him. He was my best friend. And you're right, everybody did love him, and it always made me wonder why someone who had the entire school to choose from would pick me for a best friend. He was such a big deal, but that made him kind of reckless. He thought he could charm his way out of anything. He was kind of a... you probably don't know the reference, an Eddie Has."

"Eddie Haskell from *Leave it to Beaver*."

"Yeah, how do you know?"

"Dad used to call me Eddie Haskell, so I Googled it and started watching the show on Nick at Night."

"Yeah, well your dad was like Eddie Haskell but sincere. Not a prick at all. But, you know, high school kids are stupid sometimes... even your dad. One time during junior year, he picked me up from play rehearsal. He had a crush on Kathy Vines, so he used me as an excuse and would show up at rehearsal to get a chance to talk to her and pretend he was genuinely interested in theater. One night, he drove us all home. We cruised around for a while so he could flirt with Kathy while I sat in the back seat. We eventually dropped off Kathy at her house, and while he was driving me home, he ran a stop sign with a cop sitting right there. The cop flashed his lights, and your dad looked at me and said, 'I'm not gonna stop,' and he took off."

"What the...?" I was getting really comfortable with the guy I was named after, but I stopped myself before I forgot myself too much. "Dad ran from the cops? Why?"

"God, I freaked out when he took off, but he kept going, and I was like, 'What're you doing??' He said there was a bottle of peach schnapps in the glove compartment. I couldn't believe we were *going* to jail for stupid peach schnapps. He was driving through all these back streets, trying to lose the cop, which he did for a little bit. He finally stopped when I told him to pull over or I was going jump out of the car. He was freaking out when we stopped, so I told him to get out and switch places with me."

"Wait, what? Why did you do that?"

He shrugged his shoulders and says, "For a couple of reasons. One, it was football season, and your dad was a starter, team captain. He would have lost all of that. If you were in any extra curriculars back then, you signed a 24-hour contract, so if you got in trouble outside of school, you were in trouble at school, too. So, when that cop caught up with us, I let him think I was driving and that the schnapps was mine."

"Wouldn't that mean you wouldn't be able to act in a play?"

"You're quick, like your dad. Yeah, I got cut from the play we were rehearsing. The director and the whole cast were pissed at me."

"Why would you give that up for..."

"I loved your dad," he says and pauses as if he doesn't know how to continue. "I was in love with your dad."

Holy shitbombs! What the hell am I hearing?

"I had a crush on your dad through most of the last half of high school, but he never knew it. I never said anything. I just kept my feelings to myself. I preferred keeping him in my life as an unrequited love rather than risk losing him by saying anything."

"But he let you take the blame for him."

"He wanted to come clean, but I wouldn't let him."

"But..."

"We do dumb things when we're kids. Your dad did something really dumb, but he didn't deserve to lose everything over one moment of being a dumbass."

I try to interrupt again, but Ethan Matthews continues, "Hey, I'm not a saint either. I know part of me did it thinking your dad would feel like he owed me something. Maybe it would have worked in my favor, but he was so torn up over it, I could never try to manipulate him that way. We were beyond solid after that, but wow, did Honey and Huck want me out of Tripp's life. Your grandmother can get really set in her ways."

"Oh, believe me, I know."

"Ethan-Matthew, I'm going to tell you some things, and some of it's going to be hard hear," he says, changing his tone of voice to almost stern. "I'm going to say some things about your grandparents that are going to stun you.... But if you so much as change what you think of them one scintilla because of what I tell you, we're done. I will get up and walk out the door, and you will never hear from me again. Are we clear?"

My heart thunders inside my chest, and my legs tremble in fidgety nervousness.

"Yes, sir," I mutter.

35

Ethan Matthews pulls another beer from the cooler, pops the cap, leans back and draws in a deep, contemplative breath before leaning forward and looking me directly in my eyes. "I'm sorry to be so blunt, but I know you have questions, and I want to answer them for you. You just have to be aware of what you're getting yourself into, and you're going to have to decide for yourself what to do with it. So, do you want me to go on?"

"Yes, sir. I do."

"Okay, so, first off, it's not as bad as anything you've already been through—nothing could be, so you can handle this. I know you must be thinking a million different things, but you are going to be okay, I promise. All right?"

"Yes, sir. I'm ready."

"To begin with, the whole reason I'm a part of any of this is because I crushed pretty hard on your dad in high school, which as weird as that is for you to hear, it was even weirder back then. Let me tell you, if you think this place is kind of uptight now about things, it's nothing compared to growing up here in the '80s. Using hair product or even combing your hair differently was enough to get you called a faggot and shoved into a locker, or worse. So, me doing theater and choir instead of sports... you can imagine how weird that looked.... Especially when your dad was a major jock and the big man on campus.

During the last half of senior year after the peach schnapps incident, I secretly put up flyers around campus petitioning the school to allow same-gender dates for prom, so I could ask your dad to go to prom with me."

"You started *Faux For* ?" I ask, the look of incredulity on my face impossible to miss.

"Well, I didn't start it, but I put the posters up that eventually got the whole thing going. Things were different back then. There weren't cameras all over schools in those days, so it was easy to put them up without getting caught."

"Did you ask my dad to prom?"

"No, I was never that brave, and he never knew I put up the posters. I was too afraid to come out, and as I said earlier, I didn't want to do anything to jeopardize our friendship. Plus, your grandparents already couldn't stand me. They all but ordered him to stop spending time with me. So, we had to sneak around to hang out. Asking your dad to prom would have brought all kinds of hell and hate down on us, so I just let it go."

"But when did things change between you and my grandparents?"

"Not for a long time after high school. When we took off to college, your dad was at Northwestern, and I went to this little private school outside of Cleveland that was really big in theater. I had Broadway dreams before I decided on law school, but we hung out all the time during our first two years of college. He'd drive up to my school one weekend, and I'd go up to his the next. We'd spend Spring Breaks together—all without your grandparents knowing. You could get away with that kind of thing in the pre-iPhone, pre-social media days. We were having the time of our lives, and I started thinking that we could do this forever and that maybe your dad just needed a little push. One Spring Break while lounging on a beach in Florida, I told your dad that I was in love him."

"What did he say?"

"Oh man, your dad."

"What? What did he say?"

"I told your dad I was in love with him, and he looked at me and said, I kid you not, 'Dude, I know.'"

"No kidding?"

"Yeah," he said with a chuckle, "and then he told me I was his best friend, that he would always love me and that he figured I'd come out when I was ready, but he didn't feel that way about me. That's when he told me about meeting your mom, about this gorgeous *mexicana* he met who he imagined being married to the first time he saw her. I knew your dad would be the love of my life I would never have... and that would have to be okay."

"Nothing changed between you two?"

"Oh, things changed. Your dad looooved having a gay friend. It was constantly, 'What about him?' or 'How about that guy?' He was annoying and relentless."

"Yeah, I know. Like he would never let things go on anything. Always a thousand questions."

"So, nothing was ever going to happen between us. The best thing about that was it brought your mom into my life. The first time I met her, I was so nervous because I knew your dad told her about my profession of love on the beach."

"Did he really?"

"Oh, hell yeah. And, I never had anything to worry about with her. We became as good of friends as me and your dad were."

"But I still don't understand. What's the big deal with Grams and Gramps? And why did my dad want to get away from here so badly and never come back?"

"Well, a lot happened after high school, but I want you to remember what I said about your grandparents. Got it?"

"Yes, I understand."

"When your parents got serious and your dad brought Marisol home to meet Honey and Huck, it didn't go well."

"No? But they loved Mom...."

"Not at first." He then holds up his hands in a whoa pause before I can protest. "You gotta know they were different people back then. They were products of their upbringing. I'm not excusing anything... I'm just telling you where they were coming from and that they did not like their son dating 'that Spanish girl.'"

My heart sinks at hearing Mom being referred to that way.

"Your grandparents really kind of worked against the relationship, so your dad started coming home less and less. By the time college graduation rolled around, things had really gotten strained between them. Honey and Huck insisted on having a just-family graduation weekend, which really set your dad off. But your mom was awesome. Your dad wanted to cut Honey and Huck completely out of his life, but Marisol wouldn't let him. She was fine hanging back and stepping aside so Honey and Huck could see him. And your mom made Tripp promise to be cordial or she would dump him."

"I can't believe that about my grandparents. That just doesn't seem like them."

"It's not who they are now, but when your dad asked your mom to marry him, the relationship with Honey and Huck was pretty much non-existent. Tripp was trying to get started in his career and was barely making any money, and he would not ask for or take anything from your grandparents. When he showed me the little chip of a diamond on the engagement ring he bought your mom, I was like, 'Hell, no. You aren't giving her this piece of crap.' So I gave him the money for your mom's ring, and I helped him pay for the parts of the wedding Marisol's family didn't cover."

"Wow, that's... I don't even know what to say... nice seems so not enough."

"I figured I was never going to get married, so why not do this for him? Plus, I had the money. Your dad meant everything in the world to me. I lost a lot of friends and even some family members when people found about me, but it never mattered to your dad, or your mom. If he had to pick someone else over me, I was glad it was her."

"Wait, did my grandparents not go to their wedding?"

Another long pause hangs in the air, and I can tell Ethan Matthews wishes he could answer differently.

He just looks me straight on and says, "I know it's the biggest regret of their lives, but no, they didn't go."

I've never thought about their wedding before. Sure, I've seen the framed wedding picture of the two of them, but that's it. I've never stopped to think or ask who was or wasn't at their wedding. How could Grams and Gramps be so opposed to the marriage that they wouldn't even go to the wedding? How am I supposed to think of them the same way again, knowing how much it must have hurt Dad... hell, how much it hurt Mom!

"I know you want to be mad at them, but..."

"I just don't get how Mom being Mexican could be such a big deal to them."

"I know it doesn't seem like it should matter, but they grew up in a very different time. Hell, downtown San Antonio was still segregated into the 1960s. Mexicans and blacks weren't allowed downtown, and if it weren't for the Hemisfair coming to town and San Antonio not wanting to be an embarrassment on the world stage, there's no telling how long it would have stayed that way."

"So that's why my dad got away from here? Is that why he hated this place?"

"Aww, your dad didn't hate it here. He loved this community. He knew it had its problems and that it could use a swift kick in its prissy elite reputation, but he never hated it. He always wanted more for it, and there's still a lot of work to be done here. What you're dealing with now, what those assholes were pulling at the game... it comes from people who've spent their lives in this bubble and want to keep their myopic little vision of this corner of the world as it always has been to them."

"It feels like they're getting their way."

"It does, but they aren't. People like you and your friends, you're going to change this world... you are changing this world. And there are more people like you and your friends in this community than you realize."

The way I hang my head must signal my disbelief because I feel his hand on my chin, lifting up my head. "I know it seems really dark right now, and you've already gone through enough hard times in your life that you shouldn't have to deal with any of this. I'm here to tell you that you've already changed the world."

"What have I done?"

"You gave your grandparents back their son."

36

Reid is blowing up my cellphone the next morning.
Reid: so?
Reid: so???
Reid: so ???????????????
Reid: you alive?
Reid:???
EM: hey
Reid: hey????? wtf????
EM: um, sleeping
Reid: omg y
EM: up talking til 2
Reid: be right over
EM: its 5:15
Reid: my mom wants to know wut happened
EM: its 5:15
Reid: i have a key

Sixteen minutes later, Reid slinks into my room wearing a hoodie, a pair of boxers and his cowboy boots.

"Scoot over," he says, kicking off his boots. "Tell me what happened. Who the hell was that guy?"

By the time Ethan Matthews left, I completely understood why he and Dad were such good friends. And every time I thought he couldn't blow me away any more than he did, telling me about being in love with my dad or how Grams and Gramps didn't go to their only son's wedding, he just kept dropping one shitbomb after the next. He told me about how Grams and Gramps didn't see Mom or Dad until I was born, and that's how I changed the world. When they saw me, they fell in love with every part of me, and that's when they began to see the world differently. He also told me that he was the first person Grams and Gramps saw at the hospital when they got there just before finding out that Mom and Dad had named me Ethan-Matthew Cruz Canton.

"No way! Ethan Matthews is a baller," Reid blurts out.

Then, I tell him about all the stories he filled me in on and how Dad told Grams and Gramps about the wedding and ring stuff and that Ethan Matthews started a college fund for me as soon as Dad told him that Mom was pregnant.

"It was his secretary who called Grams and Gramps to let them know Mom had gone into labor."

"Dude, he's like your fairy godfather. Oh, shit. I didn't mean that to sound all homophobic or anything."

"I think you're good," I assure Reid.

Next, I tell him how Ethan Matthews was the one who put up all the posters for *Faux For* because he wanted to ask my dad to prom.

"That's awesome! I thought my family was Pearl Heights royalty, but you guys are like Beyoncé famous."

I fill him in on how Ethan Matthews had been around a lot when I was a toddler but just got so busy traveling all over the country defending students who were getting crapped on by their schools over prom policies, bathroom ordinances, dress codes and other discriminatory policies. Nevertheless, he and Dad would go on a yearly trip and even come back to visit the school for milestones, like when the football team won state a few years back.

"So, your dad didn't hate it here?"

"He really didn't. He hated a lot of the shit that goes on here, but he stayed really tight with his core group of friends from high school."

"Why didn't he tell you any of this?"

"Ethan Matthews…"

"Are you always going to call him by his entire name?"

"For now, I am."

"So Vonschniklebutt of you."

"Is that my screen name this week?"

"Until tomorrow, but don't change the subject. Why didn't your dad tell you any of this?"

"The best I can figure is that he wanted me to live my own life. You know, not have to be what everybody expected me to be or have to be the fourth Sawyer. If I knew all that stuff, I might have felt pressured to be a copy of my dad."

"That's some Dr. Robles-worthy analysis there, Vonschniklebutt."

"Yeah, all that therapy's paying off, I guess."

"Still, I can't believe you didn't know anything about this guy."

"Do you know your dad's friends from high school?"

"*Touché*, Vonschniklebutt. Changing the subject. What about being suspended?"

"Oh, that may be the best thing about Ethan Matthews. He went to college to be a theater guy but kept hearing all these stories from theater kids about how their schools were constantly screwing them over… not letting them perform certain shows, not letting them try anything progressive with casting and, of course, the bullying, so much bullying, and—oh, oh, oh—he kept meeting all these athletes who were too afraid to try theater or choir because of what people would say and athletes whose coaches would threaten to bench them if they tried theater. So, he decided to be an advocate for these kinds of kids and sue the close-minded racists and bigots who tried to get in the way of kids being who they wanted to be."

"Damn, that's crazy. You're gonna be like a supreme court case that kids learn about in school someday."

"I'm sure it's probably going to be one of those things that gets settled behind closed doors, where I have to promise that I won't discuss the case with anyone."

"And what about your grandparents?"

"God, I don't know. I mean, I'm not mad at them or anything, but I'm also not not mad at them. I can't pretend I don't know all this crap went on. Ethan Matthews will drop my ass so fast if he gets the slightest hint that I'm holding anything against them."

For the next few minutes, we stare silently at the ceiling, both of us trying to absorb everything that has happened in less than 24 hours. And then, I remember that just because I don't have to go to school because I've been suspended, Reid still has class in about a half an hour.

"Um, you going to school today or are you hanging out with the high school troublemaker?"

"Gee thanks, Dad. Yes, I'm going to school."

"Wearing that?"

"Nah, I'll just wear some of your lame stuff. But you gotta go be nice to your grandparents, because if you're not, I'll dump your ass, too."

So Reid. So Reid.

37

Sometimes you don't really have to say anything. You just know. When I go downstairs for breakfast and see Grams and Gramps having coffee, it's as if I've never heard anything different about them. They're the same two amazing people they've always been to me. And my love for my parents is the same. Dad did some messed up shit when he was my age, and he could have kept me from having a relationship with Grams and Gramps. I know what it feels like to lose people in your life without the possibility of ever getting them back. It gives you a perspective and a peace about leaving the past where it belongs—in the past.

I can feel the apprehension coalescing with the aroma of coffee and *pan dulce* as their conversation comes to an awkward pause. For most of the last year, they've overcome their loss in order to take care of me. They've sacrificed their normal, quiet routine to have a teenager in their home once again and all that comes with it: the smell of sweaty boy, the noise from video games and the sound of legs bounding up and down stairs, the late nights, long days and early mornings, the never-ending laundry, the grocery bills to fill a bottomless-pit stomach, the angst and mood swings of a teenager trying to navigate a world of boys, girls, friends, teachers, sports, grades, college... getting suspended. They've done it all because they fell in love with me the moment I was born and because they loved my dad and my mom. I have to casually and nonchalantly let them know nothing has changed. So, in the most routine of routine moves I can muster, I stroll in, kiss Grams on the cheek and I say, "Good morning," and walk across the kitchen to pour myself a cup of coffee. From the corner of my eye, I see Gramps squeeze Grams' hand.

"There's a new bottle of that cinnamon-caramel creamer in the fridge," he says.

I pour a heaping dose of creamer into my coffee, grab a *marranito* and say to them, "Thanks for the creamer. You guys are the best," and I go upstairs to eat my breakfast in bed.

I hear Grams down in the kitchen call out, "Tell Reid to just drop off your clothes sometime. I'll wash them when he does."

A grin stretches across my face, and I know we're okay.

Ethan Matthews has come over for lunch after an early morning meeting with the school administration. We spend the afternoon reviewing all the editions of the *Blue Dawg Alt*. He wants to establish a pattern that we've been responsible, ethical and fair with what we've been producing. And sure, he was my dad's best friend from high school, and sure he's clinically examining every article I wrote, cross examining every comma and dissecting every word for intent and implication, but he's also impressed, proud of me and what I have created.

"Your dad would have loved this," he says to me as he scrolls through page after page. "He was such a great writer. Your mom, too. Words were music to them, beauty, something you had to use artfully."

"Yes, it was a definite advantage in all my English classes that my parents were professional writers. Even though they both moved to television journalism, they were still writing all the time."

"I remember the first time I saw your dad doing a story that got picked up by the network. It was the coolest thing ever. I started yelling and screaming in the office. People thought I had lost my mind."

"Oh my God, I never got tired of seeing them on television. It was pretty cool."

"And your mom.... I remember when Tripp called to tell me Marisol was going to have a piece air nationally on NPR. God, he was so proud of her. And when she got a call from María Hinojosa commending her on the piece and telling her how much she appreciated that your mom didn't anglicize her name, it was like getting the blessing of the queen of Latino journalism."

It feels like I'm getting to know my parents in a whole new way, especially Dad. Mom's life before dad was the stuff of bedtime stories and early morning chats when Dad was away. She told me all about her time in high school. Her life and school were so different from the world Dad grew up in. She grew up surrounded by poverty. The Rio Grande Valley, she would say, often felt like the rest of Texas thought of the area as another country. She told me about how she had friends she started out with back in elementary school who got pregnant or had dropped out by ninth grade. She also told me about her friends who could have gone to college but got convinced by their families to stay close to home. Then there were the stories she told me about my *tías* and *tíos* growing up, how they all took a hand in raising her because they were so much older than her. She remembered the altars she helped set up for Día de los Muertos and dancing *cumbias* and how my *tía* Anita couldn't carry a tune but that never stopped her from singing morning and night. Mom always said, I got my looks from Dad, but I got my ambition from her.

Ethan Matthews seems to be getting as lost in nostalgia as I am. Just as Grams and Gramps had put aside or hid their grief from me, it dawns on me that Ethan Matthews had to be feeling an immense grief for the best friends he lost.

Just when it seems he's about to sink back into that grief, he snaps out of it and says, "Oh, I forgot. I have all the newspapers from back when your dad and I were in high school. All your dad's stories are there, plus all the stories written about him as a high school jock."

"You saved them?"

"Guilty. It was like being friends with a celebrity in the making, so I hung onto them. Now I'm glad I did. I'll send them to you when I get back."

"That's awesome, but I don't want you to..."

"Just stop, they're yours," he says and then goes back to perusing the work of the last six months of my life.

Ethan Matthews summarizes and comments on every piece of writing I've produced and then examines the article that caused all the trouble. He parses the language, and he grills me about everything that happened that night. He is so thorough, asks a ton of questions and takes pages and pages of notes. He asks about the assault in the hallway. I say "assault" is a little strong, but he wants the loaded legal language in order to send the message that attacking someone and using homophobic language is stupid and will cost the perpetrator. He asks about the first meeting with the principal and my interactions with Ms. Gillis, and then about my sessions with Dr. Robles.

Ethan Matthews is thinking about more than getting me back in school. He wants to make sure that this mess with the school doesn't hurt my college acceptance, regardless of how it all turns out in the end. He has temporarily stopped the school from contacting the colleges I had applied to and telling them I wasn't in good standing. He wants to be prepared in case any teachers decide to rescind their letters of recommendation. He's not only my legal counsel but also a kind of PR agent for me. Reid was right, it's like having a fairy godfather who has come ready to kick some ass.

38

Kids think they hate school and that getting to stay home is the best thing in the world, until it actually happens to them. Sure, the first day is fun. You sleep late. You stay in your boxers for hours, eat whenever you want to, watch TV, play video games. It's a minivacation, but that gets really boring quickly. You think you don't want to see your teachers but when you realize that's also where you see your friends, you start to miss the very thing you think you can't wait to get away from.

I actually like all of my teachers... except for Ms. Gillis. Coach Barajas has texted me several times to check up on me. He says I can meet the guys away from campus for their off-season runs, but I don't want to risk causing trouble for him. I thank him and say I just might, even though I know I won't. I miss my English teacher's awfully corny jokes. I thought his class was going to be so uber traditional, and it was in some ways, but he also challenged the traditional ways of approaching literature. He always challenged us to look at literature from the lenses of race, power, gender and contemporary world views. Right now, we're supposed to start reading these quirky little novels by P.G. Wodehouse about Bertie Wooster and Jeeves, his butler. My group is supposed to read *The Code of the Woosters*. Some days, we're supposed to meet with our group and discuss the book, and some days we break up and meet with students from other groups who are reading different Wodehouse books. I'm missing all of it.

Three days into a seven-day suspension, and I'm ready to get back to school. I'm ready to see my friends, at least the ones still talking to me. CC still hasn't returned any of my texts, and Reid says she's been avoiding him at school. Out of all of this, hurting CC sucks the most. We were stupid, careless. Touching hands or anything that happened between me and Reid is our business, and trying to shame us over it and outing us via group chat is wrong. But we were also wrong to keep it hidden from CC. She deserved to know. But to be fair, I didn't want to do anything to hurt her. Telling her would hurt her but not telling her hurt even more. From the day we met, I wanted her to like me, and, when it started to become clear that she did, I chose her life-long best friend instead of her. I wouldn't blame CC if she never speaks to me again, but that doesn't stop me from wanting her to respond to just one little text.

Ethan Matthews has clearly been working on putting together a plan of action, even before showing up for dinner. Our first step is to address the school board at the next meeting. Grams and Gramps have friends on the board, but this issue calls for more official action. We'll only have three minutes to speak at the meeting. Ethan Matthews is busy compiling a very fancy and very legal-looking packet of all the trouble he'll put the district through if I'm not reinstated to my regular schedule and issued an apology. Plus, there has to be no disciplinary incident documented in my school record. Ethan Matthews will take no prisoners. He's a hard-ass, promising to press charges against Jonathon Barstow, the guy who shoved me into the lockers at school. Jonathon's bad luck is that he's already turned 18 and used anti-gay language, so he's also looking at having to contend with hate-crime allegations. Ethan Matthews says it's all about leverage.

For now, it's just another day of sitting at home and waiting. Grams has already made me take a shower, threatening to dump me into the pool and withhold food if I "don't get out of those nasty ol' clothes" I've been moping around in for days. I take a shower, grab the remote to the television in my room and settle back to reward myself with a well-deserved morning of Phineas and Ferb, brown sugar cinnamon Pop Tarts and a Dr. Pepper, the true state drink of Texas.

And then my phone buzzes.

Reid: omg u dressed
24601: no booty calls during first period
Reid: ha ha seriously
24601: mostly why
Reid: omg!!!!!!
24601: what??????????????
Reid: put on some not dorky clothes
24601: huh
Reid: just do it. Cya soon
24601: ??????
24601: ?????????????
24601: ??????????????????????
24601: u suck

I put on jeans, my red Chucks and a Northwestern fleece pullover and head downstairs. Grams and Gramps are having coffee and watching *The Today Show*. They look surprised and pleased to see me up and in normal clothes at a decent hour.

"Well, you like nice," Grams says.

"Reid just texted and asked if I was dressed."

"That boy is such a horn dog," Grams tsk-tsks.

"Grams, he told me to get dressed."

"Oh. Well, you know he's always welcome here."

We're interrupted by my phone.

Reid: come outside—all of you

My mind races thinking about Reid and how much he's come to matter to me in such a short time. Less than a year ago, I thought nothing would ever feel good again. I thought nothing would ever matter to me again. I thought I could go through the rest of my life just going through the motions. I was wrong.

We hear them before we see them. The Blue Lacy Drumline is approaching. Any team that makes playoffs gets a send-off from the drumline. Any local dignitary making a visit to the school gets a welcome from the drumline. So, to step outside and see the drumline beating out cadences as they parade to the front of my house, makes me definitely glad Reid texted me and told me to get dressed. But I'm even more surprised by what follows behind the drumline.

Try not to cry. Try not cry. Try not to cry. The thought bounces around behind my eyeballs and ping-pongs throughout my head. CC, with a bullhorn in her hand, is leading a group of hundreds of students up the street to my grandparents' house, to our house. It's literally a parade, complete with signs and posters, marching up the street in my honor!

I try to take in all the sights unfolding before me. Reid's truck is parked in front of the house with a large wooden box in the bed. There are vans from two different local news stations parked across the street, and I begin to see messages on some of the signs coming into focus. Some read, "Bridges not Walls," "Free Einstein," "Hate Speech Sucks," "Love is Love," "We ♥ EMC^2" and "No Einstein, No School."

Chants of "No hate here" grow in volume and intensity as the crowd draws closer to the house. Reid comes up and stands behind me, his hands on my shoulders. Grams and Gramps stand on each side of me in the front yard, their arms pulling me in close between them. I can see tears gathering in Grams' eyes as I scan the faces of the students gathered in front of my house. Some of them I know, some I recognize, but most are strangers to me. I have no idea what I'm supposed to do. Everything in me wants to run to CC and hug her, apologize to her, convey to her that hurting her was the last thing I would ever want to do.

I'm clueless about the spectacle in front of me. How did they get out of class? How did all of this happen? What's going on here?

And then the pieces start coming together as the crowd reaches our house. Reid takes my hand and pulls me over to his truck, releases the tailgate and climbs aboard. He pulls me up behind him and, before I even realize what's happening, Reid and I are helping CC and a girl I don't know climb into the bed of the truck with us. When CC hugs me, I don't want to let her go. I want to hug her for as long as it will take to make the wrong, I've done her go away.

I whisper into her ear, "I'm sorry."

"I know," she whispers back and then she takes over.

Reid helps CC climb onto the wooden box in the truck bed and addresses the crowd through the bullhorn she holds.

"Most of you know me as CC. Some of you probably even think that's my actual name, but my name is Carmelita Selena DeSoto Cortínez... and I am a proud Latina!"

Hoots, hollers and woohoos of support roar up from the crowd.

"I am a proud Latina who barely speaks Spanish, but that doesn't make me any less Latina. It doesn't make me any less proud of my heritage, of my mother and grandmother, two proud Latinas both born in Mexico. They raised me in English and *amor*, taught me right from wrong, to speak up and speak out with power, *con fuerza y con ganas*, in the face of injustice, against the ugly face of racism. So we say: 'NO HATE HERE!'"

The crowd roars its enthusiasm while Reid, the girl I don't know, and I stand by CC and applaud.

"The ugly face of racism came to our community, to our school with chants of 'Build that wall.' It came to belittle, to intimidate, to divide, but we say: 'NO HATE HERE! NO HATE HERE! NO HATE HERE!'"

The crowd chants in unison with CC.

"They sought to divide us with bigotry and bias, with walls and whiteness, but we don't need to build walls. We need to build bridges, bridges of diversity, bridges of understanding, bridges of love because there is NO HATE HERE, NO HATE HERE, NO HATE HERE!"

CC was born for this, leading the chanting crowd, holding her hand up in the air, waving and gesticulating, fighting for justice.

"But what did our school do when the voice of bigotry and bias came calling at a baseball game? Did they shut it down and say, 'No, no, no, don't bring that here?' Did they stomp it out and say, 'No, no, no, that's not who we are?' No, no they did not. They ignored it, and they punished the messenger."

Boos from the crowd fill the morning air. Signs bounce up and down in protest and support.

"Ethan-Matthew Cruz Canton, Einstein, as I call him," she says, pointing to me, "did the brave thing, did the right thing, the noble thing.... He called out that bigotry and bias and said that kind of hate has no place here. Instead of celebrating his brave voice, our school silenced him, punished him, took him away from us. And what happened to the jerks who brought their bigotry and bias?" CC asks the crowd, cupping her hand to her ear and awaiting the answer she already knows.

"Nothing!" the crowd bellows back.

"Nothing," she continues. "All those guys are sitting in class free from the responsibility of the real damage they did, while Einstein got suspended for telling the truth. That is not right. So today, we walked out. Tomorrow, we will walk out, and we will walk out day after day until our school does right by Einstein. Does right by all of us!"

"Do the right thing! Do the right thing! Do the right thing!" the crowd chants until CC raises her hand to silence them so she can continue.

"Einstein was not the only victim, and we were not the only ones to blame. We alone were not responsible. We alone are not the ones who need to learn, we alone are not the ones who need to break down walls and build bridges. I want you to meet my new friend," CC says.

Then, she and Reid help the girl I don't know step up to the make-shift dais.

Her hair, long and straight, is a beautiful mixture of golden highlights woven into a deeper auburn, her skin is a glowing hazelnut. Sporting a Toros letter jacket crowded with patches from mariachi, academic decathlon, choir and FFA, she looks like a girl who smiles with her entire body and commands attention wherever she goes.

"This is my friend Mitzel Pacheco-Santos. She is student council president at César Chávez High School. We've come together because we want the same thing for our schools: NO HATE HERE!"

"No hate here, no hate here, no hate here," the crowd of students chants back. CC hands the bullhorn to her new friend, who holds her hand up bidding silence from the crowd.

"*Hola*, my new *amigos*!" Mitzel says, waving. "My name is Mitzel Pacheco-Santos, and I, too, am a proud Latina." Cheers rise up from the crowd. "But I'm more than that. I am a proud Chávez Toro, a proud senior, a proud Texan, and I am also a DREAMER!"

Whistles, whoops and woo hoos rise up all around us as Mitzel continues, "I came to this country as an eighteen-month-old baby. I am Latina. I am Americana. And. I. Am. Home!"

Roars of unfettered support rise all around.

"My friends, my classmates, when confronted with bigotry and bias, behaved badly. That was wrong. I am here to apologize that we let bigotry and bias determine our actions. We are better than that. You are better than that. This is not who we are. This is not who we choose to become. The adults in our lives, the leaders of our country have chosen to allow hateful language to become the norm of our discourse. That is not who we are, that is not who we choose to become. We choose bridges over walls, love over hate, diversity over bias."

Mitzel turns to look down from the dais at me. "I don't know you, Einstein, Ethan-Matthew Cruz Canton, *pero te apoyo con cariño*—I support you lovingly. The Toros of César Chávez High School support you and stand behind you. We promise that we will learn from your courage and speak out. We demand that the Pearl Heights administration welcome you back to school and denounce the bigotry and bias they have ignored. Thank you, *mis amigos*," Mitzel says as she blows kisses, waves to the crowd and steps down from the dais.

I haven't had a panic attack in months. Even when I was shoved into the lockers, my emotions stayed in check. When I was called into Dr. Caldwell's office—again—to learn I was suspended for the week, my emotions stayed in check. The past week has been a jumble of raw emotion, discovery, enlightenment, understanding of my mom and dad, my grandparents and even myself from a new perspective.... Even through all that cavalcade, I have kept my emotions under control. It's not that I fear my emotions or that I think I have to become some kind of macho guy to prove I'm tough. It's that I don't want to be ruled by them or held prisoner by them.

I cry.

It isn't an ugly cry—thank goodness—just big drops of happy tears, tears of disbelief, joyful tears. And as the tears continue to flow, a new chant rises from the crowd: "Ethan, Ethan, Ethan, Ethan, Ethan…"

Reid looks at me and nods for me to get up there. So I do. With a hand on Reid's shoulder, I push myself up to the dais and try with everything inside of me to memorize the scene in front of me.

I scan the crowd. Malibu, Carlisle, Gage and Wiley are right up front. Toward the back, Kelly from the advanced journalism class stands near Victoria and the rest of the cross-country team. I don't know when he showed up but standing in our front yard next to Grams and Gramps is Ethan Matthews, along with Reid's parents.

I don't know how they managed to be here supporting me when they should be teaching class at the moment, but clustered in the back are Coach Barajas and Mr. Shoenborn, my English teacher. Their faces seeming to say, "We're proud of you."

Standing to the right of them is Ms. DeSoto, who has been such a champion for me. I had worried that after breaking her daughter's heart I might have lost one of my most ardent champions. No worries, her smile is bigger than I've ever seen it before. I'm sure most of it is for her cheerleader daughter turned activist-protest organizer, but I can't help thinking some of that smile is for me, too. Next to her is Mr. Ruddell, the librarian who rescued me on numerous occasions and was my go-to resource for all things research.

And so, I take it all in. Teachers, friends, acquaintances, kids I only recognize from passing them in the hallways are chanting my name…well, chanting part of my name.

"Ethan, Ethan, Ethan!"

I stand before them all, humbled, overwhelmed, awed by how any of this can be for me. I raise the bullhorn to my mouth and say exactly what I'm feeling: "I LOVE Y'AAAAAALL. ALLLLL Y'ALL!"

The crowd roars its approval as the humble me kicks in. I wait for them to quiet down and find a way to thank them. "Just a few months ago, I came here after losing my parents. I had no friends and didn't think I needed any. I planned to go to my classes, keep my head down and leave without anyone knowing I was here. That didn't happen because I met a girl, this girl, and I'm a better person because of it. I'm a braver person because of it, and I have a place to call home because of it. I don't know what's going to happen to me, what the school is going to decide. I hope I'll be back in class with you soon. I hope I'm seeing you guys in passing periods, in practice, and I hope in a few months, I'll be walking the graduation stage with some of you. Most of all, I hope that we will keep standing up for what is right. I hope we will keep speaking out against bigotry and bias. And I hope we will be friends for years to come. Thank you. Woof, woof rah!"

39

The rest of the morning sweeps by me in a blur of hugs, hellos and handshakes. Students and teachers make their way back to class, but CC has accomplished her mission for the day. She explains a little bit of school funding to me, how schools receive ADA, or average daily attendance funds. The state pays a daily per pupil rate to schools based on the number of students in school that day. When kids are absent, schools lose the money from the state for that student. At our school, the attendance count happens at 9:45 AM, during second period. CC arranged for the walk-out to happen when first period ended. Hundreds of kids were not counted present this morning. The plan is for that to keep happening until the school ends my suspension and punishes the students who started this whole mess.

CC started planning this from almost the moment I was suspended. She was pretty put out with me and Reid, not because we ended up together, but because we hadn't told her. She says her mom talked her through it, helped her understand how I hadn't not chosen her but had simply chosen her for another role in my life, that this was new for Reid and me, so we were bound to make some mistakes along the way. Her mom said that the world is too ugly a place to let go of good people because they found someone else to love. CC found out who the student council president was at Chávez and reached out to

Mitzel almost immediately. She even went over to César Chávez High School with her mom and met with their administration. Organizing the marching band and the rest of the demonstration was easy after that.

After we get down from the truck, Mitzel takes me aside and says, "Seriously, Ethan-Matthew, we've all got your back. That was such an ugly night, and you did the right thing calling those guys out. You just keep speaking out for what's right. I know I will never get to meet your parents, but I know they're proud of you. And you," Mitzel says, looking over to Reid, "you're definitely cute."

Somehow, we end up at a local Mexican restaurant. Reid, his parents, Ethan Matthews, Grams and Gramps are sitting around the table as the events of the morning dominate every conversation. Two of the local news stations that sent crews interviewed me after the event, and Ethan Matthews was sure the others would call after the story aired. He also plugged the story to the local paper, and a reporter has already called me to schedule an interview. But the big, actually huge, thing he has been working on is an interview with CNN, which will happen later this afternoon. I can't believe after all the years of watching my parents conduct interviews for media like CNN that I'm going to be one of those stories.

Maybe it's the aftereffects of too many chips and salsa at lunch, but all of this is starting to feel overwhelming. I wanted to *tell* people's stories, not *be* the story. This is all part of the plan Ethan Matthews has to get me back into school, have my record cleared and get accepted by whatever college I want to attend. He didn't plan or know about CC's walkout but says it was more ingenious than anything he's come up with in his plan. He's an expert on student protests and says you can't manufacture student movements. They have to grow out of a genuine passion, or they fizzle and gain no traction. CC was able to seize the moment and bring the protest to life. She saw the larger issues boiling under the surface and decided they could no longer be ignored. I may have posted the story online that set events in motion, but CC is the one who really put herself out there and took a risk.

The school is arguing that I disrupted the learning environment with my article, but there's no doubt that CC disrupted the learning environment. She completely upended it. What's more, she's planning to upend the learning environment every day until I get reinstated and the thug who assaulted me gets punished, which is what she boldly proclaimed to the two news stations that interviewed her. I'm thinking about her as I mentally prepare for my interview.

When I sit down with Polo Morales, the reporter from CNN, he does what I saw my parents do so many times. He reassures me and tries to make me feel comfortable. He lays out what will happen, how he's going to start. He wants me to know he's there to tell my story.

"We're just going to have a conversation," he assures me.

Before the interview, he was able to shoot "B-roll" footage in my bedroom and of family pictures on the mantle. After that, he walks with me up the block toward school, asking me questions along the way.

Polo Morales cannot possibly know how much it feels like I'm talking to Mom and Dad as he asks his questions, poses follow-up questions and talks to me like I'm more than just a story. By the time we finish the interview, I feel like I've just come out of one of my sessions with Dr. Robles. I started to tear up once and had to pause for a second when he asked me what I wished my parents could know about me. I told him that I wished my parents could know that any happiness I have in my life and every good thing I've ever done or will ever do is because of them and the kind of people they were.

When we finish the interview, Polo Morales hugs me and gives me his business card and cell phone number. He says that if I ever need anything, to call him. He also promises to help hook me up with internships and shadowing reporters whenever I'm ready.

"Keep writing the hard stories, Ethan-Matthew. I'm sure your parents know exactly the kind of kid they raised. They'll always be proud of you," is his parting advice for me.

Things are moving fast. Polo is rushing his package through to run tomorrow, and we're all anxiously awaiting the attention, good and bad, we know is headed our way.

We arrive at Reid's house about 5:30 to watch the 6 o'clock evening news and have dinner afterwards. The Tibbitts want to do their part to contribute to the cause and whip up a viewing party to commemorate all that CC has accomplished. I wonder if they probably envisioned their son with someone more like her than me, but, if that was the case, they've never let on, never made me feel anything less than a person worthy of love and respect. I've always felt like they really liked me, but now I'm pretty sure they love me.

When CC and her mom arrive, they look subdued, something I have never seen in either of them. There's a coolness tamping down their customary warmth. It seems, CC and her mom have been driving to and from school together these days while CC's car is in the shop. Today, when they got home after school, they arrived to find their lawn completely covered in tortillas. Some jerks—we have a pretty good idea who—caused CC and her mom to spend nearly an hour picking up tortillas from the lawn, porch, driveway, shrubs and tree branches.

"Why didn't you call us to go help you?" Reid asks.

"That's sweet of you, but it's okay. It was a lot easier to clean up than toilet paper," Ms. DeSoto says, the warmth of her personality beginning to return.

"I swear, I'm gonna kick someone's ass!"

Ms. DeSoto takes Reid's face into her hands, pulls his face in close to her and says, "You're a beautiful boy with a good heart. Don't let the hatred and stupidity of others change who you are. I know you want to defend us, but don't you do anything stupid on our behalf, or I'll kick *your* ass."

Reid slowly nods in the affirmative.

That little drama is interrupted when the TV anchor teases the walkout story about to air after the commercial break. The Tibbits' den looks more like our super bowl party from last month than a simple gathering of friends. Assembled together are Ms. DeSoto and CC, along with Grams, Gramps, Reid, Malibu, Gage, Wiley, Carlisle, Victoria, Kelley, Ethan Matthews, Coach Barajas, Mitzel and, of course, me. Looking around the room, you would swear we've been friends all our lives.

As soon as the commercials end, there's a mad combination of omgs and shushing.

"Good evening and welcome back. This morning, students from a local high school staged a..."

A collective groan issues from throughout the room.

"You mean, Pearl Heights... don't let the admin get off the hook!"

"...walkout to protest the suspension of a student over an article he published in an unsanctioned online newspaper. Our Montana Méndez has more."

"Thanks, Crystal. That's right. In a move inspired by her namesake, the little-known teenage Mexican protest leader Carmelita Torres..."

"*Órale*, Montana, tell that story," Mitzel whoops out.

"...a modern-day teenage protest leader led a walkout that was nothing short of inspirational."

The coverage goes straight to CC speaking to the crowd of students gathered in front of her. It's a good thing we're recording the news to watch the story again later because the cheers and celebration in the room sound as if the Dallas Cowboys have actually made it to a Super Bowl and scored. When the story ends, and Montana Méndez throws it back to Crystal in the newsroom, our living room is engulfed in cheers, hugs of support and the retelling of our favorite parts. We will definitely watch this news story again and again.

By the time we finish the dinner of fajitas, frijoles and Spanish rice the Tibbitts had catered from the restaurant Mitzel's family owns, we have relived the walkout, the news story and my interview with CNN so many times that all of us feel like we're historians documenting a critical moment in time. While Reid, the other guys and I gobble down the handful of *polvorones*, CC's mom baked and brought over, CC fills us in on the details of the meeting she had with Dr. Caldwell. She threatened disciplinary action if CC does not cease and desist her disruption of the learning environment. She warned her that disciplinary action can negatively affect her college application process and that she's seriously jeopardizing her role as head cheerleader. I am beyond stoked that my friends are willing to champion my cause despite personal risk, but I don't want to be responsible for screwing up their future plans.

"CC, you've done enough," I tell her. "Maybe you should back off. Let Mr. Matthews take care of things from here. This is getting serious. We all got a robocall from the school reminding us about the student code of conduct and how dangerous and inappropriate it is for students to leave class without permission."

"That's such bullshit," Reid chimes in.

"Language," Mrs. Tibbitts calls from the dining room, where the adults have migrated for their adulting, which basically means they're having margaritas.

"Sorry, Mom. I forget you're the only one allowed to swear in the house."

"Don't be cute, dear."

"I can't help it, I'm fuc..." but he doesn't get to finish because Mitzel has slapped his arm.

"*Oyes, Flaco*—don't be disrespecting your momma that way," Mitzel says with every impression that her edicts are meant to be heeded.

"All right, girl. I hear you," Reid says with a wink.

Mitzel gives him a smile and head tilt as the two of them share an unspoken conversation that speaks volumes.

"Okay, you two, he's kind of spoken for," I say and get back to the subject at hand. "Anyway, as I was saying, the school said it's going to crack down on any students who leave campus without permission. You guys are looking at not being able to participate in any of the activities you love just because of me."

"Excuse me," CC says, turning to me but speaking to the group, "you're special and all, and we love you Einstein, but this is bigger than you, now. This is about standing up to hate speech, about sending a message that we don't have the time or patience for racism and homophobia. So, it's sweet that you're concerned about me, about us, but I made this choice because it's the right thing to do. Some things are bigger than cheerleading, bigger than 'looking to perfect a college application.' Bad-ass women have been changing this world for long time without worrying whether someone would take away their damn pom poms because of it."

"Mom, CC's using bad language."

Mrs. Tibbitts doesn't respond, just raises her margarita glass in our direction.

By the time we go home, our faces hurt from laughing. We feel like Mitzel is our new best friend, and there isn't a single *polvorón* left.

40

I feels like I haven't slept a bit, but when the alarm on my phone chirps to stir me from sleep, I wake up in a panic, like I've missed the very reason I set the alarm in the first place.

6:15 a.m. Still plenty of time. Polo Morales, the CNN anchor, has let us know the story will be aired during the 7 a.m. news hour for the first time and will be dropped into several other news programs throughout the day. The piece will also be available on the website sometime later in the day.

By the time I shower, dress and head down for breakfast with Grams and Gramps, my phone is on fire with text messages from friends wishing me good luck and telling me they're going to watch CNN for the first time in their lives. Ethan Matthews shows up around 6:45 with breakfast tacos, just as Gramps has put on a fresh pot of Taste of San Antonio coffee. Everyone's doing their best to act normal, but there's a palpable buzz of energy, excitement and apprehension in the room.

"And this morning, we have a story from Texas that will warm your heart on a chilly day like today and give you hope in this next generation of kids. Polo, what do you have for us?"

"This is it, this is it," Grams announces, not even trying to hide the giddiness in her voice as we all instinctively lean in closer to the ridiculously large television screen.

"Good morning, Jon. Yes, that's right. This is definitely a story that will 'give you all the feels,' as the kids say. I traveled to San Antonio, Texas, where I met Ethan-Matthew Cruz Canton..."

Grams and Gramps hoot like they're at Friday night football.

"...which even he admits is a lot of name. But for someone who's lived and lost so much in only seventeen years, it's a name you're not likely to forget."

The screen cuts from Polo to video of Polo and me walking onto the back side of the campus. The football stadium fills the background as Polo's voice plays over the video.

"Last May, Ethan-Matthew Cruz Canton was a typical high school student but that all changed on a horrific day when his parents, Tripp Canton and Marisol Cruz Canton, both correspondents with the Foreign News Network in Spain, were killed in a terrorist attack in the building where they worked."

The video cuts to news footage of the day. Black plumes of smoke rise into the sky as sirens blare and the chaos of the scene floods into the living room. I see Gramps reach out for Grams and put his hand on top of hers. I can feel Ethan Matthew's eyes on me as I audibly gulp and swallow.

"The attack, linked to three terrorists, killed fifteen, injured eleven others and forever altered the course of Ethan-Matthew's life."

The video transitions to footage of family pictures on the mantle in the house before settling on a baby picture of Dad and a baby picture of me in almost the exact same pose. Grams' voice plays over the video. "He was always such a good baby, just like his daddy. We only had the one son and one grandchild, but they have filled our lives with more joy than anyone has a right to." The video then cuts to Grams and Gramps at the dining room table leafing through a photo album with Polo. "He spent every Christmas with us. We couldn't wait to have him in the house. He looks so much like his father," Grams says. "But he also has so much of his mother in him," Gramps adds. "The boy is the best of both of them."

The video cuts to Grams, Gramps and me getting lunch ready with Polo's voiceover explaining my situation. "And now Ethan-Matthew lives with his grandparents and attends Pearl Heights High School, the same high school his father led to the state championship semifinals as quarterback before graduating. But Ethan-Matthew isn't living in anyone's shadow."

Next, there's video of me running in my first cross country meet. "He's a great kid, so coachable and just the kind of athlete you wish you could have a whole team of," Coach Barajas says. "He would have gone on to state if he hadn't fallen. But this kid got up and finished the race, limping and bleeding the last mile to the finish line."

The video then cuts to Polo standing in front of the school. "Ethan-Matthew also made a name for himself following in both his parents' footsteps. He created his own online news magazine." The video cuts to me and Polo sitting at the desk in my room scrolling through *The Blue Dawg Alt*. It cuts back to me, and I say, "We try to cover a wide range of topics. Tell the stories of people who rarely get to have their stories told. And we want to do it in a fun, contemporary way, kind of cutting-edge, but also keep it professional but not stodgy." I couldn't believe I used the word "stodgy."

The video then cuts back to Polo doing a walk and talk and using his hands to convey a sense of earnest credibility. "It's that cutting-edge that landed Ethan-Matthew at the center of controversy and suspended from school."

The video then shows some B-roll from cell phone footage of the baseball game. It looks like just any other high school baseball game. "At a baseball game between two of the state's top ranked teams, Pearl Heights and César Chávez High School, things got out-of-hand between the mostly white Pearl Heights team and the all Latino team from César Chávez...."

"These white guys kept shouting all kinds of rude and offensive things throughout the game, like 'Taco Tuesday' and 'Isn't your dad our gardener?' And they kept making all these Mexican *grito* sounds. It was super-annoying, but we also understood it was intentional, planned," Mitzel says as she sits across from Polo. "But students from Chávez weren't completely innocent, either. There were students yelling 'Pearly Whites' and behaving really immaturely, as well. It was pretty awful."

The next scene is Polo standing in the middle of the Pearl Heights baseball field. "It could have been nothing more than a little mean-spirited taunting between two rival teams, but when the game ended, things escalated. A controversial close call gave the Pearl Heights team the win, and the taunting reached a new low." There's more B-roll taken from a cell phone footage, showing the guys repeatedly yelling, "Build that wall," as the coaches and some other parents I hadn't noticed before try to get them to stop.

The entire evening floods back into my mind as Polo explains about the chaos that followed the chanting. Then he reports on my editorial calling for the school to suspend the students who chanted and set the chaos in motion. He makes it very clear that the school did not discipline any of those students but suspended me instead. Next, there is footage from the walk-out, an interview with CC and a shot of me visiting Mom and Dad's gravesite while he explains that I'm still not allowed back on campus and have to wait for the decision of whether I'll have to finish the year at the alternative school after my suspension ends.

I don't realize I've been holding my breath until I exhale as the CNN story ends and the camera cuts to the two news anchors in the studio.

"Polo, thank you for that. And, what an outstanding young man Ethan-Matthew is," Jon, the male anchor says.

"Polo, I am just so impressed by all those kids. Wow, what an incredible story, and oh, my goodness, he lost both of his parents. What a tragedy. Do we know anything about what decision school officials are going to make?" Leslie, the female anchor, asks.

"Ethan-Matthew and his grandparents are hoping that he'll be back at school next week and that all of this will be cleared from his record. We'll keep you updated" Polo answers.

"Well, thanks for this great story on a really amazing kid. Keep us posted," Jon adds and then continues on with a tease to breaking news after the commercial break.

Somehow, Grams just knows what everyone needs and when they need it. She doesn't say a word when the story ends but just gets up from her seat, walks over to me and hugs me in that way that tells you everything is going to be all right.

41

After watching the story air again on the next hour's news program, Grams, Gramps, Ethan Matthews and I walk over to the school. We're on our way to observe and support the second-day walkout. CC anticipates a much smaller group will join in today and that there will probably be pushback from the administration. The school has been issuing all manner of disciplinary threats, from suspensions to canceling extra-curricular activities. I know that most of our students are applying to top-tier and highly selective colleges and universities. The pressure is on them to not do anything that could jeopardize their college acceptance. School walkouts on the first day are cool, but walking out on a second day is the stuff for true believers. Putting skin in the game takes lots of kids out of the game.

Nothing has prepared me for what comes into focus as we get closer to the campus. In the student parking lot in front of the school, there are at least ten trucks with big-ass Trump signs and American flags furling in the breeze. Shoe-polished in white on the windows of at least a dozen more cars are the letters "USA." There are parked cars lining the streets all around the campus. It looks like Friday night football. I assume the cars belong to parents of students, but there are adults of all ages standing on the lawn in front of the school and on the sidewalk across the street from the school. As we make our way closer to the front of campus to look for CC, people wave to me, shooting thumbs up and taking pictures of me like I was some kind of celebrity.

"Oh, my God, oh my God, oh my God," CC squeals, running up to hug me as we make it to the front of the school. "This is crazy! The CNN story was so good, people have been talking about it all morning. My phone has been going off like crazy with people calling and texting me.... Granted, lots of people are calling me a wetback bitch on social media, but there are like news stations, reporters, old teachers, people from church..."

I have never heard CC speak so excitedly.

"Almost everybody has been so supportive and positive, and like they can't believe that any of this is real, like how could the school be so wrong, and 'You go, girl,' and 'We got your back, anything you need.' Seriously, I can't believe how big this whole thing has gotten."

"That's awesome. I'm so proud of you," I say to CC and hug her again.

"Oh, my gosh, that's not even the best thing. Like, look at all these people.... No, no, not the deplorables over there with their MAGA crap," she says, pointing away from the people in clothes they must have bought at a post-Independence Day half-off sale. "All these other people coming onto campus.... I thought we might not have anyone today because the school was being all hardcore. But parents started calling the school and showing up to sign their kids out of school. The lady in the attendance office really likes my mom, so she's been texting her to tell Mom how many parents and kids are signing out. So far, like 65 parents have called to sign their kids out and like 80-something seniors who turned eighteen already signed themselves out. Oh, and she's texting Mom because my mom and like 27 teachers all called in sick today," CC says as she turns to wave to her mom, who's standing not far away talking with a group of parents holding signs I can't quite make out.

I wave to Ms. DeSoto, and she blows kisses to me, then turns back to the group of parents she's with. I know she's telling them about me from the way they turn to gawk at me with that proud-parent look you can't mistake.

"I'm going to text a walk-out message in just a little bit. I'm just waiting for..." CC says and suddenly pauses to look at a yellow-dog school bus inching its way toward us.

CC beckons me to follow her as she moves toward the sidewalk and flags down the bus. As the occupants begin to disembark, I'm once again in awe of all that CC can accomplish. The first person off the bus is Mitzel. She's followed by Jesús Sepúlveda, the principal from Chávez High School. I recognize him from the local news stories. The group of guys who unload after them are all sporting their Toros Baseball T-shirts. I marvel at this exceptional friend who is under the threat of her own suspension. Who knows if even her mom's job is in jeopardy... and CC still makes all this happen.

Then, the magic of the morning blossoms into something wild and wonderful.

CC sends the walk-out text and, like a hero riding in on a white horse, Reid, who I haven't seen or heard from since he texted me before the interview, rounds the corner in his truck and pulls into the parking lot across the street from the campus entrance, where we have all gathered. Gage, Malibu, Carlisle and Wiley are in the bed of the truck with a set of huge speakers blaring Enrique Iglesias singing *"Duele el Corazón."*

Just then, students start exiting from doors all over campus and crossing the street. Guys from the Toros baseball team are shaking my hand. Parents are coming up to me and telling me who their children are, telling me what classes we have together, telling me how they saw the CNN story and are proud of my conviction. Other parents are holding up signs that I'm finally able to read: "Teach Love Not Hate," "No Hate Here" and "Free Ethan." Other parents come up to me and tell me how much they love and respect Grams and Gramps, and that's why they have to come out and support me.

Guys from the Pearl Heights baseball team show up in their Blue Lacy Baseball shirts and are busy offering me their support and taking selfies with players from the Toros baseball team. And Reid, Reid is like some kind of social events coordinator. He's schmoozing with parents and the teachers who called in sick and with those who have walked out with the students. The whole thing looks like a giant block party. There's an aura of joy and unity mixed with purpose and conviction.

Nevertheless, there are also guys wearing MAGA hats walking out and chanting, "USA, USA, USA." Their chants soon fade, however, when they see how outnumbered they are. One sight more than anything silences their chanting: There are reporters everywhere. All four local television news stations have trucks in front of the school, and there are numerous reporters with and without video cameras taking photos and interviewing people.

Suddenly, as if they had rehearsed it, Reid drops the tailgate of his truck, hoists CC up and hands her the mic connected to the speakers in the truck bed.

"Y'all are awesome!" CC booms into the mic as she surveys the crowd that has turned toward her. "Thanks for coming out today. I know you are risking a lot to be here today, but our message hasn't changed: NO HATE HERE!"

The crowd echoes back: "NO HATE HERE, NO HATE HERE, NO HATE HERE!"

"Y'all are proof that we are better than all the hate and division around us. Y'all are proof that when we stand up for what is right, people listen and things change. My friend, our friend—Ethan-Matthew—give the people a wave, Einstein," CC calls to me and points at me. I wave my arms above my head, the way I saw Mitzel and CC do. I feel pure joy stretching across my face. I didn't think anything could overwhelm me more than yesterday's walkout but knowing that everyone out here is risking something to stand up for me, fills me with the most intense happiness I've ever experienced.

"Ethan-Matthew has shown all of us that we have to stand up to those who would seek to divide us with bigotry and bias. Our school needs to do the right thing and bring Ethan back to school. Yesterday, we walked out. Today, we walked out, but we need more for tomorrow. We need all of you to speak out and speak up. Speak up when you see bigotry and bias. Speak out when something is not right. We are the future, but we have to start today. Thank you for what you've done today and for what you're doing for tomorrow. You're the best!" And with that, she hops down from the back of the truck to ovation and admiration.

Looking across the crowd, I can see the doors that I walked through the first time I came to Pearl Heights for Gear Up Day. I remember how I wanted to be anywhere but Pearl Heights. I thought about how all I wanted to do was get my schedule and get out of here as fast as I could. Then I think about this bold, confident, gorgeous cheerleader who pep-stepped up to me and inserted herself into my life. Now, I'm watching this same girl, multiple microphones shoved at her, orchestrating a social-justice protest like a boss. I can't think of any other place I'd rather be than here.

42

"Hey, Mom. Hey, Dad. I'm eighteen today. I know, I can't really believe it either. I'm sorry I haven't been by in while. I've kind of had a lot going on. I mean, I know you know. Still, I'm sorry. I got my driver's license today."

It probably looks pretty weird, but I show it to them.

"It's just the paper copy, but it's pretty cool. I'll come by and show you the real one when it comes in. My friend Reid took me. That's him over there."

I turn and wave at Reid, who has stayed back to give me time alone with my parents. He waves back.

"Um, he's also not just my friend. Reid, is, um... well, he's my boyfriend."

I turn and wave at Reid again. I'm not really sure why I do this. It just seems like the thing to do, and I'm a little nervous about telling them. Reid, humoring me as usual, waves again.

"I know you guys would be cool with all this. I guess it just sounds funny saying it out loud. Boyfriend. I've never actually said it before."

In my mind, I sort of feel like a fifth grader again, when dad pulled me out of school for a day to have "the talk" with me. I bury my hands in my pockets and nervously digging at a pebble on the ground with my foot.

"You would really like him. He's super smart and funny. He's an awesome runner and an amazing singer. He's only a junior, so I don't know if we're going to do the long-distance thing when I go to college...

"Oh my gosh, I can't believe I didn't start with this. I got into Northwestern."

I've actually been accepted by a lot of schools. I even heard from schools I hadn't applied to. Between the CNN interview, my parents being journalists and the story getting picked up and basically going viral, I started hearing from lots of different schools of journalism trying to recruit me. After the second walkout and rally, the Pearl Heights High School administration had no choice but to relent. Principal Caldwell was catching heat from parents, alums, teachers and students—lots of students. I still hear under-the-breath comments from some of the MAGA crowd, because sometimes that kind of hate just doesn't go away. I won't let it steal any of the joy that's come into my life after so much hurt and hate. And in the best twists of fate, the punk who shoved me into the locker is the one finishing the year at the alternative school, which his family saw as a better option than the assault charges he was facing. Ethan Matthews, as he said he would, put the fear of Jesus in them.

"I guess I'll probably learn about not burying the lead in journalism school, but I definitely picked Northwestern. Oh, I met your friend, Ethan Matthews... which, by the way, I'm kind of pissed at you guys for some things you never told me. We'll talk about that another time. Anyway, he's really cool, and I can tell he really misses both of you, but especially you, Dad. He's like super-stoked I picked Northwestern. Told me I could stay with him anytime I need to and that he'd be there for me if I ever needed anything."

I pause to caress the watch weighing heavily on my wrist. "He said it was a promise he made to you a long time ago."

A San Antonio Spring breeze wafts around me and levitates the leaves curling around my feet into a whimsical dance that heralds the passing of one season to the next. Despite a valiant effort to remain, the chill of winter mornings continues to lose its battle with the warmer days of Spring. My senior year is ending, and I'm finally getting to write for the actual school newspaper. That's because a circle of close friends literally went to battle for me. In two and half months high school will end, and I will move on to a new season of the closest thing I know to a normal life.

"We're having a big party tonight. Grams and Gramps are going all out, like they do for everything. I told them we could have a combo birthday-graduation party, but Grams looked at me like I was crazy."

From behind me, I can hear Reid's soft steps as he comes up to stand beside me.

"So anyway, I just wanted to say I love you and I'm glad you are my parents and that I'm going to be okay."

Reid takes my hand and squeezes it the way he did at that first varsity meet. I know it's time to run the next race.